TRAVELS IN DEATH: DESTINY

By James Piansay

Day fades to Night

1.0 | The Hero & The Archer

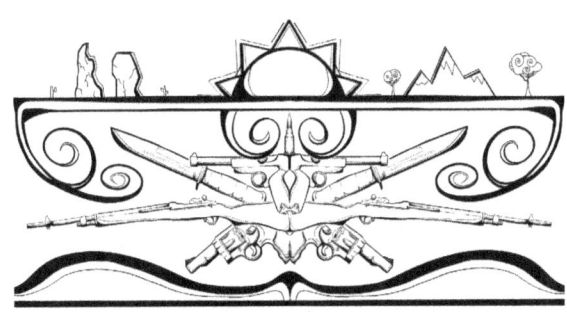

A dead man stares forward, back resting on a short wooden wall as the background passes him by. The tattered cap on his head flies off as the wind grabs hold of it, tossing it down the train on which he died. It flipped and turned while flying down the iron beast, sailing just beside the windows of the carts as its passengers ducked in fear. In the reflection of the goggled hat, a younger man sprints down the aisle. His head is turned back with a shaky smirk plastered on it, suddenly bullets fly past him as he dives forward – breaking through the door and exiting the cart.

Soren Prahl, a young man who cheated his way into the army, now runs away from bounty hunters. Cart after cart he sprinted, and chasing after him is a hunter who he has some unfortunate history with.

"I DON'T SUPPOSE YOU'LL LET ME GO THIS TIME RIGHT?!" Soren yelled out to his pursuer. Hearing the idiotic attempt for a ceasefire, an agitated expression formed on the Hunter's face. He then scoped in with his rifle. A loud metal clutched noise shot out as he pulled the bolt handle. Firing at Soren, the bullet whizzed through his short and scruffy black hair – snipping the long braid he had at the back of his neck. "YOU KILLED MY BROTHER, YOU IGNORANT **FUCK!**"

"OKAY, WELL TO CLEAR THINGS UP, **I** DIDN'T KILL HIM!" Soren yelled back while dodging the bullets. Seeing the barrel aimed at his back and looking around to see nowhere to dodge, he grabbed a random man's suitcase and used it as a shield. The bullet shredded whatever was inside as he handed it back. "Sorry bout that! I'll uh– pay you back at some point. Promise."

Sprinting off, Soren dug into the interior of his large hoodie-like trench coat and took out a pistol. His arm snapped up like a whip as he aimed and fired at the metal shelves above the seats. This caused an avalanche of luggages to fall between them, blocking any clean shots the Hunter may have had. Running toward the door, a bullet surprisingly grazed Soren's cheek as he exited the cart. And as blood trickled from the scratch he looked back to see who had shot it.

"Now how the hell did you do that?!" he said to himself, amazed by his marksmanship. Closing the door behind him, Soren looked around and found a broom stick in a small closet to his right. Using it to lodge the door shut, he then ran forward – quickly ducking after realizing the door had a window. A bullet shot through the glass and whizzed over his head, and after narrowly avoiding it, he continued. Now between carts, he looked around and eventually up. Climbing to the top of the train, he ran while frantically swinging his arms – at the same time the broom was snapped in half as the hunter kicked the door in. "FACE ME YOU DAMN COWARD!!"

"WHY WOULD I DO THAT?! YOU HAVE TWO GUNS, DON'T YOU CARE ABOUT THE ALIVE BONUS?!"

"TO HELL WITH THAT SHIT! I'M TAKING YOU IN **DEAD**!"

"This guy is really damn persistent huh? How long has it been, two cities?" Soren said aloud while running. Looking over to the horizon, all he could see was the open desert. A place with a crumb of flora and fauna spread across its copper sands, barely even any sources of water either – this place had more giant spires of sandstone than people who were willing to cross it. Even just thinking about surviving in the Dratari isthmus put a sour expression on Soren's face. "Yeah, that's not happening. I'd rather just turn around. . ."

Climbing onto the top of the train, the Hunter laid on his stomach to immediately take a shot at Soren. Not realizing that he was in the man's scope, Soren was shot in his right thigh. From the impact alone he fell from the roof, dropping down into the next segment of the train.

His face planted onto the floorboards of the open cart, and as he picked up his head Soren made eye contact with the dead body. It still seemed fresh with the color that remained in its skin, especially from the bullet wound in their chest. Blood still slowly leaking from it. With the way he was dressed and the weapons he had on him, they must've been a criminal or at the very least on the run. That means one of three things – 'he had a shoot out with a ranger or maybe a hunter.' Soren thought while trying to stand.

"Drop the pistol and turn around, I wanna see the look in your face before you die." Listening to the Hunter who spoke out from behind him, Soren turned slowly to see them on the roof – scoped in with their rifle already. His eyes stared down its iron sights as a gunshot went off. The Hunter's right shoulder was thrown back like it was punched as blood spewed out of it. In reaction to being shot, the Hunter pressed down on the trigger. Ducking down, Soren managed to avoid the bullet as it went straight into the wooden boards beneath him. As he looked back up with comically wide eyes, he saw the hunter fall off the train as he landed in the sand. Peeking over the edge, Soren made sure he wasn't able to hop back on before taking a moment to breathe.

"I see you've met my target." Said the man on the other end of the first shot. He had dark brown, seemingly black eyes even on the brightest days. And unlike Soren who spoke with a myriad of emotions, Cypher spoke with barely any, indifferent with every sentence.

He carried a Myzer rifle, a common gun used by those who need a reliable weapon. It has a sleek wooden exterior and carries up to five shots in each magazine – but more than being reliable, it's known for being malleable. Thus, the Myzer has given birth to nearly a hundred different types of rifles. So understandably, there's a large influx of buyers from across the world. Military, mobs, hunters, rangers, and criminals – all marksmen in their own right. But from the most recent war between nations, the rifle is in no better hands than Cypher.

"Welp, all my guesses were wrong. The secret fourth option of 'soldier' got me. And yeah, I've briefly met buddy ol' pal over here. Not really a talker though." The two then stared at each other – there was an odd intensity in the air. Breaking the tension, Soren laughed as Cypher slightly smiled. Walking closer to one another they shook hands and hugged, reuniting after however long it'd been since the battle on the shore.

Being cartoonishly emotive, Soren asked how he'd been and while standing like a statue, Cypher responded. "It's been nice. Getting paid for a single kill has been more profitable than the war. At least for me. Now all I have to do is guard the body till we get to the 13th station at Printon. The money is practically in my pocket already."

"Interesting. I tried the hitman business for a bit, but then I realized that some of the targets weren't ya know – *bad*. Learned that the hard way, went on my second mission and didn't know that I had to kill a kid. Couldn't stomach it so I just walked away – SHIT! Speaking of which–" Soren then turned to look through the carts and noticed rangers going up and down the aisle.

Putting on his hood he tucked himself into it, trying not to be seen despite standing beside a dead body. But the rangers easily noticed the suspicious looking figure outside and walked toward him – opening the door and stepping onto the flat cart. However, once they saw Cypher the rangers paused. They then silently walked away as beads of sweat dropped from their brows, pretending not to have seen anything or *anyone*. "Damn – what kind of reputation did you cook up since we last met?" Soren asked with a smirk and look of genuine concern.

"A very good one." Cypher replied while cleaning his gun.

1.1 | The Enchanted Town

Pushing the view upward, we look down to the sleek exterior of the plated train while the locomotive spews black smoke from its piping. Gliding across the metal tracks beneath it, the hundred screeching wheels spin as its patterned noises echo out. Waiting for their stop, an entire day and night would pass before Printon appeared on the horizon. The city stands right outside the Dratari desert, on a massive grassy glade spanning miles upon miles. Buildings and city blocks extend across it as thin roads carve through them, creating a smooth pattern – one that can be seen from above. And because of its unique shape, many have called Printon, 'The City of Dawn'.

As the train begins to slow and eventually stop at station 13, both Cypher and Soren make their way onto the patterned stone brick streets – looking for the person who had hired the *Void Hitman*. Meanwhile, the contractor stalked them from the shadows of a nearby alley. Only leaving once more people had gathered around the train. So as a large crowd appeared, they made their way over, bumping into Cypher amidst the chaos and slipping an envelope into his jacket pocket.

The pair would then blend into the exodus of people that were leaving the train, making their way deeper in Printon as rangers scoured the streets. Dealing with hunters is one thing, in all intents and purposes you're legally allowed to kill them – but rangers are enforcers of the law.

Getting rid of a single one could mount your bounty to an even higher pedestal, at the moment, neither Soren nor Cypher wanted that. Thus, they continued to skulk through the streets with avoidance as their top priority. But as those two faded, the contractor appeared.

The mysterious appeared walking onto the flat cart, going to the body and taking out what seemed like a golden cup. It had an intricate and almost flawless mural etched into its sides, but with the person's hand around it, there was no way to tell what they were. Ignoring the aesthetics, the cup was brought underneath the slow leaking wound of the dead man. Blood then trickled down into it as the mural began to glow, illuminating one of the three designs around its exterior. Pulling away, the cup appeared to be empty once more – despite this, the one symbol was still shining.

"*Destiny*? **Fate**? Words given *definition* and *meaning* by man, and by man they will be rewritten. I say it will be done in my lifetime, yet as long as it's been the others say longer. But soon we shall find the je ne sais quoi that makes a maker. Chains will rust, flowers will wilt. I will be free soon enough." – The Contractor

2.0 | The Trails of a Quest

Lurking in the tight alleys of Printon, Cypher and Soren climb up winding stairs that gradually rise above the passing buildings. Looking around for a  safe place to open the envelope, Cypher spots a demure street. The alley was a bit small for Printon standards, just enough for three people to stand side to side if they touched shoulders. In here was a bookstore and a flower shop, both had items placed outside that were meant for interior decoration. Tables, seats, and even paintings were scattered about in the tiny street. A quaint and quiet place, far from any main roads – a true gem in a city this big. Walking into the bookstore, Soren yelled out to an older gentleman who worked the desk. "Aye, Rocco! You don't mind if we stick around do ya? Got some things to look over, nothing to worry about."

The man turned and pushed up his glasses from the edge of his nose, while sitting down behind the desk he replied. "Yeah, yeah – just don't bother me with any of ye illegal nonsense, nephew." His voice was awfully deep and every word resonated in the big beer belly he had.

"I wouldn't dare!" Soren said while saluting him. The two then made their way to the cramped corner of the store. Sitting at a table with books stacked all over it, towers of literature were between them. Trying to speak, Soren tilted his upper body in a weird manner to get around the novels.

"So. . . how much did you make?" He asked excitedly, his leg bouncing up and down in anticipation. The same one he bandaged after getting shot. However, Cypher didn't say anything for a moment – instead he opened the envelope and took out the blue bills. An eyebrow raised as he dug his fingers in again, taking out a handwritten note. "I should've been paid around 10 thousand ren, but there's a lot more in here. And then there's this–" He said while holding a piece of paper. "–I assume it's a follow up job, or extra steps." After getting up and moving his chair closer, Soren asked why he didn't just open it to find out which.

"Such a thing was never in the contract. This is random – completely new. It can't be good news, I'd rather just move on." Cypher was then about to tear it apart, but before he could Soren snatched it away from his hands. "OKAY! Hold on, *I'll* take a peek – that way you never even have to know what it says." Cypher didn't respond and Soren took that as a go ahead and opened the note. The childlike excitement faded from his face, it sank into a worried and confused look as his eyes slowly rotated over to Cypher.

This was the letter.

"I apologize for the sloppy handwriting. The original letter became void once I saw your friend there. I needed to quickly make another. So let me cut to the chase. You have been a great asset to me, so much so that I cannot let you go. But I know there is no material gain in the world that would keep you by my side. Yet I still need you. So at the very least, I'll give you a warning. I've attached your name to mine. My deeds are now yours, and yours mine. Best of luck, my ally." –The Contractor

"Did you guys get married or something?" Soren asked Cypher. His head then tilted as he looked out the window to see several rangers walking down the alley. "No. But I have a feeling those men are after me, maybe even *us* if you're unlucky. Hand me that letter."

"With how many bodies I keep stumbling on, yeah – they've gotta be after me too." Soren sadly stated as the both of them hid their guns in the piles of books on the table. Soon after the rangers entered the shop, taking a quick look around before interrogating the owner. In a quick and succinct way, he simply waved them off and pointed over to the lads in the corner. The duo looked at one another as the sunlight shined through the nearby windows, illuminating the dust that wandered in the air. The four rangers then approached, rifles in hand and pistols on the hip. One of them stepped in front of the others with a question on his tongue. "I don't suppose you two are gonna come along peacefully?"

Trying to pry out any information, Cypher asked what charges were held against them. And in an almost dismissive way, the ranger scoffed before answering. His head turned to the others as if he couldn't believe what he'd asked. Seeing that Cypher was serious, the ranger's shoulders loosened as he looked at him puzzled. "Wait, you're bein forreal?" He asked.

"Yes, I am. What charges are we being held with and how did you find us so quickly? It's hard to believe that you found us this fast without being tipped off, we just got here."

The two groups stared at one another, a tension tightening between the both of them. The rangers held onto their guns with trembling hands as the soldiers were unarmed, yet somehow the duo was calmer. There was a very clear gap in experience between them, with that alone the disparity of victory for the rangers widened. Seeing their unwillingness to answer, the duo realized something was wrong.

Initiating the fight, Soren sprinted forward – dodging enemy fire even with the limp in his leg from being shot. Grabbing the closest ranger's rifle, he swiped it away and slammed the stock of the gun onto the man's nose. His head was thrown back as blood spewed up from his nostrils like a fountain. Quickly after, though they were a bit timid to approach, the other rangers closed in on Soren. As they did, Cypher grabbed the gun he hid in the stacks of books and immediately aimed at his enemies – his sights hung over the center mass of a ranger, seemingly not caring if they died or not.

"WAIT-" Soren yelled to Cypher. He knew that saying 'we don't have to kill these guys' wouldn't work – he also understood that Cypher already believed that killing them would just be easier. He had to convince him that it would be to their benefit if these men survived.

"Let them live. . ." Soren said as he grabbed one of the other rangers, placing a knife to their neck and using them as a hostage. "We can get information out of them, plus – only more will come after us if we kill these guys. The two of us won't be enough if that happens, you know that." The two rangers who were still up and fighting pointed their rifles at Soren as he backed up with the hostage. Noticing that they were frightened, he probed them to respond and hopefully lay their weapons down.

"How does that sound to y'all? You get to live and all you have to do is answer some questions. Damn good deal if you ask me." The two of them didn't say anything, and in the silence only one of them lowered their weapons. Instantly, the one that still held their gun was shot in their dominant arm – rendering the shooting hand useless. Cypher then walked forward and placed the hot barrel on the other's chest, threatening him to speak. "He'll die before you can make it to any hospitals nearby, unless you tell us what we want to know – quickly. Is that clear?" The ranger who had given up nodded as the hostage was knocked out by Soren, he realized that there was no point in holding the man anymore.

"Wonderful." Said Cypher as he pulled over a chair. The whole time his rifle was aimed directly at the man's chest, even in the relaxed pose that he sat in. "What were you told about us, and don't bother lying." Not wanting to have his chest caved in by a bullet, the ranger spilled the information he was given.

Apparently, he and the others were previously briefed about a gang named Destiny's Call. A new group that was meant to meet up in this very city. Rocco's Library just happened to be on the list of places they were meant to check. That's why only four of them came over. If they knew that some of the members would actually be here, then they would've sent a lot more.

"Huh?! Other places to meet? **Some** of the members?" Asked Soren. "Okay, how bout we start with you writing those addresses down." He then looked over to Cypher. "I say we go meet our other 'friends'. There's bound to be something there for us, right? I don't suppose you ever got a name for that contractor did you?"

"Of course not." Cypher sighed. "I did what I was told and nothing more." Turning his head to the ranger, he questioned him. "Last one and you'll be on your way. Clearly you knew about us, there's no reason trained rangers should've been fearful of some startup gang. The others must be famous in some way too, who are they?"

It was at this point where the ranger hesitated to speak, seemingly more afraid of ratting out the other members than the city that they worked for. A completely illogical way of thinking, after all the man has no ties to these people. However, he'd eventually give in as he stared into Cypher's eyes – knowing that he'd spend his last moments in this dusty bookstore if he didn't.

"For starters, there's you two — soldiers from the 7th division of Mystcalls armed forces. Cypher, better known as Heartless Cypher and the Youngest Hero, Soren Prahl. Out of all the members you two are the most famous amongst the rangers — most of the department, myself included, idolized your victories during the war against Mastonov. Most memorable though was the valor earned in the mountain city, Yeleshi. I always dreamt of meeting you two, just never thought it'd be like this. . ."

Soren sighed while looking at him. "If it means anything, I really didn't do any of those crimes — except the stealing allegations, most of those are true. But can you blame me? Prices skyrocketed ever since we got back. As for the bodies though, I stumbled upon 'em. I swear on my mothers grave that I just have terrible luck." The young man then put a hand over his heart. Afterward he went over to the ranger Cypher had shot, using his own shirt he made a tourniquet and bandage for the man. Turning to his statuesque buddy, he did a 'gimme' gesture with his hand. "Hm?" Cypher uttered.

"C'mon man don't play stupid. The antidote, I know you have it on you." Soren knew this explanation was gonna be long as fuck. Cypher then rolled his eyes and tossed him a small glass vial. Popping the liquid into the wounded man's mouth, Soren looked over to the ranger.

"This'll keep him alive, he'll still need medical attention but he should last much longer now. Carry on." And so, with a bit of relief and suspicion, the ranger continued.

2.1 | The Knight

"The other soldier in the group is Uval Lotrensky, better known as the *Stagnite Brawler* from the 9th Division. He hails from a small village on the coast of Mastonav, but he defected once they showed how little they cared for his home. While working with Mystcall, Uval rose through the ranks and easily became an Ogre – with his massive frame there was no better job suited for him. But what made him truly remarkable on the battlefield was his unique ability, he could instantly weld materials to himself. I always heard stories of Uval mending his armor or giving it upgrades on a whim. And every time, it depicted him in the Southern theatre of the war where the last battle was fought."

As the ranger spoke, his words continued outward. Following his voice into the winding streets of Printon, we enter a busy cafe tucked away in an alley. Inside the Tasse Dor, several customers are seen frantically fleeing. Their heads turned back constantly to look at the four rangers that stood in front of the hulking figure. Uval had short hair and shaved sides with a striking mustache to boot. Atop his even mix of fat and muscle, the Ogre wore a large coat – but the thin fabric easily outlined the armor he had on beneath it.

"Hands behind your back, big guy. Don't make this harder than it has to be." One of the rangers said, approaching Uval with a set of handcuffs that clearly weren't going to fit him. Looking at the Ogre, it was hard to believe that he managed to get into this quaint establishment without breaking anything.

But in reaction to their request, Uval smiled without knowing much of what was going on. All he knew was that he was being threatened, nothing more and nothing less. He cleared his throat before speaking with a powerful bass.

"You think you are able to beat me? If not, I suggest to run – I am afraid this will not be painless." Despite the thick accent he had, Uval spoke clearly for someone from the countryside of Mastonav. And though one of them heeded his warning, abandoning the others and sprinting out of the cafe, the rest of the rangers stood their ground. Seeing their bravery sparked a flame in Uval's heart, this warmth passed through his body as his smile grew brighter. You could tell he was about to have fun. "Very well then." He said under breath. Grabbing the helmet on his waist, Uval placed it on his head and twisted it like a cap to a bottle. A puff of gas spewed out from the seam and his voice echoed out from the power armor. It was a bit muffled with radio static behind it.

"Hold! I do not want to harm my wonderful coat. Please allow me to take it off before we start." Uval put a hand out while speaking, as he did they could see the metal gauntlets he had on. A bit confused by what was happening, the rangers obliged and allowed him to place his coat onto a nearby chair. Unveiling what was beneath, he showed a custom made beauty. A gunmetal suit of power armor that fit him like a glove. Though most ogres rely on their armor to tank most of the damage that comes their way, Uval is a bit different. Instead of the usual clunky models, he's fitted with a 'slimmer' build – one fit for his fighting style. It was sleek in most areas, but very rigid in places he would block with. Arms, legs, even his chest had sections that were designed to do the opposite of deflecting blows – after all, Uval wanted each attack to stick to him.

"Now I am ready. Let us start the ritual of combat." Uval said as he paused for a moment, giving them ample time to prepare themselves. Despite the leeway they were given, Uval managed to charge forward before they could react. Swinging an arm at the closest ranger, they were sent through the front window. The other two panicked and opened fire upon him, their bullets ricocheting off his head as he put up his arms like a shield. Their lead began to combine into his vambraces while the Ogre slowly stomped forward. His gauntlets gradually grew larger as the rangers poured more bullets onto him, and when he was close enough Uval slammed his fists down like a hammer. His enemies stared up with wide eyes. One of the rangers managed to dodge out of the way while the other was crushed beneath his hands. A large crater formed in the mosaic tiling of the floor as the last ranger started to run away, exiting the cafe after seeing their friend get treated like an empty can of pop.

"Where are you going?" Uval said as he picked up a chair, tossing it at the guy and breaking it against his back. Once they dropped to the ground Uval deeply sighed and took off his helmet. "Oh! I should have asked this before we fought–" He said while looking down at the person in the crater. "But what am I in trouble for?"

Understandably so the ranger didn't reply, they were unbelievably deep in sleep. So in the silence Uval turned his head to notice an older lady getting up from behind the register. She peeked her head over sheepishly as she trembled like a wet dog. Walking to her, Uval looked back to all the damages he caused in the store. Placing a stack of cash in front of the woman, he says, "I am sorry for tha noise. Have a blessed day, ma'am." He then walked out of the cafe, looking down to a loose note while stepping over the ranger who was trying to run. Picking it up, he curiously read the addresses written on it.

"I wonder who else is here. Might as well see, my time in Mystcall has been boorish since tha war."

2.2 | The Rogue

"Then there's the least interesting of the bunch" Said the ranger as he looked at Soren and Cypher. "Nobody knows too much about the guy, honestly we kinda laughed once we figured out who he was. Apparently he's just some petty thief and a part-time con artist. He usually circulates in Vola, that damp kingdom and all their cities are his playground. But apparently he's been having some trouble getting used to Mystcall – especially Printon. Word has it, the so-called 'Greatest Showman' has already gotten himself thrown into one of our cells. I wouldn't even bother with him if I were you."

Suddenly, in the middle of him talking, the radiopack of the other rangers was turned on. A voice shot out through the speaker that hung over the unconscious man's head and everyone in the room turned to listen. Abruptly, a woman's voice called out for all rangers near Carstin Ave.

"I repeat! Calling all rangers nearby Cartsin Ave. Criminal, Orwin Trinket has escaped!"

Looking down upon the city, we can see Uval slowly making his way through the tight streets as he looks around confused. Passing him by, we arrive at a ranger station deep into the sunlike pattern of the city. The building stood tall at the end of the street. Black lamp posts lined the structure with its gentle swirls and curves. Then leading up to the station, mosaic stone tiles fill the sidewalks as old-timey automobiles occupy the streets – their engines purr as black smoke puffs out during their clicks and clacks.

The message from the radio then repeats again as it spews out of the speakers inside the station, the voice is muffled but becomes clear halfway through as the front doors burst open. Nearly forty rangers march out and onto the streets of Printon, each one with weapons in hand as they scan about. In the middle of the pack, two of the rangers look to one another and softly whisper – not wanting the others to know what they were saying. As they spoke, the large group began to split up into pairs.

"So, do *you* know what this guy looks like? I didn't pay attention to his part during the meeting – SUPER boring compared to the others ya know?" Said one of the rangers. He looked to the other while waiting for a response, donning an awkward smirk as the two of them searched an alley. "Well, you should've paid attention!" The other sarcastically demanded. "He may not have a crazy background like the rest of them, but I'm sure he has a winning personality!"

The first ranger shrugged. "Definitely a better one than the rest of those monsters and heroes, that's for sure!" They laughed as they spoke. "Can't believe we're even lookin for this guy. Probably would probably be easier for all of us if we let 'em go."

"I don't know about that, he might have something pretty cool up his sleeves. You never know! Could end up actually being a problem to us policemen!"

In the middle of the dark alley, the two of them suddenly stopped walking. Turning to one another as a tense, but an actually more awkward, stare down occurred. The first ranger looked to the other and questioned him. "Policemen? You transfer in from Vola? We don't call Rangers that." They then paused for a moment, not knowing what to do or how to respond – the other ranger then suddenly punched them in the nose. Taking off the ranger cap, he slicked his short sandy blonde hair back, exposing his bright emerald eyes.

"Sorry man, I'm just a tourist – calling your law enforcement rangers just ain't stickin." Orwin said while taking off the uniform, however in the middle of that process he realized that the ranger hadn't been fully knocked out. "Shit, sorry." Lifting up the rifle, The Showman slammed the gunstock against the man's head to fully put him to sleep.

"Hope you get some good rest though, rootin for ya buddy." He then crouched down, searching his pockets and finding a list of places on a piece of paper. "Can't believe I missed that meeting, now I don't know shit about these other guys. Man, I probably won't bother. I just need to find *him*."

Orwin then fully took off the uniform, sporting *most* of a three piece suit. He was missing the blazer and had the sleeves on his dress shirt rolled up. Looking around, he scratched his head before heading off to these 'other places'. "I should get me another cap, forgot that one of them policemen stole mine — rat bastard. I'll get that shit back. Just watch." He said while wagging his finger at the empty alley in front of him.

As he walks off, our view pans back out into the city as it swoops back over to the bookstore several streets away. The ranger tells Cypher and Soren about the other members and seems to hesitate for a moment before speaking, almost having to force the words up his throat and off of his tongue. "There's almost too much to say about this next fella. I'll keep it short and sweet if I can, but I'm sure you already know him."

2.3 | The Mage

"The Wandering Mage. He has platinum hair and golden eyes, always seen wearing a white robe that hugs his silhouette yet remains flowy. It's said he's often spotted from afar, standing atop a distant hill or faraway building. Every time he's just seen standing there, observing the world through his tinted glasses as he jots down notes with a pen and paper. Never does he touch either items, letting them float and write for him. *Huruk Rem*, the man who has no place of origin but a destination that no one knows. He travels the world in a pursuit of the arcane, and in that quest he's been known to do anything to reach his journey's end. Castles, criminal groups, even small battalions of several armies have been vanquished as they stood in his way – it's a bit hard to believe you guys even managed to get him on the team."

"We didn't." Cypher said. "If I had to assume for the others, we were all tricked into this little group – and with names this big, I doubt disbanding will smooth anything over." Thinking about it for a moment, Soren sighed and nodded his head. "We'll have to meet up with these guys. Figure it out from there."

Pushing out from the bookstore once more, the perspective soars over buildings to reach a huge Victorian clocktower. Standing on the metal spike at its highest point, Huruk looks upon the city. His gaze scans Printon as large shadows pass him by, shifting his head up he sees the belly of a manmade beast. Several blimps of various sizes glide upon the winds. Their extended layers of hinged wings flap and shift to guide them through the open air. In awe Huruk stares at them, not noticing the vast amount of rangers beneath him until they yell out with their speaker, gaining his attention. One of them, a young woman, pops her head out of a carriage like car and speaks into a handheld radio – her voice booms out from the vehicle and finally reaches him.

"Sir!" She said confidently. "You can't be up there! We're gonna need you to come down the way you came! If you're unable to do so, we'll send up some men to assist you – is that clear!?"

Huruk had a calm facial expression and a soothing glare within his sunrise eyes. Looking down to the rangers, there were around ten of them as more were soon to be called in. Understand that though they couldn't see him that well, a random man who peeked his head out from his hotel window did. About to hang up his laundry upon a thin line, this person suddenly looked up to see Huruk — yelling out immediately after with wide eyes. "IT'S HIM!" He screamed. "**THE WANDERING MAGE.**"

Immediately after, reinforcements were called in and the nature of the situation had drastically changed. The well mannered suited men became frantic as they sprinted away. Even the demure women in their large puffy dresses began to run. Every single person in eyesight of him had become madly frightened in a way that was odd, for it isn't the fear of death which scares them – but the ambiguity of what the Mage can and is willing to do. The rangers lifted their rifles to aim at him and the woman in the car yelled out. "HOLD YOUR FIRE DAMN IT, THERE ARE STILL CIVILIANS NEARBY!" However, their fear had gripped them too tightly. Their fingers wavered just off the trigger, and in that hesitation Huruk waved his hand and whispered something to himself. Reacting to this motion, all of the rangers excluding the woman shot their guns. A hailstorm of bullets began to shred the burgundy tiles that lined the roof of the belltower – slowly they even broke down the metal spike which the Mage stood on. As Huruk was shot at, every bullet which hit him carved a fist sized hole through his body – however, it seemed like the man had been made of smoke. As they shot more, Huruk was dispersed into nothingness.

Feeling as if they'd won, the rangers lowered their weapons and were taking it all in. They relished in the fact that they had felled the great mage. The only person who knew that wasn't the case was Aurelia, the unfortunate lieutenant of this group. As the others yelled out in false victory, she looked around with bated breath in an attempt to find him.

"WE DIDN'T WIN, YOU **IDIOTS**!" She screamed out at them, but they didn't listen. 'I knew they were stupid, but something doesn't feel right. . .' Aurelia thought to herself while sprinting out of her vehicle. As she ran away, a heartstring tugged at her to not abandon them. Skidding to a stop, she made her way back and grabbed the closest person. They didn't respond to her touch, so naturally Aurelia turned them around to make them look at her, but what she saw made her realize that wouldn't work. Their eyes were glazed over with a thin white mist, tinted by the facade of triumph.

Aurelia tried her best to wake them up, but neither shaking or hitting them worked. That's when suddenly she turned her head to see him, walking in the midst of the rangers without a worry in the world. "What the hell did you do to them!?" She asked while speaking through the crowd and in response, Huruk stopped to look at her. "I'm letting them believe they won."

"Why?" She asked with a bit of anger riling up in her voice. "Why are you still here?!" At that moment, Aurelia had a deep pit form in her stomach. Her line of thinking was 'if he immobilized my men this easily, he could've escaped already – so there must be a reason he's still here. And if he wants bloodshed, I'll have to fight. There's no chance I'll win though.'

Her eyes then wandered off to the left and right. She saw more rangers piled up in the nearby alleys, slowly approaching as they suddenly raised their guns – pointing into the crowd which Huruk stood in the middle of. "So that's why you're still here. . ." She said to him, then without saying a word he just nodded.

If the other rangers shot at Huruk there was no chance they wouldn't kill their own men. This forced the reinforcements to stay at a distance, outlining the street he stood on. In this standstill, Aurelia looked over and asked "So what now? How do you plan on getting outta here, *great mage*." She spoke while being a bit irritated, walking right up to Huruk and staring up into his eyes. "I can't stop you from casting a spell. But you should know, if your next magic trick doesn't involve *me* – I'll take the knife that's on my hip and jam it into your throat before you can whisper your little words again."

Seemingly taken aback by her unwillingness to back down, he responded simply. "Fine, have it your way." Waving his hand, Aurelia waited for something to occur. But nothing did. Taking out her knife, she held it to his neck. "What the hell did you do to me?" She asked.

Tilting his head, Huruk leaned forward – his nose almost touching hers. "Apparently nothing. You really are strong, aren't you? Say, what's your name?" Though she hesitated for a moment, she eventually gave him what he wanted.

"Aurelia." She cautiously stated while leaning away from him. "Can you back up please, I can smell the magic coming off of you."

"And what does that smell like?" He asked curiously, leaning in more as he took a step forward.

"It was a joke, but you do smell nice — like flowers I guess. . . and coffee. Anyways, I assume you won't let me put you in cuffs and I doubt I'd be able to subdue you. It's not wise to hold back when fighting somebody strong, I'd have to try and kill you if we fought – I don't really want that on my conscience right now so here's a deal. Since you haven't hurt anyone, technically, I'm gonna help you get outta here. That's the only way I can see this ending peacefully, I don't want my men to die for no reason."

Leaning back, Huruk took her up on the offer, asking how they'd go about such a plan. She then started to explain while looking around to see if the far off rangers could see what was going on. All they saw was the two of them abruptly beginning to fight. Aurelia swung her knife and attempted to jam it into his neck as she promised. However, it seemed Huruk was a bit more physically competent than he gave off – being able to ward off attacks from a trained combatant. Each time Aurelia stabbed or slashed at Huruk, he'd avoid the blade entirely or pushed forward to control the swinging arm. As he grabbed onto Aurelia, he managed to disarm the weapon and then grab the knife she dropped — holding it to her neck while grabbing onto her shoulder. The two of them began to walk out the golden eyed crowd of rangers, using Aurelia as a hostage and ticket out of the situation.

They approached a nearby alley and all the rangers were visibly hesitant to fire — knowing their bullets would tear through the unaware crowd behind them. With that the pair managed to make their way into a nearby alley as they were let through the line of reinforcements. However, they were suddenly stopped. Out of view, many of the rangers moved in to secure the safety of the ones who were bewitched – meanwhile, in front of Aurelia and Huruk stood the current chief of the Printon Rangers, Constable Leander. The grizzled man stood tall as his medals adorned his boulder-like shoulders. While he took a military-like stance with his hands held behind his back, Aurelia looked over to him relieved — realizing now that her father was here, they'd be able to take Huruk in without needing to sacrifice so many people.

She smiled while looking toward the group of rangers and Constable Leander, she then said "I'm glad you made it in time, I almost had to let this guy escape to save my men." Immediately after, without hesitating for even a moment – the constable ordered his men to fire, even with his own daughter in front of their guns. And though the rangers from earlier wavered and chose not to fire, these men were different — hand recruited and trained by her majesty's own royal guards. A wave of bullets came barreling down the alley, heading straight toward the two of them. Aurelia, clearly shocked, slowly lost her smile as Huruk waved his hand and whispered.

"Tesaso Irbum Unvas"

In Aurelia's point of view, everything slowed down as she had to bear witness to the bullets of betrayal sailing toward her. In these fleeting moments, the only thing that moved as normal were her own thoughts, so what would normally take a person an hour to mentally process took her a fraction of the smallest conceivable second. In those tiny moments, indescribable by numerical value, the world flickered between two places in her eyes. The first was the one alley she and Huruk were in, and the second was atop a building – one faraway from any of the dangers that pose against them. These two still images flickered back and forth, speeding up until it blurred into a single reality. In that moment where distortion became clear, everything went black as if the sun had disappeared. Once it reappeared in her vision, they were gone.

In the fraction of a second after Huruk waved his hand, the two of them disappeared and teleported several city blocks away. They now stood on a tall tower as sweat dripped from their heads. Huruk seemed to be fatigued from the magic he had casted and Aurelia was coming back to terms with reality, both with what she saw and what she felt. Dropping to her knees and hands, Aurelia heavily panted while staring at the ground. Slowly she lifted her gaze back toward the city, scrunching her brows as Huruk began to take his leave.

"I'm sorry that you had to hear that, but I hope it'll help you come to terms with your father." He said softly, trying to find the words to give comfort to her wounds. But no matter what he said, Aurelia wouldn't have responded. Her mind was completely on her father, it raced with questions but more than that — it had broken and rebuilt her resolve. Seeing that she wasn't going to say anything back, he whispered to himself and waved a hand – walking off the edge of the tower and floating down to the streets below.

Now sitting alone, her breathing slowed as she calmed. Standing up, Aurelia wiped the sweat from her forehead and looked down to the badge she had on her chest. With furrowed brows she ripped it off, tossing it to the ground and looking at her uniform next. "I don't know what the hell I'm gonna do now. . .but let's start with a new outfit." She then began to make her way down the stairwell. "He loves his duty more than his own daughter, he always has hasn't he? *sigh* I need a new outfit."

3.0 | The Search

With the grand stage set within Printon, all of the actors make their moves, each walking their own paths as they inevitably cross. "Hold the fuck up." Soren said, interrupting the next scene. He looked

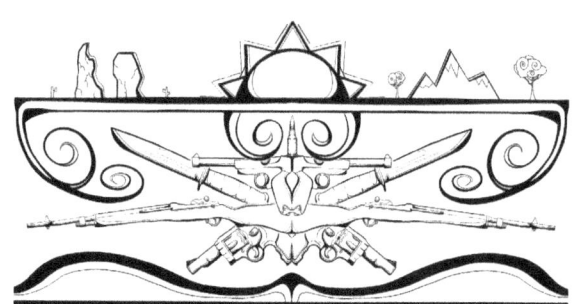

to Cypher and asked if any of those guys could've been the Contractor. Thinking about it for a moment as the two walked down the alley, away from the bookstore, he replied. "Possibly, I'd have to hear their voices to confirm if they are or not — otherwise there's no way for me to tell without meeting them. Knowing the Contractor, they'll try their best not to speak. They're cunning, hopefully to a fault."

"Then I guess that's where we'll start, finding each of these strangers and having a chat with them — surely it shouldn't be too hard right? We have a list of places, it'll be a cakewalk." Soren then began to eat his own words as the minutes passed by.

Getting to the first location, they found a bakery on one of the main streets – a tourist attraction with dozens of people exiting and entering with every passing second. Laz Pierro, a bright shop with pink walls and a comically large bakers hat above their lit sign. The both of them stared at the spotlight of a meetup place, knowing this was clearly not where they were supposed to meet. Showing a bit more emotion than usual, Cypher had the slightest frown as he snatched away the list of names from Soren. After reading it he looked at him with a disappointed glare, "This says *Pez Lienno*. How did you even mix these two places up. . ." After asking he followed it with a deep sigh. "Can you not read? How did you manage to read the letter from earlier?" Pushing his lips together, Soren looked to the left and right to avoid eye contact. Meanwhile, Cypher stared at him, waiting for an answer.

"Listen! Sometimes the letters just get jumbled around ya know?" Not giving Soren any breaks, Cypher immediately interrupts.

"No. I don't understand. Fix your brain, idiot. It's a miracle that you tricked the examiners." Groaning as if in pain, Soren roughed up his own hair in frustration. Cypher ignored him as he did so.

"It's not that simple! My bad though, I thought I could do it. But hey! At least we know of a good place to buy cupcakes right?"

Not even entertaining him for a moment, Cypher slowly turned on his heels and walked away. Jogging for a second to catch up, Soren looked at him and went, "So, that letter really wasn't a marriage proposal was it?"

He was then smacked on the head with the rolled up list of places.

3.1 | The Rogue and his vanity

We find Orwin stumbling into a fancy store, mannequins line the front window as they are adorned with elegant suits — the fabric they use are posted up on the interior walls by the roll. All the patterns mix together to become a colorful and almost over stimulating room. Turning to look at everything, he smiled and waved over to one of the well dressed staff members. "Bit too much to look at." He chuckled. "Could you point me over to y'all caps?" Speedily walking over to Orwin, the older gentleman greeted him and returned the smile. "Indeed we do! If you'll follow me I'd be happy to guide you to them." And so he did, following the man toward the back of the store as an array of hats awaited him there. Orwin then began to happily roam through the selection, at least at first — he slowly got more and more upset once he remembered the hat that had been stolen from him.

"None of these are like my baby. . . *sigh* maybe I just gotta go and find that bastard. Gotta break them fingers when I get to you."

His angry eyes slowly faded to sad and pouty as he lazily looked about. Suddenly he looked over to the changing room as the staff worker made his way through its velvet curtains. After some short exchanges, Aurelia walked out of it with a new suit tailored to her figure. The suit retained a masculine silhouette while fitting snug to her waist, additionally it was a three piece with a long flowing tailcoat that hovered over her rear like twintails. With colors of burgundy and gold to align with her dark brown hair and eyes, she looked around before going over to pay the owner of the store.

Orwin's eyes opened like a deer in headlights, watching her go over to the register as he held onto a random hat. "Fuck." He whispered to himself. See, the large group that Orwin was a part of when he was pretending to be a ranger was actually led by Aurelia – that's why he knows exactly who she is. Snapping out of it, Orwin quickly turned all the way around and placed the hat on himself, calling over the older gentlemen afterward. "Yes? Need help with anythi-" Interrupting the man, Orwin spoke hurriedly. "I'll take it."

The worker stood there a bit confused, staring at the floral patterned hat and the striped pants he had on — not to even mention the clashing color palette that he saw. "Are you sure you're satisfied with this hat, good sir?" He asked. "I can help you pick another out if you'd like! I'd be delighted even!" It was obvious that he was just trying to make Orwin not commit a fashion sin. Sweating a bit, he just agreed – keeping his back turned to Aurelia at all times during this process. "Yeah, yeah. Just uh- make it quick will ya?" He said nervously, his eyes constantly looking to the left and right to see if he had to turn away more. However, sadly for him – Aurelia already saw him. She was just paying for her outfit first.

"Ooo! I think this striped bowler hat would go perfect with your current clothes. What do you think, sir?" The staff member asked Orwin. In an attempt to get this over with as fast as possible while still looking good, he took the hat and placed it on his head. Turning quickly to a nearby standing mirror, Orwin took a glance at himself and got distracted — smiling as he looked surprised to see how good it looked on him. "My good man, you have outdone yourself this day." Still looking at the mirror, Orwin asked how much it was, and responding instead was a woman's voice as Aurelia stood behind him. "The price tag says 150 ren, but it'll cost you nothin if you plan on running out of here with it — Mr.Trinket."

He didn't dare to turn around in case that provoked her, instead he continued the conversation while looking at her in the mirror. "Of course not, ma'am. I would never do such a crude thing." As he spoke, the anxiety he had was immediately buried by a masked confidence. Even the slight accent Orwin had faded. "If you'll allow me to do so, I was *just* about to pay the man." He said while hovering his hand over his pocket. At the same time Orwin stared at her doing the same thing, but there was very clearly a handgun in hers.

Aurelia then nodded, giving him permission to reach into his pocket without her shooting him in the back. Taking out a large amount of rolled up bills, he licked a finger and took out two one hundred rens — holding it out for the staff member to take. As they did, Orwin spoke aloud. "Going shopping while on duty, Lieutenant Leander?"

"Do you see me in my uniform?" She said mockingly. "I don't represent the badge any longer."

"Sorry — is that a term for quitting? Did you retire from being a policeman?" Orwin said, looking genuinely confused — even turning around to look at her as he responded.

"It's complicated. I just know that as of right now, I won't be working with them." Aurelia said while letting her gaze lower for a moment. Seeing her eyes drop down to the ground, and realizing that she can't legally bring him in, Orwin took off running.

"AYE! COME BACK HERE." She yelled while trying to take out her pistol, however the front sight of the gun got hooked onto the inner lining of her pocket — preventing her from stopping Orwin as he ran out the store. "I should've kept the holster at least. . ." Aurelia begrudgingly whispered as she chased after him.

The two of them sprinted down one of the main streets. Weaving in and out the crowds of people, Orwin was constantly looking back to see if she was keeping up — and she was. In an attempt to shake her off, he sprinted through the street. Grabbing the top of a car, he swung himself through its interior — narrowly missing the woman that was in it. Running forward, he jumped onto a hood and then to a roof, treating the hazardous busy street like a jungle gym. Reaching its end, Orwin leapt upward and grabbed onto the railing of a balcony. While he scaled the building, Aurelia simply ran across while flashing her gun like a badge. Just like that, she had a clear runway.

"CAN YOU STOP!" She yelled up at Orwin. "I JUST WANNA TALK, DON'T MAKE ME SHOOT YOU TO SLOW YOUR ASS DOWN." Aiming up at him, she was able to secure a clear shot as he climbed to the rooftop. Sighing to herself, she didn't take the shot and started to sprint the same direction he was going, quickly running up a set up stairs tucked in an alley. As she ran down the cobbled back streets, the shadow of Orwin casted down in front of her as he sprinted atop the rooftops. Knowing that she wouldn't be able to catch up, she yelled out again. "I WANNA MEET YOU AND THE REST OF THEM!" Confused by her words, Orwin yelled back.

"WHAT?! WHY THE HELL WOULD YOU WANNA DO THAT? WE'RE ALL CRIMINALS AREN'T WE?"

"WELL, IT'S NOT LIKE I CAN ARREST Y'ALL — C'MON, JUST STOP RUNNING! THE ONLY ONE THEY WANT ANYWAY IS YOUR LEADER!"

Confused, Orwin stopped to ask a question. "What? I thought he was captured already. Is- is that not the case?" Aurelia finally caught her breath as she looked up at him. "It's complicated. . .we don't know how his powers work. But yes, he's still in custody."

"Huh?! How did he even set up this group then? Don't tell me you guys gave the man his phone call." Orwin was visibly upset by the revelation.

"We think he has a way to escape on his own, there's been sightings of him across Mystcall but every night he's in our cells. It doesn't make sense, but why don't you know any of this shit, aren't you part of the Abbot's group?"

"Listen, I've never even met these guys. But I have met *him* once, I thought I could meet him here but apparently that's not the case." Orwin said while slowly climbing down. "So I guess I wanna meet them too. The other people that got wrapped up in all of this must be interesting. At least enough to gain the Abbot's attention."

Looking at him walking toward her, Aurelia says "Not afraid I'm gonna arrest you anymore?" She was clearly winded, leaning forward onto her knees as sweat dripped from her face. Laughing a bit, Orwin replied. "You serious?" He chuckled. "No. Clearly you don't wanna shoot me, and you damn well ain't catchin me — oh and for future reference, wear something a lil loose fitting when you chase somebody. It helps with the climbing." After a mixture of a scoff and chuckle, she replied "Yeah, I'll keep that in mind next time."

The two of them would find a nearby place to sit, lounging upon crates while talking with one another. They surprisingly got along well considering what they both used to do. A renowned thief and a well known ranger, talking about finding a group of other strange individuals. Then, just like all the others, they figured they'd go after the list of places. As their conversation continued, a group of rangers began to patrol the streets beside them. Orwin immediately ducked behind a corner as Aurelia, not accustomed to avoiding law enforcement, stood there like nothing was happening. "The fuck are you doin, Lia?" He whispered over while pulling her behind the corner. "Ain't your daddy tryna kill you? He probably don't like loose ends, and in his eyes you might still need some snipping. Get your head in the game, you gotta start playing differently."

Realizing her mistake she apologizes. "Sorry, I'm not used to *your* kind of life. This is all just **very** new to me. . ."

"I was gonna get offended with how you said 'your', but actually that's pretty fair." Orwin then peeked around the corner, staring at the rangers that passed them by — and despite being several car lengths away, he could read the pieces of paper they had in their swinging hands. Orwin saw that they had already marked off several places on the list — shortening the locations that Aurelia and him had to go to. Closely following, they could hear them talking as one of them shouted out to the others.

"UVAL THE OGRE IS RAMPAGING AT THE PEZ LIENNO RESTAURANT, SPLIT UP AND START MAKING YOUR WAY OVER — I WANT THE **ENTIRE** STREET SURROUNDED!" As the officer yelled out his commands, all the rangers shifted from a march to a sprint — their thunderous steps overtook the noises of the bustling city. Loud banter between mates, even the purrs and roars of engines were drowned out. Looking to one another, Orwin and Aurelia knew where they needed to go.

"Well, I guess we'll have to beat them there." Said Aurelia.

"Just try and keep up this time." Orwin said jokingly.

3.2 | Troubled Deals for Troubled Deeds

The sound of splintering wood and shattering stone blasts out from a shopping district. As the sun lowers to give way to the moon, its fading light scatters across the rooftops, interlacing itself through alleys and streets just to reach the broken windows of a noisy restaurant. Casting its

radiance upon the shards of glass, in the reflection we can see Uval as he thrashes about, fighting rangers to his left and right with his mighty armor. He suddenly yells aloud. "**MORE!**" His bellowing voice was akin to a war drum, the type of noise that resounded in your chest and ears. All consuming in its wake. Grabbing a ranger with a single arm, he lifted them up and tossed them at those who shot at him — their bullets crashed into his armor and mended its damages.

"I'VE MISSED THIS SOUND! THE NOISE WHICH SHAKES THE BED OF THE GODS!" Stomping into the ground, Uval crushed the tiles beneath him as he rushed forward like a bull — breaking the formation they had as he sprinted out into the streets. Nearly a dozen men flew away as if hit by an explosion, landing in nearby walls and vehicles as Uval continued forward — rushing toward the line of rangers that surrounded the entire street. The wind strangely began to pick up as a wall of gunfire surrounded him. With so many guns, Uval was stopped from going forward. Instead he was forced to put up his arms to protect himself as the bullets started to take chunks off of his armor. Sparks and ricocheted gunfire bounced off of his metal exterior. In these holes, some lucky fragmented bullets pierced his skin. Blood poured and they shot more and more, but those who had to reload backed up as a replacement line approached. This way they were able to constantly keep pressure on the beast of a man.

He then yelled out with a hearty laugh, it was obvious that he was having the time of his life. "IT HAS BEEN AGES SINCE DEATH'S HAND HAS REACHED FOR ME. YOU'VE BLESSED ME WITH COMFORT!" Uval then ran to his left, jumping up and landing flat on a random car that was nearby. Welding it to himself, he made a temporary replacement to his armor. Rushing forward once more, Uval would continue to slam into random metal objects. Cars, streetlights, benches, even fire hydrants were not spared in his pursuit for battle. As they chipped his metal flesh, he added more. Eventually this led him closer toward the line of rangers, seeing this however, they backed up. But Uval had anticipated this, the next car he approached did not become one with his armor. Rather, he used it like a projectile. Launching it toward the fleeing rangers and throwing them into disarray. With their formation temporarily stopped, Uval had space to finally breathe. In these moments where the lieutenants failed to command their men, Uval would use this small opening to wreak havoc.

Viewing the scene from a distance, you'd be able to see the nearby buildings crumble as gunfire randomly shot out like fireworks. In this chaos, Uval screamed out.

"I WAS PROMISED MY ARMOR — *WHERE IS IT!*" Watching all of this occur a couple of blocks away, Orwin and Aurelia looked to one another — questioning if they should even go over there.

"You sure this is the guy?" Orwin said while taking several short glances back and forth. "Who the hell else would be *The Ogre?* Stop being a pussy, let's go." As Aurelia dropped down from the rooftop they were on, Orwin deeply sighed before following. "You got real comfortable real fast, huh?"

The two then ran down staircased alleys, rapidly approaching the muffled thunderous booms that echoed out. As they turned one final corner, the noises became awfully clear. Staring down the open street, Uval bursted through a wall, grabbing a man and tossing him like a shot put. They crashed into the second floor of a building as Uval turned to Orwin and Aurelia, at this point the rangers had been taken out — a group of nearly fifty of them, rendered useless by a single man.

"You should not be here. It is a battlefield." Uval says to them as a rickety street light falls to the ground. The crashing of it makes him realize how silent it is. "Well, there *was* a battle here but I think you get it. Carry on with your shopping, I am sorry for tha mess."

"Actually. . ." Orwin hesitantly says as he begins to walk toward the large man. "I came here to meet *you*, big guy. This lady too. Names Orwin, can I safely assume you're Uval the Ogre?"

In a sad way, Uval's shoulders lowered as he looked down to the ground. Sitting on a broken fragment of a building, he stares up to the fading sky as it shifts to black. "I am no Ogre without my armor." He despondently says, clearly losing the fire that was in him during the fight. Walking up to him, Orwin sat to his side and laid a hand up to his shoulder.

"Is that what the Abbot promised you?" In response, Uval nodded his head while holding a winged badge made of gold. "I'm coming to think that he can't give us what he promised, but there *might* be some truth to those empty deals. I can feel it in the air, the person I'm looking for — she's here. So maybe your armor is too, we'll just have to look for it. There's no doubt in my mind that we've been tricked into this, that's been apparent since I took that first job in Luminel. But that doesn't mean we can't make the most out of what we've got. And not to say anything bad about it, why do you want this armor of yours so bad anyway?"

Looking down to his medal, Uval sighed. "It was what I used in tha war, but that alone does not make it special. Tha mechanic that took me in during my transfer was the only man that treated me like an ally, the rest only saw me as Mastonov scum. He's the one who made me that armor, I very much need it back. It made me who I was before, strong. And if you'll help, I can help you find this lady friend you look for — I happen to be quite the romantic." Towards the end of his ramble, Uval smiled a bit. Throwing his large arm over Orwin's shoulder as he responded with a groaned voice. He now had the weight of a young adult on his back.

"A romantic? I'm looking forward to workin with you then." He said with a smirk "Oh! By the way, do you mind if I call you Val? I have a thing with shortening people's names." Chuckling a bit, Uval patted him on the back. The force of it was enough to make a man cough up his breakfast.

"I don't mind at all, my friend."

3.3 | The Good, then The Bad

As Orwin introduces Aurelia to Uval, the three of them begin to have a rather heartwarming conversation — just speaking on random things about their lives as they walk away. Panning out and going up toward the clouds, we look down to see them going deeper into the city as more rangers approach the Pez Lienno. Accompanying the huge group of nearly one hundred, there are armored vehicles with large barrels attached to their tops, appearing like smaller tanks. Leading this group would be none other than Constable Leander. Using the radio transmissions from the battle, the constable would gather the necessary information and supplies needed to take down the Ogre. So as the rangers approached, they were prepared to end this.

Meanwhile, a couple of streets away from all the commotion, Cypher and Soren race to where all the noise came from, but at this point everything had long died down. However, that didn't stop them from at least trying — this was the only lead they'd had all day.

"You think he's still there?!" Soren asked as they ran, struggling to speak while trying to catch up with the dying commotion. "Who?" Cypher asked. In his mind the obvious hadn't connected since there was no information in front of his eyes. Confused by his confusion, Soren said something along the line of - "Huh?! What the hell are you talking about, it's OBVIOUSLY UVAL!" But what he actually said was more like gibberish, almost utterly incoherent except for the emotion and hand gestures he 'graciously' exaggerated. Despite that, Cypher somehow understood, likely from how long they'd known one another. "I see. Then I doubt he's still there. The rangers taking him down with an impromptu force simply isn't on the table. Seeing that it's quiet now probably means someone else from Destiny's Call got to him first. We should've been faster."

Soren then said that they should stick to recon then, "No point in dirtying our hands if there's no gold to grab. How bout we head up to a rooftop? Get a good vantage point and see what's going on — could be good intel on where the others are going and what this city has in store for us in the future. I've heard about the Constable of Printon, he's a nasty fellow. Used to be in the military just like us, but he climbed the ranks before the war happened and ended up being a royal guard for a bit. So he's here now, craving the battles that he missed. He also hates my guts. . . actually, can we just go to a hotel or something? Now that I'm thinking about it-"

As they climbed onto the roof, they saw a person already standing atop it. They stared across the ruins of Uval's battle, even tracking those three as they made their way further into the city. Turning back to Cypher and Soren, Huruk looked a bit surprised to see them.

Almost immediately the two soldiers stopped talking, looking over to the magic looking fellow fully knowing he was the wandering mage. Glancing back to one another, there was a silent exchange of words. They agreed to not shoot or attack the man until he seemed hesitant to speak. Testing if he would or not, Soren asked Huruk a question.

"So uh- how's your day been?" Soren said with a meager voice, he had no idea what to actually ask. Then, as Huruk stared at him confused, mere seconds passed in silence before Cypher raised his rifle as if it had no weight at all. Firing before Huruk could even react, his eyes lowered and turned to his shoulder as blood spurted out from it. Immediately after getting shot, he waved his hand and whispered something. The prussian blue tiling of the roof then lifted individually and created a wall in front of him, blocking the four bullets that Cypher had left before reloading.

"I THOUGHT WE WERE GONNA KNOCK HIM OUT OR SOMETHING, NOT **SHOOT** HIM!" Soren yelled at Cypher, clearly confused about the silent exchange they had. Meanwhile, not hesitating for a moment, Cypher ran forward as he stowed his rifle and took out his pistol — responding back to Soren without losing focus. "I left him his head for a reason."

The rest of the tiling then suddenly tilted at an aggressive angle, causing the both of them to start sliding off the roof. As they dealt with that, Huruk jumped down to the streets on the opposite side of the wall he created. While falling, he felt the arm he got shot in go numb. Feeling the numbness travel to his chest, he knew a normal bullet couldn't have caused the effect that he's feeling. 'This is poison' Huruk realized.

Landing on the street, it was mostly empty from the havoc that Uval had caused — so in the emptiness he could hear Cypher and Soren land. Turning his head, just up a set of stairs the two of them landed safely. They then took off in Huruk's direction, Cypher lifting his pistol and shooting several times as Soren caught up and pulled his hand down. "RELAX!" He yelled out, trying to calm the emotionally void looking man. While being chased down the street, Huruk scanned through hundreds of memorized spells in search of something he'd be able to use. His current dilemma was that he was far too tired to use the ones that he would normally rely on, teleporting Aurelia and himself had been far more taxing than he anticipated. Now with this poison running rampant in his body, anything that required his concentration was out of the question.

'What does that leave me with?' He thought to himself.

Yanking his own arm away from Soren, Cypher continued the chase while swiftly reloading. As he did, Huruk waved his good hand and whispered something. He then suddenly came to a sliding stop while turning to face them. Pulling back his arm, a glossy white pearl appeared on his palm. Thinking it was a harmful attack, Soren and Cyper frantically split apart, sprinting to opposite sides of the street and diving into separate buildings. As they did, Huruk released his spell as a thick white smoke blasted out. Using it to obscure their vision, he continued to run. Ducking into an alley and heading toward the rest of Destiny's Call.

Running back out into the smoke covered street Soren looked around confused. Calling out for Cypher to see if he was in here too. Not hearing a response, he deeply sighed before hearing the sound of a hundred footsteps approaching him. Turning his head he could see a crowd of silhouettes in the smoke, and behind them rolled an armored vehicle — its barrel already pointing down at him. "Shit. . ." Soren said while putting his hands up.

Back in the alleyway which Huruk ran down, a handgun suddenly emerged from a corner in front of him. Coming to a stop, he turned to see Cypher walking out while aiming at his head. "You were already sweating before we got up there. You must be tired. . . I heard a rumor that it's hard for mages to use their tricks when they're fatigued. Humor me, try one now." Cypher said with a cold expression, waiting for him to make a move.

During this standstill, Huruk knew of a couple spells that didn't need a somatic component. Meaning he could cast one without waving his hand — only his verbal whispers would be needed. But the ones Huruk knew wouldn't work in this situation, he was too far. So the Mage waited in these silent moments, hoping he wouldn't just be shot and that he'd be able to surprise him. Sweat dripped from his brows but he kept his composure, on the other hand Cypher seemed unnaturally still. When he's described as a statue it truly isn't too far off, you could barely even see his chest move as he breathed — it was almost like he wasn't even alive to begin with. But as Huruk saw the man blink, that's when he did it. Lifting his hand he waved but quickly realized that Cypher was still one step ahead. Throwing a knife with his eyes closed, the blade flew into Huruk's palm, stopping him from finishing it. Cypher then sprinted forward with a hunter-like focus, pushing his forearm against Huruk's neck as he placed the barrel of his gun to the side of his head. Slamming him into a wall, he stared into his eyes and said a single word. "Speak."

Obliging him, Huruk did just that. "*Extav Inti.*" His skin began to glow from within, turning himself a vibrant sunset color to match the fading light in the sky. As the illuminance shone before Cypher's eyes, he realized that this wasn't the Contractor. "Shit." He said as the explosion went off.

The thunderous boom cracked out into the air, sending a shiver down everyone who could hear it. However, it was more loud than dangerous. As the dust settled, Cypher got up from the wall he'd been thrown into and looked awfully confused. 'That hurt-' he thought to himself. 'But other than minor bruising and some internal injuries, I'm alive.'

Walking over to Huruk, who struggled to stand due to everything that's happened, Cypher stood in front of him. "The only reason I didn't shoot you was because I thought our fates were sealed. But you're still in one piece and so am I. Did you account for how little energy you had left? If so, congrats — your thought out gamble or ignorant pride lucked out. Here's your reward." Reaching under his army jacket, Cypher threw Huruk a small glass vial. "Drink up, I need you alive. That'll nullify the poison, so hurry up while you still have motor functions. The heart is always the last to go."

Biting down onto the sealed tip, the Mage spat out the glass — drinking the concoction right after. Trying to get up and failing, he then looked over to Cypher and said, "I can't walk. You'll have to help me." And though Cypher felt like it would be easier to just kill him at this point, he helped Huruk up. "You're lucky you do magic." He said while acting as his crutch. "The least you can do is lend me your shoulder, you shot me in mine." Huruk responded.

The two would continue forward in mostly silence, only speaking once Cypher randomly brought something up. But before that happens, our view pans out to look at Soren. He stood in front of nearly a hundred rangers and several armored vehicles. Walking forth from the smoke, Constable Leander approached first. Greeting Soren with anger in his eyes.

"The Youngest Hero. . ." He said with a mixture of hidden jealousy and pure scorn. These feelings were masked behind his commanding voice and proper way of speaking. "You faked your age to get into the ranks of the Mystcall army — a noble effort indeed, many looked to you as a symbol of honor. Especially through your deeds and victories, young man. You were truly what we needed for the war, **inspiration**. But I've heard that you've been having your fair share of fun since then. Three murders, each with you at its crime scene. Though there aren't any witnesses to prove you've done them, there's plenty of other evidence that claims such a thing. *How do you plead?"*

Keeping his hands up high so no one had the excuse to shoot him, Soren replied without moving a muscle — though, his face was expressive enough to show what he wanted.

"Last time I checked, **sir** — you aren't a judge. But don't get me wrong, I plead innocent. I just happen to have the worst luck imaginable. Promise."

"Your best excuse is that it's **luck**? You truly do act your age don't you, Soren? *sigh* No matter, I'll have you escorted to our finest cells — only the best for a big name like yourself. And fear not, *Youngest Hero*, your friends will be joining you soon. "

A couple of rangers put Soren into handcuffs, while being walked away he thought of something to ask the Constable.

"Oh! By the way, what crime did we commit to have all of Printon on high alert? I find it hard to believe that you simply just hate me that much. You got WAY too much honor to let your pride control you."

Hearing him, Constable Leander turned and raised a brow. Lowering it, his confusion turned to a hearty laughter. "*Printon*? You and the rest of Destiny's Call have the entire **country** coming after you. After all, you stole her majesty's prized possession. *The Linking Chalice*."

Soren was then taken away, utterly baffled by what he heard. As he sat in one of the armored vehicles that they used to transfer him to jail, he whispered to himself. "What the fuck is a linking chalice?" He paused to think more. "What the fuck is a chalice?"

4.0 | Nightfall.

The Archer and Mage made their way farther from the sound of rangers. During this Cypher suddenly broke the silence between them. This question had been lingering in his mind. "Those strange visions, 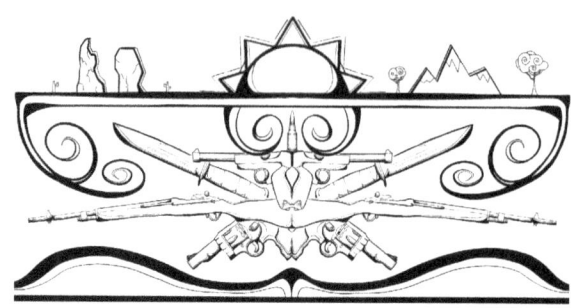 the ones that happened right after those weird words you said. Was that because of you? And if it was, *did you see what I saw?"* The way he spoke was odd, though he lacked emotion as he usually did, you could hear a hint of fear and anger coming from him. If Huruk answered wrong, Cypher would go against the logic which he lived by. He'd no doubt kill him.

"No. It wasn't me." Huruk said. "The language I use for the spells is Ancient Tongue, it's very powerful. Just hearing its words will put a burden onto your psyche, its effects are often random — the same can be said about what you see. But there's a single through line, you'll always know what the visions are trying to tell you. It's hauntingly apparent."

"So that's why you whisper. I thought it was to hide your hand, but you're really just putting away a weapon.."

"Yes. I only ever let others hear those words when there's no other choice. I've forbidden myself from using it as a weapon, as my teachers have instructed. It will only ever remain as an unfortunate side effect of my craft."

The conversation paused for a bit. The two could hear the approaching steps of rangers. So focusing on escaping, they managed to swiftly get away. Continuing the conversation once they were safe again.

"Do you get those visions every time you use your spells?" Cypher asked, feeling a bit remorseful for the mage.

"No, I don't think I'd be able to proficiently use my spells if that were the case. It only happens when you hear each word for the first time, the visions worsen with how many your brain intakes at once. But learning what they *mean* is far worse. I've spent several days and nights struggling to comprehend a single sentence. Rummaging through cultures and books for a mere phrase. But I have spent far longer **recovering** from when I succeed."

"Tell me, just how many words do you know?" Cypher said with curiosity.

Pausing for a moment, Huruk stared up at the stars, giving a moment of silence before speaking. "It would be far easier to recount every breath I've taken today, perhaps even this year."

Following their conversation came another wave of silence, the movement of the rangers alerted them once more — forcing them to focus on evading them again. Continuing forward, the two worked together to try and escape. Though Cypher didn't know the city very well, he knew how an experienced force this large would operate. With him leading, they ran through tiny gaps between buildings as lights swept through passing streets. They climbed up copper pipes as rangers ran underneath them. And they ducked into sewer grates, waiting for the rumbling wheels of their vehicles to pass. Each time Cypher made sure to stay on the move, always doubling back into places they've already checked in order to evade them. A 'one step back, two steps forward' kind of approach. However, Cypher's lack of experience in Printon would eventually stifle this procedure he'd made.

Finding themselves trapped in an alley with no exit high or low, they turned to see approaching lanterns in the white fog of the night. Not wanting to leave Huruk behind, Cypher knew there was no way for them to escape, thus, he reloaded his gun. Planning to kill whoever was leading this band of enforcers, he aimed forward. Taking a deep breath in, Cypher waited for a clear shot. A wooden door to their left suddenly unlocked and opened. From it reached two large arms which grabbed both of them. Pulled into a quaint home, Cypher and Huruk looked around the living room they stood in, both completely bewildered. Staring down at them, Uval stood tall as three other people were in the modest kitchen behind him. Aurelia and Orwin both were talking, politely trying to refuse food from the older woman that wandered about with a tray in her hands. The lively grandma then looked over to the new strangers in her home, smiling a bit brighter before speaking. "Uval, let the gentlemen in — I'm sure they're hungry." She said with a soft voice.

The group then sat together at the dining table. A single incandescent lantern above them slowly swayed as all of them talked to one another. At first, Cypher and Huruk were very standoffish, not wanting to speak since they still didn't understand what was happening. The two of them just accepted the medical aid they provided and nothing more. But as Orwin and Uval talked, Cypher knew they couldn't be the Contractor. This allowed him to open up a bit more, especially after eating the nostalgic lasagna that the grandmother placed on the table. As for Huruk, his eyes often found themselves looking at Aurelia. He wondered if she was alright. With everything with her father and the words he had to let her hear, Huruk thought that she may have broken. But as she smiled and laughed with the others as they went on about their past, he realized that she was fine. A slight grin appeared on his face and he then slowly integrated himself into the conversation as they happily welcomed him.

"Wait. . ." Orwin says as he counts the Destiny's Call members at the table. "One, two, three, four. . . aren't we missing somebody?" He said with an eyebrow raised. Realizing the same thing, Uval added on. "Grandmother Leander, who did you say we were missing?"

"Hun, for the last time we're missing Soren. That young man is somewhere in this city, that's for sure. My son wouldn't be so stir crazy for nobody else."

Being a couple of drinks in and trying to catch up to the others, it took Cypher a long time to remember what he saw back during his chase with Huruk. With a statuesque face, he goes, "Oh yeah. He got arrested." Immediately after, the rest of the people at the table looked appalled that he didn't say anything sooner. "My bad." He says once seeing everybody's reaction.

4.1 | The Loathing Heart beats in Hatred

A mound of copper sand bursts open in the Dratari desert. Getting up in a feral and hazed state, bounty hunter Dario grabs the shoulder he'd been shot in. Without it being tended to, the bleeding had somehow stopped and the poison nullified. The wound was already scarred over. Scratching it, his face twisted in anger as he began to run forward. While sprinting, the rails to his right began to shake on their own. Looking back he heard the rhythmic thumping sound of a train as it rapidly approached. Gritting his teeth, Dario ran like a madman as he screamed out for Soren. "THIS ISN'T OVER, 'HERO'. YOU OWE ME AN EXPLANATION, YOU FAKE!!" His voice echoed out, it curdled with rage as his heart began to pump harder. The beating of it was like an engine with far too much coal in its furnace. And as the train passed him by, Dario jumped up and landed between the carts.

Leaning off the train as he held onto a metal bar with one arm, his eyes stared forward as tiny specks of light glimmered in them. Reflecting upon his gaze, Printon and its city lights could be seen on the horizon.

"I don't care what the world thinks of you. My brother promised me he'd come back from the war. None of this makes sense. . .**you** should've died. Not him." Dario the Hunter whispered.

Under Rainy Clouds

1.0 | The Hour Glass Tilts

An entire week would pass before Destiny's Call would make a move. They spent most of this time planning a way to break Soren out of Granite Gate, a temporary holding ground for prisoners who'll be moved to the main prison. And by any means, they'd do their best to avoid having him sent to the Damned Heights. It's a ruthless place with a single rule that solidifies its name — after a year of being kept in their cells, no matter your sentence nor charges, you **will** be executed. There have been many escape attempts and some were even successful, but only ever pulled off by those with enough resources to spend — mob bosses and people of that status. Thus, while these big names try to break out before their due date, chaos ensues year round in this forsaken prison tucked in the ocean.

"If Soren ends up there, ain't no savin him." Orwin says, explaining the Damned Heights to the other members. Looking at one another, each one had varied opinions on the mission ahead. Some were hesitant to join while others were enthusiastic. But the one thing that held them together was their anger for the Contractor, better known to the rest of them as the Abbot. Cypher then explained how terrible Soren's luck is — they considered it notable since the man bound to logic was the one who brought it up. This unnatural phenomenon even intrigued the likes of Huruk. After hearing the unfortunate track record Soren had been having, the Mage seemed to lean in — pondering if it was the works of magic which hindered him. Regardless, he had to know.

As for Orwin and Uval, they were fully willing to join Cypher in his quest to free Soren. Seeing it as extra help with their own missions. But oddly, for those two it slowly became a bit more than just getting him. They felt good about this group, a feeling that wasn't necessarily shared with everyone. One of them yearned for a bond that they lost in their homeland, where the other missed the friend he'd lost in the war. Without them having to say it aloud, they felt as if they could finally fill the gap that was left those years ago.

However, Aurelia wasn't technically on the team. She'd been a ranger until a couple of days prior to the meeting. Yet she somehow found herself working alongside a band of criminals, sharing laughs and stories. This feeling was utterly new to her, something that she'd never experienced in her time as a ranger — especially not from her father. He was a stubborn man who did his job as a parent, but nothing more. Not raising Aurelia with personality but efficiency, creating the soldier that he never had the chance to become. Raising her glass to the others, she salutes sloppily with a smile. "I don't give a damn what y'all say, I'm joining." Scanning the group, she looks over to Uval and Orwin as they laugh.

"I do not hear any objections." Uval says as he stands.

"Shit. Neither do I-" Orwin follows as he takes a sip from his drink. "Guess that settles it then. Let's save this hero, I've been dying to meet him anyhow. I hope he's as fun as you say he is, Cypher."

Replying to him, Cypher raises a brow. "I don't remember using the word *fun*. But I certainly did call him stupid. Admittedly though, his presence can be a little helpful."

"See!" Orwin excitedly says. "You just said he was fun!" And with lowered brows and a grumpy look, Cypher immediately corrects him. "Not what I said. **At all.**"

The group would then gather their stuff when the week ended. Using Aurelia's knowledge of the rangers, they staked out on a large tower overlooking the route that Soren would travel via caravan. With that, they waited for their moment to strike.

1.1 | Bonds in memory & making

The air was turbulent this morning, especially around the massive clock tower which Cypher stood in. Leaning against a wall, he peered through an open panel of the clock's face, staring down below to the winding  streets of Printon. Scanning the city, Cypher felt as if he could see it in its entirety; the walled buildings that had tiny streetlike alleys tucked behind them, the floral embellishments which adorned every store, lamppost, and fence, even the streetcars that carried people by the dozen. An odd sensation came over him — he actually enjoyed the view for once. Seeing his eyes glimmer with more than just the task in front of him, Aurelia looked to Cypher while leaning against the window with him. "You didn't strike me as the type of guy to take in a view like this, or has something changed? I don't usually get my profiles wrong."

Still staring out into the city, Cypher peeks his head out the window, letting the wind run through his short black hair. Breathing in deeply for the first time while not holding a gun, he breathes out without having to pull a trigger. A sense of relief comes over him as his mind wanders.

"I didn't think I was either-" He says in response. "But something strange happened to me, and I'm thinking you know what I mean." His head turns to look at her, knowing that she'd understand. Taking in the view while thinking for a moment, Aurelia responded.

"Huruk explained it to me too, but my visions didn't seem nearly as bad as he said they could be. I'm pretty certain I just lucked out. They were oddly serene in a way. I can't recall every detail, but- but I think there were things guiding me — floating lights, filled with emotions. It was hard to tell what they were saying, but I knew what they meant. The throughline Huruk mentioned is true, I'm just hoping your message was good too." She spoke in a sincere way. In her attempts to recall these visions, though she struggled, you could see her being in those moments again.

Grabbing his rifle from a suitcase which he clicked open, Cypher attached a lengthy scope to it — scanning the city afterward. His gaze swung across Printon as he searched about and at the same time, he responded.

"It was. . .interesting. I can't tell if what they told me was good or not. But what I do know is that I'm starting to look back on what I've done. Whether any of it was worth it or not, because I hope it was. Without those choices I made — I wouldn't be here."

As Aurelia responded, Cypher locked onto an alleyway. In it stands Orwin and Uval in matching striped suits, both in a dark blue color and a hat to boot.

"I won't bother with asking what you've done, but I know that you're here now, doing something for someone that isn't you. If anything, the title you've been given is starting to fade. And I'm glad I've joined you crazy lot. I'm interested in seeing how all this works out."

"Thankfully one of us is. I'm starting to miss that coldness already." Cypher then swung his line of sight away from the other two. Tracing the street next to them, the Archer spots the caravan. A large armored vehicle with a boxy shape. With iron plates all across its body and highly tinted windows, it'll take nothing less than an explosion to open it up.

Five of these transports are moving together at a slow pace with a crowd of rangers at their sides. Once they reach the outer gate of the city, the caravans will separate from the group and start moving at full speed. At that point it'd be too late to catch up.

Down below, Orwin sips his coffee as Uval takes a huge bite out of a large donut, an item that was meant to be shared with a family of five. Hearing the rumblings of marching and the roaring of several engines, the two quickly finished their breakfast and peeked around the corner. Spotting the infantry making their way toward them, Uval attempted to step forward. Grabbing his arm, Orwin reminded him that he no longer had his armor.

"Only thing stopping them bullets from diggin into your skin is that expensive suit I just bought you. How bout we take it easy, stick to the plan and all?"

"Yes, BUT! I can make armor easy. Throw myself into a couple metal benches, maybe some street posts and bam. Armor." Uval acted out his plan as he spoke. He then shrugged afterward.

"I know we were sent to distract, but THIS-" Orwin exclaims while looking back at the hundred men and their armored cars. "THIS IS A LOT MORE THAN WE THOUGHT! Like holy fuck, Lia's dad must really hate Soren to add this much security. Anyway, all this to say that you're gonna get shot before you can even do any of that, Val."

Immediately after, Uval placed his forearm on a nearby wall. Welding the bricks to his suit, he rips off a large chunk of the building and holds it like a shield. Through the exposed hole is a showering man, looking up surprised to see the new window that Uval so graciously installed for him. Almost in a way where you'd think this is a normal occurrence for him, the man simply says, "Can I get that back? I ain't showering with my ass n balls exposed to the streets." Staring back down, Uval ignores the guy as Orwin replies. "Uh- shit, sorry but you're gonna have to deal with the draft — enjoy your new window!" As they ran out into the street, the man just sighed and continued to scrub himself clean.

Jolting out in front of danger, one of the rangers calls out to the others. "IT'S THE OGRE AND THE SHOWMAN!" Following his voice came a swarm of bullets which swept down the empty street. The gunfire gnawed at the makeshift shield that Uval held up as the two of them charged forward. Catching them by surprise, the rangers didn't have the time to set up the same line of fire they used to pressure Uval last time. All they had to do was outlast the first barrage. As soon as the hailstorm stopped the Ogre dropped the shredded shield and ran forward. In the middle of them reloading, other rangers attempted to sprint toward the front of the pack to shoot. Getting to the front, one of them quickly knelt down and scoped in — but before he could shoot, a knife had landed in the lever of the gun. Pulling it back via a chain connected to its base, Orwin caught his weapon as it retracted under his sleeve.

"Would it not be better for you to use a gun at your size?!" Uval yells out as he jumps up, diving into the engine of the foremost caravan. The driver and passenger leapt out as Uval rose from the black smoke, donning the front of the armored car as crude armor — it appeared like dense and crumpled tinfoil.

"I like throwin knives but it's a pain to- wait, you can't even hear me. . ." Orwin brushed off Uval's comment while facing off the rangers which approached him with bayonets. Meanwhile, the Ogre screamed aloud as bullets tried to pierce his new iron skin. "AHAHA, THIS IS A **FRACTION** OF WHAT I WAS IN THA WAR — YOU COULD NEVER TAKE MY LIFE, BUT I WELCOME YOU TO TRY!"

Using a mixture of elegant tactics and brutish strength, the two continued to fend off the front lines of the transport. Several rangers thrusted their bayonets toward Orwin, in reaction he leaned back and threw out his chains. Wrapping it around one of the rifles, he yanked it away then spun around. As the chains sped up several runic engravings began to appear through a sky blue illuminance. Slamming the rifle into the rightmost ranger, a large shockwave exploded out on impact. The force of it was enough to topple the dozen men which surrounded him. Turning his head toward the sound of gunfire, Uval suddenly leapt upward and landed in the middle of another crowd. A handful of rangers were thrown up into the air as Orwin sprinted forward to push up with him. Spinning two separate chains with both hands, the runes shined blue.

Jumping forward, Orwin slammed the ends of his weapon to the ground and created a shockwave which sent him flying to Uval. Landing beside his large friend, they continued rampage throughout the vast number of the enforcers. With so many rangers around, it was hard for the transports to escape — but though it took time, they slowly opened a way for them to leave.

The rangers parted to create a clear pathway toward a nearby street, it was thinner but just wide enough for the armored cars to squeeze through without scraping the buildings. With no other choice, they lined up and drove in as Uval and Orwin trampled through their troops in the front. "WHERE ARE YOU GOING?!" Screamed Uval as he stood atop one of the transports that couldn't escape in time. He opened his arms, welcoming any challengers to approach him. On the other hand, Orwin did his best to avoid getting shot — forcing the rangers into close combat knowing he could comfortably win in that range.

Treading up stairs and tight corners, the three caravans left did their best to escape the onslaught that occurred behind them. Taking an escape route they'd planned in case something like this happened, they were nearing an open street that they cleared preemptively. The end of the alley was near and just past it was a huge stone brick street with indented rails riding the middle of it. But in a sudden shock to the front driver, a random citizen walked in front of the alley — stopping like a deer in headlights, they turned toward them. Slamming down onto the brakes, the caravan stopped as the others rammed into one another like dominos.

Pulling down the window, the driver peeked out and yelled at the person. "GET OUT THE FUCKIN WAY! UNLESS YOUR ASS WANTS TO GET ARRESTED!"

Not responding, the person opened their mouth and whispered. At that moment the driver realized who they were, turning his head back to the other transports behind him, he screamed out for them to back up. "IT'S THE WANDERING MAGE, BACK THE **FUCK** UP!"

Huruk then waved his hand as dark clouds appeared above the front caravan. Azure lights then flickered in their shadows and lightning suddenly struck down, caging the vehicle and blocking the exit. Throwing the cars into reverse, the last two caravans sped backward as they stared at their side mirrors yelling to one another in an attempt to figure out what to do. "WHERE THE HELL ARE WE SUPPOSED TO GO!?" One of them screamed, clearly shaken up by the whole situation. The one who was calmer, yelled back. "RELAX, HEAD TO CASINOVA." Taking a sudden sharp reversed turn to the left, they continued to talk.

"BUT THAT STREET HASN'T BEEN CLEARED! WE'LL RUN INTO CIVILIANS!!"

"DO YOU SEE ANY OTHER CHOICE?! DRIVE GOD DAMN IT."

"I- I CAN'T. . ." He said while slowing down. This caused the other caravan to do the same, there was nowhere else for him to go.

"DO YOU KNOW WHO'S IN THIS FUCKING CAR?! **MOVE GOD DAMN IT!**" Not hearing them respond, the driver became frustrated. He knew that letting this man out would only spell danger. It was a stroke of luck that they were willingly let themselves be captured in the first place. With no other choice, the frustrated ranger stepped on the gas and rammed into the other caravan. Pushing them past the turn they couldn't force themselves to make, the ranger drove forward and took the sharp angle to the right. Zooming out the alley and toward a street filled with citizens, the wheels of the caravan screeched aloud as it barely missed them. Shifting sideways while entering the packed street, the driver slammed on the gas. Maneuvering between fancy automobiles and streetcars, they looked around with anxiety lurking onto their shoulders. "He's waking up." The driver says as he leans forward, trying to get away from this odd feeling. "We were supposed to sedate him again at the gate. . ."

The entire car suddenly spun out of control as a loud popping noise shot out. The tire exploded and the metal wheel sparked against the stone. Taking a look outside, the ranger looked up toward a clocktower to see a glint in its face. Cypher then reloaded, taking another wheel.

Standing next to him, Aurelia looked out the open panel with a pair of binoculars. She stared down at the caravan which swerved out of control. Sliding sideways, the vehicle slammed into a streetcar causing both of them to come to a sudden halt. The dramatic stop in speed shot the driver out through the window and onto the stone streets. Rolling into a nearby crowd the ranger became protected by the civilians nearby. Despite this, Cypher could still deliver a killing blow to them — all he'd have to do is shoot through the crowd. But he didn't.

His finger hesitated above the trigger and Aurelia took notice of this. She didn't know how far Cypher was willing to go, but she was glad that he was starting to change. As the ranger got up, the keys to the caravan jingled about on their hip, they sprinted through the crowd while yelling for them all to evacuate the premises. All Cypher could see was their face.

"Dark brown short hair, oak wood skin, and a scar running down his right cheek." Aurelia says, making sure he knew who the ranger was.

"That doesn't help me." He replied, and in confusion Aurelia reacted with a question. "What do you mean that won't help you? You've got eyes that can **actually** spot a needle in a haystack, I know you fuckin see the man."

"I can't see his **face**. Tell me what he's wearing." Still confused, Aurelia takes a moment to try and process it but quickly moves on. 'There's no point in arguing, he's about to exit the crowd anyway.' She said to herself. "He took off his ranger uniform, but he's running toward the northern gate. White dress shirt with dark blue slacks and brown boots."

A shot echoed out from the clocktower.

Falling down to the ground, the fleeing ranger fell limp onto the floor. Blood trickled from his body as dark clouds slowly formed in the sky. The waking drizzle began to descend, washing the blood from the man and into the nearby drains. Though the city became dull in color, the keys attached to the ranger still shined with luster. The quiet footsteps of Cypher and Aurelia trailed down the clocktower as they moved with a mouse-like silence.

At the same time in the opposite direction, the chaotic crashes and screams that Orwin and Uval created began to fade. And in the middle of both, Huruk walked toward the last caravan. Steam and black smoke spewed forth from its damages as the side of the metal vehicle laid in the crevice of a cable car. Raising his hand and whispering, the keys lifted off of the ranger and though not dead, the man was far too injured to do anything to stop him. His leg had been shot with a bullet of poison, a weaker dose than the one Cypher usually used. He wouldn't die from it.

Grabbing the keys which flew toward him, Huruk opened the back of the caravan. Slowly the double doors swung out. A hand then pressed against the inside of it, their eyes staring into Huruks. "No hard feelings for the other night right?" Soren says as he sticks a hand out, hoping that the Mage would take it. With his hand extended, the two stared at one another. Unmoving. The rain then began to pour much harder, obscuring any and everything farther than a couple arm lengths away. Several thoughts came into their heads, for Soren it was mostly, 'I hope he doesn't have a grudge with me. That'd be how many now?'

But on the other hand, Huruk was waiting — he wanted to know if it was true. To his surprise, it was. Soren truly had bad luck. Peering over his shoulder, Huruk saw a man who twisted his own heart with hate. The Mage's hands balled up to fists as he looked at the Abbot. Grabbing Soren's hand and helping him down, Huruk tossed him the keys to his cuffs then stared at the man inside.

With a snappy cadence, one akin to icicles breaking at the end of winter, the Abbot sat with his hands bound by chains while speaking. "How *long* has it been, Huruk? You've grown lots since then. I hope you've been taking care of yourself."

Huruk took a moment before speaking. He looked at his buzzed head, it had a stroke of white running from forehead to nape, going just slightly askew from the center of the man's skull. Staring at his eyes, he noticed how remarkably dark they were — but because they weren't fully filled black, Huruk became cautious. He **had** to be careful, and yet his curiosity still drove him to speak. "How many of you are left?" The Mage asked. "Can't be that many."

The Abbot stood, hands in front of him and still cuffed together, he walked toward the opened doors and looked down at Huruk. "I fear *both* of our people are the rarest of us now. Quite the turn isn't it? I can still remember the days when Mages maintained the Arcane world." He took a deep breath in and out. "A shame I had to kill most of them."

Huruk stood his ground not with confidence, but anger and revenge. His usual calm and proper way of speaking was filtered through gritted teeth and a stammering voice. "I- I don't get it. How could someone like you get caught? Put in a cell with four walls and nothing more to stop you. Why are you letting this happen, what's your goal?"

Jumping down onto the street, the Abbot took a deep breath in and out while looking around to the fleeing citizens. "That smell of rain, it's delightful isn't it."

"Answer me, Rakesh." Huruk opened his hand, ready to fire a spell at him.

"*sigh* I have the same goal as I had before. All I want is to be free, to stretch my legs after all these years of being chained down."

Huruk then took a step back, his fingers growing tense with anticipation. "I've done my fair share of research, but I still can't tell what a Seraphic would ever want. But now that I can look you in the eyes again, something tells me that I know."

The Abbot smiled as he looked at him. "Do you now?" He then spoke aloud. His voice was whispery like a specter and chilling like the wind. "*Utar Hahso.*" Layered right behind those words, were ones you could clearly understand. *"Enter the Veil."* Before anything else happened, the mind of the Mage fell back — falling through the street and into darkness. There Huruk went, into the visions he'd purposely plummeted into before. But this one was different. It was afflicted not by a Mage, one who seeks magic's end for the love of it. It was by a Seraphic.

1.2 | Silent Sleeps the Mage

The tongues of flame lick against the temple of knowledge, bright does their light brim in the dead of night. Swallowing what took lifetimes to forge. Grass and stone, flesh and mind, everything was eaten. The  Academia of Terox, an institution set upon a cloud piercing mountain — one that boasts such a great height that it was said to overlook each nation and their people. Peering through the flames as their fingers dig into buildings and crawl through halls, a young Huruk stands amidst the blazing glow — it's heat tickling his flesh. Barely taller than a nearby table in which he hid under, Huruk cupped his ears to avoid the noise. Through the fiery crackling shot screams every so often, warped and squeamish to hear. The sound of them was like a warning from the oppressor which walked the halls. Memories then flashed into the boy's mind, remembering what his teachers had once told him, he then ran out from beneath the table.

Frantically scanning around, he struggled to breath as smoke filled the room and his lungs. The inferno gripped the bottom of every wall around him, slowly scorching the books of Macrocosm that his predecessors worked so hard to create. In mere seconds, the collective lifetimes of a hundred mages were destroyed — and with each passing moment, many more.

Wanting to preserve even just a single book, the young Huruk ran toward a sliding ladder that stayed affixed to the wall. Jumping over the flames, the fingers reached up and burnt his legs. Wincing at the pain as he landed, the boy climbed, as did the fire. A hundred years. Two hundred. Three hundred years. Gone. Burnt to ashes that will blow away to nothing given a mere day.

Reaching the top of the ladder, the boy grabbed as many books as he could. Seeing the flames approaching on his left, he grabbed onto the wall and pushed the rolling ladder to the right. The wheels screeched as it came to its end, the sudden jolt of force threw the boy off of it as he fell down toward the ground. Falling into the fire, some of the books were let go as the impact sent a shockwave into his chest — but worse was the flames which gripped onto his back. Rolling out of the fire, the boy frantically searched the last two books he had left as the flames stayed upon him. In the heat of the moment, the boy's mind flashed with words he'd been taught. In a single second he remembered hours of lessons.

"*HUSHO INTI!*" The boy screamed as a blast of wind shot out in all directions, extinguishing the flames which latched onto him. Turning head, he looked to a clear path toward a window. Though he was a couple of floors up, he knew it was the only choice he had. But as he shifted on his heels to run, a man sprinted down the hall then into the door which was blocked by pillars of flame. An adult mage could be seen with blood trickling from his head, it covered his eye which he quickly wiped off. Heavily breathing, he stared down the hall from which he came — coming to a stop just in view of the doorway. Shifting his eyes only, he peered inside. Seeing the boy there, his eyes widened in fear and surprise. Steeling his nerves, he quickly looked back down the hall.

Suddenly, the flames turned black. No light shined from them as the building suddenly went dark. In the moment the mage was distracted, a hand reached out and grabbed hold of his neck. It was dark burgundy leather and had engravings on the top of it — the symbol looked like a draped cloth, pinched at the top but flared at the bottom. Though its current nature was uncanny, the flames still emitted black smoke. It choked both the man and the boy as it entered their lungs with every breath. The mage was lifted in the air by a single gloved hand at his throat, and poor young Huruk was paralyzed by fear — unable to look away. His small legs trembled as he stood there, slowly breaking at the grip of fear which stopped him from moving.

Lifted up from his feet, the mage struggled to breath. Air barely squeezed through his narrowed throat as he was being choked. Slowly his eyes drifted, fading into unconsciousness. Feeling his body go numb, the mage's arms began to droop down. Then suddenly he was slammed against a wall as a whooshing noise shot out into the hall, pushing both him and his attacker. Helping him up from the ground, the boy pulled the mage toward the window with all his might as he regained balance after being saved.

Grabbing the boy, he placed an ornate ink pen upon his chest, pushing him away and yelling at him to run. Though it pained him, the boy did as he was told — sprinting at the window. As he did, the red gloved hand reached up from the shadow beneath the windowsill. The whole arm extended out, revealing a sleeve of blood all the way to the shoulder. The arm then bent at the elbow and reached back into the shadow, grabbing at something — the hand then pulled out a mass of black vines. Throwing them over the window, they riggled around as if alive. They were as dark as night and as liquid as ink. It was hard to tell if there was something under that watery substance, or if that was all there was. Coming to a sudden stop, the boy fell to his back as he crawled away.

The mage, seeing this occur, ran toward him with whispers on his lips. Waving his hand a blast of fire erupted from a sphere that formed above his head, from it shot a spire of flame directed at the black wall. As it made contact, the wall slowly began to retract back into the shadows. And at the same time, the figure clad in red rose from beneath the window.

The Abbot wore a burgundy cassock with onyx buttons and obsidian lining. It was finely layered from shoulders to feet with a black sash around his waist, it draped to his side just like the symbol adorning his gloves. However, the man who emerged at the window had pure black eyes, no white in them at all. Otherwise he looked exactly like The Abbot. Then the original walked into the room from the doorway behind them. His eyes were normal except for how exceptionally dark his irises were. At this moment, the mage grabbed the boy and wrapped his arms around him. A desperate attempt to keep him safe.

"**All** I want is freedom-" Said the Abbot. "To be unleashed from the chains *your* forefathers placed upon **my** brethren. If you relinquish the secrets I seek, the one held close by you mages, I promise the lives I've taken today. By me they **will** return." Both the Abbot and his Husk near the window put a hand out for him to grab. Gritting his teeth, the mage held the boy tightly. Though he was told by his masters not to utter a word to the Seraphics, he couldn't help himself. "You worship a corrupting practice, and now you're rotten to the core. You think highly of the shadows and what lies beneath it, but that loyalty only masks how truly wicked you've become. Even death will not lend you a welcoming hand. . ."

The Abbots' hands lowered and so did their eyes. "I **yearn** for what I was promised at birth, the *right* to explore this world. The same thing you were born with or any other man. And if you will not help me reach that goal, I'll simply **make** you."

The one in the doorway then walked forward, a hand reaching out once more but not with its palm facing up. He wanted to **take**. The mage's eyes then suddenly spotted a book nearby, one of the ones that the boy had dropped from his fall. Scanning the pages with his eyes, he saw something he could use — but he needed more time to learn it.

"I don't understand. . ." The mage whispered. His head was staring at the book, reading it as he spoke aloud. "We've seen many of your Husks, those empty shells of flesh with pure black eyes. You live through them, don't you? You've been across the world already, what more is there for you to see?"

Stopping in frustration, the Abbot's eyes narrowed in anger. "*scoff* You mages believe your practice to be the *highest* form of arcane, yet you are but an **amalgamation** of many — you lack *creativity*. The other users of magic have forged their systems, you all have taken the foundation from what they've made — and with it you've made this jack of all trades. Do not judge or question the arcane path I've taken. You are a master of none, you all do not reach the floor to see what we see. Explaining my perspective will fall to ears that can't hear it."

Shooting up from The Abbot's shadow, a giant hand rose as if emerging from water. It was skinny and clawed with its flesh rotten and torn. It began to slam down toward the mage and the boy, you could see the rows of teeth and gaping mouths which lined its palm. Finishing with the visions that he flashed through, the mage used the spell he'd just learned in that moment. Looking down at the boy, he smiled and whispered — knowing that the ancient tongue he was about to speak would plague him with visions. But in his heart, the mage hoped they showed him something good. Anything to distract him of the horrors which draped upon his home.

"Tesaso Irbum Unvas"

A flash of white occurred and the young boy was gone. Yet, Huruk — the one who'd fallen back into these memories, had to stay and watch. The Abbot filled in the gaps in which he did not see, showing the mage getting grabbed by the horrid hand of darkness. He was then lifted up into the air by it, forced to look at the Abbot face to face.

"I do hope you keep your mind. It's hard to communicate with the beasts that some of you turn into. Hopefully the Hollow Heart deems you worthy, but I doubt it cares."

The Abbot then took out a syringe, plunging it into the decrepit hand which poked out his shadow. Drawing a starry black liquid into it, he walked over to the mage and stabbed him in the chest. As the strange essence entered his body, the mage began to convulse violently — his veins filling with it. Screaming aloud, he began to slowly change. His skin tore and mended over and over again to make room for the rapidly growing muscles beneath it. Bones cracked and splintered to form a hairlike mane from out his spine, this growth followed up to his head to form a nestle of bones resembling horns. With a protruding snout and layers of teeth, the mage now resembled a Wendigo-like creature. It had a lengthy body, seemingly void of any water or blood. And no visible eyes where they should be, despite this the creature still stared at the Abbot intently. With his dwindling sanity, the mage screamed out — a deep howl shot forth, and behind it was his gut wrenching plea for help. He then lifted his claw, about to swipe down at the Abbot but suddenly stopped and turned his head. The mage stared at where Huruk stood in the vision, stunned by his appearance.

Confused by the odd behavior of the newly found monster, the Abbot looked in the same direction. "What caught your attention? All that anger you just had disappeared, your worry too. No matter, come — we have keys to dig up." As the Abbot walked out the room, the lingering sanity left in the mage forced the monster to stay for just a moment longer.

Staring at Huruk, he stares back. A weak and shivering voice then spoke out from the monster's chest, echoing through its maw. "Y-you're. . .safe." The mage said with his final moments. Huruk was then pulled upward, the whole world warped with the speed in which he moved and suddenly he was jolted back into his body.

The rain continued to pour heavily, obscuring everything more than a couple arm lengths away. Standing in the street was Huruk, Soren, and the Abbot. We were back in the single after those spectral whispers ushered from the Seraphics lips.

"You alright?!" Soren yelled as he shook Huruk by the shoulders. Coming back to his senses, he looked down to Soren's arm to see a large gash across it. Looking back up with groggy eyes, Soren replied before he could say anything. "I'm good, he just sent some freaky shit at me from out his shadow. I need you awake though, do some magic or something. PLEASE."

2.0 | When Rain falls, Darkness follows.

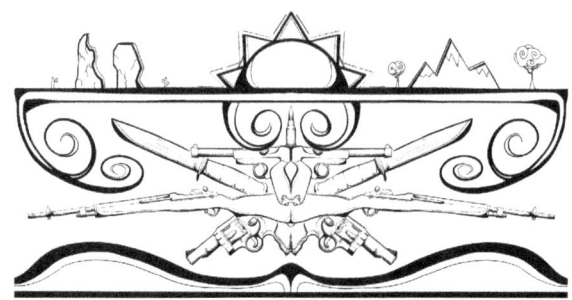

Huruk and Soren turned their heads to the Abbot as he looked down to his hand curiously. "That medicine they gave me still seems to be *hindering* my movement. Though, the numbness is fading."

He pulled his arms apart and broke the handcuffs. Placing a palm to the ground, it sank into the shadows while he stared forward. Pulling something out of it, the Abbot slowly lifted a writhing mass of tendrils and teeth. The inky heap of moving flesh wrapped around his right arm as he donned it like armor. Before he fully finished equipping the mass, Soren looked to Huruk confused as the mage stood there paralyzed. "You not gonna blast him with something? If I had a gun I would've shot him already, just sayin."

Hearing Soren snapped Huruk out of his fearful state, waving his hand he whispered under the cover of rain. A sphere of flame then appeared above his head as it suddenly shot toward the Abbot in a spire of fire. It crashed against the mass upon the Abbot's arm as he lifted it up to defend himself. Once the tendrils reeled back in pain, he raced forward and swung it at the both of them.

"SHIT!" Soren yells as he leans back to dodge the attack, so much so that he fell down into the puddles on the street. Meanwhile, the arm swung above him and slammed into Huruk. A cracking sound echoed out on impact as he was sent flying into a nearby building, smashing through the window as a huge baker's hat fell down from the logo above. "So the magic guy is dead, great." Soren says as he looks away, rolling backward as he quickly gets up. "Do you mind if I go get a gun or something? This isn't uh- this isn't very fair."

Staring at Soren, the Abbot slowly walked forward, dragging the black mass behind him. A grin smeared across his face as he swung again. Leaning back once more, Soren nearly fell to the ground but this time he managed to somehow stay on his feet. Beneath him, reaching out from his shadow emerged a pair of gloved hands clad in red. Grabbing onto his shoulders, Soren was about to be pulled into the darkness but an opposing chain wrapped around him.

A bit far away, Orwin placed his feet on the back of a bolted metal bench and pulled as hard as he could. Seeing him struggle, the stomping steps of Uval trailed past him as he grabbed the chain and yoinked Soren away from the Abbots Husk. While Soren rolled over to Orwin, Uval sprinted forward in his iron armor — pulling back his fist and the Ogre launched it forward like a cannon shooting its ball.

Shielding himself with the eldritch tendrils, the mass was blown apart by the strength of the Ogre. Uval's metal fist then dug into the Abbot's forearm, bending it unnaturally as his bones shattered and splintered through flesh. Punching again with his other arm, Uval struck the Abbot directly on his chest, caving it in and sending him backward as he slammed into a bench. It crunched and shaped around his body as he stared at Uval with an inquisitive gaze.

"I wonder who gave you that power." The Abbot questioned. "Clearly you were chosen for a reason, I can feel the desperation in your strength. You were empowered by someone who was scared of something, I wonder what that is."

Uval walked toward the man confused, wiping the red blood from his knuckles while responding. "What tha fuck are you saying? I do not know who or *what* you are, but it is clear that you must die. You are more dangerous than I thought."

As the Ogre walked closer, the Abbot's wounds became covered in a starry void-like fluid. Resembling the blood drained from the hand in Huruk's visions. It moved as if living, rapidly replacing what was broken in a brutal fashion — rebreaking and rebuilding. Everything was forcibly snapped back into place before Uval could even reach the man. Getting up from the severely dented bench, he reached in the shadows of his sleeves and pulled out blades of teeth. They chattered from the flesh which made its base.

"I learned much of you through my Husks, but you still exceed the legends. You know there are others like you, and there will be more. I wonder how you'll face them." The Abbot then smiled, sprinting at him while leaning forward. Swinging the blades, Uval managed to protect himself by meeting them with his fists — though still being overpowered, the Abbot hadn't been pushed away like he was the first time.

"It's been **years** since I've turned myself in. They've tried many times to bring me out of the country and to the Damned Heights, but not a soul figured out how to get me past the border. So I remained **here** — lingering in a *muddled* state while living lives through my Husks. Torturous it was to bring you all together, but now I'm one step closer to true freedom. *Destiny's Call was the right choice.*"

Uval's eyes widened as they filled with violent flame. "IT WAS **YOU**!" He yelled, his voice booming out like thunder. "YOU PROMISED ME MY ARMOR IF I MADE IT HERE, AND I HAVE BEEN BATTERED WITH NUISANCES SINCE I'VE ARRIVED!" His punches became heavier. The impact of each strike blew away the surrounding rain for a moment, causing a clear sphere to form. "SO WHERE IS IT. **GIVE ME WHAT I AM OWED**!" Uval then raised his fists up. The Abbot stared toward them with a grin and a glint of fear in his eyes. No matter if he died or not — this would surely hurt nonetheless. About to turn away and run, a chain wrapped around his blades as his head whipped over to Orwin. Sitting across the street, the Rogue shot him a smirk as Soren stood beside him helping pull the chains. He was also smiling.

Abandoning the weapons, the Abbot fully turned around to run — however, two bullets tore through his skull as he went limp onto the floor. The Abbot then turned to the opposite side of the street as Cypher and Aurelia stood there, both of their guns emitting smoke. Falling to the ground, Uval slammed both his fists onto the Abbot as a massive shockwave halted the rain above the street — with a deafening silent moment passing, it continued to pour.

Blinded by rage, Uval lifted his fists again and slammed them back down, but this time he didn't feel the soft cushion of flesh. Confused, everyone looked around frantically. All except for Soren and Cypher. Those two met in the middle of the street as Cypher tossed him a handgun. A strange look then appeared on the statuesque face as he asked him a question.

"Ugh," he said while being disgusted. "Have you always had that shiteating grin?" And completely ignoring the insult, Soren smiled much brighter. "Wait, you can tell what my face looks like?! What the hell happened to you?" Pushing Soren away from him, Cypher looked around for the Abbot. "I'll brief you later. But I heard that man's voice — I can confirm that it's the Contractor. This is the guy who brought all of us here."

The day grew darker as the Abbot rose from the shadow of the crashed caravan. He climbed up like a zombie emerging from their grave, staring forth at a feast of flesh. His body was mangled to all hell. Bones and entire limbs were where they shouldn't be, but slowly he was fixed. Snapping everything into place and replacing what was lost. The Abbot smirked as he reached down into the shadow whence he came from. Everyone felt something exceptionally dangerous coming, like staring at the countdown of a bomb which you can't disarm in time. Destiny's Call sprinted away into different buildings, all except for Uval who ran forward.

"Even *with* those gifts bestowed to you, Uval. You will fall short. Let me show you a glimpse at the height of power in this world of ours." The Abbot spoke proudly as the shadow beneath him grew darker — spreading out in all directions, even climbing atop surfaces where it shouldn't exist. Taking a deep breath in, he yelled his enchantment aloud for the whole world to hear.

"TESTARO IR HAHSO"

A layered voice whispered its translation.

"Brave the Darkness"

Like a fisherman pulling its catch onto their boat, the Abbot yanked his arm from the chasm of shadows. The black ink spurted out into the air as a great onyx beast emerged. It leapt up into the sky. At the peak of its jump, it slowed in the air — spreading its massive wings across the clouds. The monster opened its long beak and revealed its rows of sharpened teeth then screeched out what sounded like a cacophony of dying animals.

On the street below, everyone woke from their visions as the monstrous raven dove down. Its hollow white eyes stared at Uval as he sprinted at the Abbot, screaming at him for not keeping his promise. Everyone else shot at the monster, but their bullets simply bounced off its blade-like feathers. The Raven then landed between the Abbot and Uval, crushing the street and forming a crater with its spearlike claws. However, through unmeasurable rage the Ogre jumped up at the monster. Reacting to the man, the Raven swiped at him with its talons. The attack landed upon him as he was smashed into the fourth floor of a nearby building, but as the beast retracted its claw, Uval hung there latched onto its nails.

Ripping off the broken helmet from his own head, Uval bled from a gash just above his brow. The blood ran down his right eye as he stared at the Abbot who now stood on the Ravens back. There was only scorn and abhor which resonated through the Ogres pupils. Screaming out again, he started to climb the beast. It tried to shake him off like a bug, violently waving its wing but to no avail. Uval welded himself to the monster with every inch he climbed, gaining more confidence he stood and began to run up toward the Abbot.

"I WILL **BREAK** YOUR SOUL! **RIP** YOU APART AND **SPREAD** YOUR REMAINS ACROSS EVERY **STATE** AND **COUNTRY, TOWN** AND **VILLAGE**! YOU WILL **NEVER** BE REMEMBERED! **YOUR *EXISTENCE* ENDS WITH *ME*!**"

Uval declared the Abbot's end as he reached the shoulder of the giant bird. In a panic it began to soar upward, in a single stroke of its wings they flew beyond the nearby buildings. The Raven then turned its head in an attempt to bite at the Ogre, but before it could, Uval sent the back of his fist across the monster's beak. A huge shockwave went out as it landed, causing the rain to stop and the monsters head to jolt backward in pain. "YOU THINK YOUR PET SCARES ME?!" He said while climbing onto the back of the beast, walking down toward the Abbot. "IT SHOULD BE SCARED OF **ME**!"

Emerging from the rubble of a bakery, Huruk walked onto the street while holding his head. Staring up at the beast that flew toward the Northern Gate, he looked to the others nearby. A certain spell wandered to the forefront of his mind, one that he thought he'd never have the chance to use.

"I have an idea, but I'd normally advise against taking such a risk. The effects are like most mage spells. They're a bit random, in a controlled yet chaotic way." Huruk looked specifically at Soren and Orwin. The two of them looked at one another and sighed, turning back to him and putting a thumbs up. During this, Cypher and Aurelia gave each other a nod and then turned to them.

"We'll find a way to keep up, you guys do whatever the magic guy says." Aurelia then put a hand on Soren's shoulder. "Nice to meet you by the way, good luck bud." Her and Cypher then ran to one of few working cars nearby and hopped in. Realizing they needed help to get it started, Orwin went over and finagled with the wires — turning it on. Going back over to Huruk and Soren, the mage explained. "I'll cast a spell that'll allow myself and one of you to fly temporarily. And I already know who the other person will be, you just have to trust me."

Feeling it in the air, Soren stared at the beast that made more and more distance with each flap of its wings. "It's me isn't it. . ." He said with a cringed expression. Moments later, Soren and Huruk are soaring through the air with grey feathered wings attached to their shoulder blades and birdlike talons on their hands and feet. Yelling out to Huruk, Soren squealed about how much he hated this. "PLEASE-" He said as the rushing wind muffled his voice. "TELL ME THIS ISN'T PERMANENT!" And with a confident voice, Huruk replied. "SURELY NOT!" He then whispered to himself. "*I hope.*"

Feeling a tug on their legs, they both looked down to see Orwin attached to them via his chains — he held on tightly as they dragged him through the air. Screaming at the two of them, his eyes widened. "LOOK AHEAD YOU FUCKING IDIOTS! WHY AM I EVEN HERE!" Huruk and Soren then intently looked through the rain to see a small blimp heading directly at them. As they reacted by going opposite directions to dodge, Orwin went splat on the windshield as he then got dragged over the top of it. Shaking his head to recover from that terrible display of teamwork, Orwin looked up to see the Raven circling back toward them. Rapidly approaching it screeched aloud while opening its long beak, such a thing could easily crush a bus between its rows of sharpened fangs.

Atop it was the Ogre and Abbot who fought one another fiercely, their striking blows halted the rain with each impact. However, though it seemed like Uval was winning, he was beginning to run low on steam as the Abbot continued to regenerate at a rapid pace.

"**UP!**" Screamed Orwin, attempting to direct the hopelessly incompetent flyers which held his life. Hesitating for a fraction of a second, the two of them hauled ass as they flapped their wings furiously. But like an aerial train the Raven approached fast, its white eyes like the headlights that shone onto the three deers in front of it.

The monster then crashed into the group, snapping the binds which held them together as they split apart like bowling pins. Descending fast, Orwin's vision was dizzying with how much he was spinning. Flailing his arms he eventually steadied himself as he stared down to the approaching street. Though Orwin's mind wasn't focused on it, Cypher and Aurelia were in his line of sight as he screamed out in terror.

Driving in the car Orwin had hotwired, the two grounded members looked up as they drove with the pedal to the floor. Aurelia was on the wheel and Cypher was in the back with his sniper. With no roof on the vehicle, he knelt onto the cushioned seat and pointed his gun straight up. Peering through the scope, Cypher aimed at Orwin to get a better view of what was going on. But with how far they were and the hefty rain that drowned out detail, he was merely a smudge on Cypher's lens.

"Speed up, I need a better angle." He said to Aurelia. She then looked back at him with a confused scowl. "You know this piece of shit ain't goin any faster right? I do tighter turns and we'll go sliding." Not caring for the repercussions, Cypher immediately replied.

"Do it. I **need** a better angle." Smiling a bit, Aurelia looked forward to all the dormant cars in front of them — her grinning scowl deepened as she heard the sirens of rangers behind them. "Fine. If that's what you want, I'll give it to you damn it."

2.1 | The Northern Gate

The car whipped from left to right, its wheels barely gripping the wet streets as Aurelia drove between obstacle and obstacle. The massive puddles which she drifted across splashed up like waves. Behind them  came several ranger vehicles, their sirens blaring aloud for all to hear. Knowing that she'd need to make even more distance, Aurelia took tighter turns which caused their car to drift wildly.

Her pathing between the cars became so narrow that the sides of the vehicles began to scrape against theirs — sparks shooting out as they did. While the metal screeching of friction screamed out, Aurelia yelled out to Cypher. "How's it looking up there!" Her voice ran through the falling rain and screeching tires.

Looking up, Cypher scoped in to see what was going on — the first thing he saw was Soren and Huruk desperately flying down to catch Orwin. Reaching out with their birdlike talons, Orwin threw out chains.

A strike of lightning then lit the sky behind them, revealing the Ravens silhouette as it soared with readied claws. Swooping toward the three of them, the beast swiped at Huruk as he quickly casted a spell over himself — forming a shield which its nails cracked into. He and the shield were swooped away and slammed into a nearby tower, leaving Soren to save Orwin. The Raven then flew back up into the air as Huruk walked out from the hole in the wall. Mostly unhurt, he caught his breath — he soon realized that his birdlike transformation was gone. Staring toward Soren with wide eyes, Huruk screamed as loud as he could. **"DON'T GET HURT! YOU'LL LOSE YOUR WINGS!"**

His fearful voice echoed out through the rain, traveling to Soren as he reached out as far as he could. "C'mon. *C'mon.* ***C'mon.***" He said repeatedly, trying to reach Orwin as he reached back. Though the chain extended as far as possible, he was still just out of reach. Even in the shadows which the city basked in, a darkness loomed over them as they fell. Without looking, Soren knew the Raven was diving down toward them — he could hear the train sized beast descending. "I JUST FUCKING MET YOU, BUT I'LL BE DAMNED IF I LET YOU DIE! I CAN'T MAKE THAT SAME MISTAKE AGAIN!" Screaming at the top of his lungs, Soren reached out with his clawed fingers. Tapping at the chains, he barely managed to hook his talon into the links. Pulling Orwin close, he turned to dodge the attack but the beast was far too close. Its mouth was wide open. Behind its hooked teeth lied a white abyss at the back of its throat. Staring into it, a bullet suddenly whizzed past them — striking the Raven in its eye and causing it to screech in pain. Reeling back in anguish, the beast twisted and turned its body. Slamming its wing into the two of them, Soren held on tightly, refusing to let Orwin fall on his own.

The Raven then crashed down like a falling comet, completely destroying the northern gate upon landing. Bricks and other debris went flying in all directions as the explosion-like noise alerted the entire city. That's if they weren't already aware of what was happening.

Soaring down from above, Soren and Orwin landed on the street to see a crashed car. Flames and black smoke rose from the wreckage as they sprinted to it. But before they fully made it over, Cypher and Aurelia walked out from the smog. Regrouping, they stared back toward Huruk as he stood atop a nearby building. With a cadence akin to a poet he whispered to himself. Speaking out to the world, several strong gusts of wind passed through the streets with every line Huruk recited. Thunder boomed louder and lightning struck fiercer, it was as if this mortal man was enticing the weather to rage harder — scream louder.

He stared at the large force that amassed in the streets before him, surrounding the northern gate with nearly three hundred rangers and fifty armored vehicles. Printon gathered all they could and marched toward these indescribable threats that they harbored in their walls. No longer in the interest of capture, they moved forward with the goal of execution.

But unfortunately for them, Huruk saw violence as their only way out.

Waving his hand across the army, lightning bolts began to rain down like arrows. They struck the streets which his enemies trampled upon. Explosions of turquoise plasma trickled throughout the city. With each strike a handful of rangers were blasted away. Even the armored vehicles succumbed to the vast power that Huruk summoned.

Falling to his knees after starting the storm, Huruk suddenly went limp as he fell off the building. Sprinting toward him, Soren flapped his wings and dove forward — narrowly catching Huruk before he hit the ground. During this, the rest of the team sprinted off to what was left of the northern gate.

There they found a huge cloud of dust which began to settle. Roughly outlined in the massive rubble, the Raven could be seen sinking down into its own shadow. As everything continued to settle, a person walked out from the curtains of destruction. The Abbot approached, wounds all across his body that seem to be healing quite a bit slower — but healing nonetheless. Behind him he dragged Uval with a large mass of obsidian tendrils. Throwing the Ogre toward the feet of Destiny's Call, they could see how badly he was beaten. All of his iron armor from the waist up was gone. Bruises and deep cuts littered his skin as he took a troubled breath of air. Uval's body trembled with weakness as he tried to get up.

"With this little squabble between us, my actions alone will forever seem interlinked with yours. But Destiny's Call, this group of ours is a gift for all of us. I have brought together some of the greatest minds and hearts. Think about the things you could do now that you're not alone, perhaps this was needed for the world — the changes Destiny's Call will bring shall be written and talked about for ages. And behind your legends, I will continue to seek my freedom. That's all I want, you are free to do as you wish — all I need is your namesake."

The Abbot then stepped back into the dust, turning around and walking away. With a final statement, he solidified the nature between himself and the group before him. They were his distraction. "Do make some noise in this world, it's too quiet for me."

Knowing they couldn't just follow after him, nor even defeat him as it stands, Destiny's Call regrouped at the broken gate. Though their feelings were a mixed bag, they all knew one thing was certain. They couldn't stay here. Quickly the group found a nearby vehicle, hotwiring it they drove out through the rubble and exited Printon before any of the rangers could catch up. A silence overcame all of them, they didn't know what to do or what to say. So they just kept moving.

Broken down and tired, there was so much they didn't understand. As Aurelia drove, she steered them deeper in Mystcall's forests — hoping that nature could hide them away for at least a single night. "How's. . . how's everybody doin?" She hesitantly asked. Turning her head to see how they were, Aurelia saw a broken group. It appears his words cut deeper into them than her.

Uval, the Ogre who prided himself on strength was beaten down till he couldn't move.

Huruk, the Mage with a vendetta was powerless against the likes of a Seraphic.

Orwin, the Rogue that had his last hope shattered. The future he saw with his love was gone.

Cypher, the Archer who didn't know if his hands belonged on a weapon. He questioned himself.

Soren, the Hero that hated being looked up to. He can't see himself as the world does.

"I'll ask again later. . .let's just hope Huruk can heal you guys when he wakes up." As Aurelia spoke, you could hear the mellow hope in her voice. She wanted to make this work, this group to work. Even with everything that's happened, all the changes and broken promises.

3.0| What plagues a Hero.

Soren's eyes flash open as dirt is tossed onto his face. Lying down on the ground, the Hero jolts up to his feet with a confused look — his head twists and turns to scan through the trench he stood in.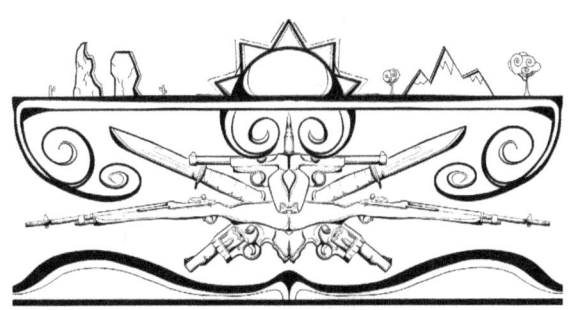

The floor was littered with corpses, some riddled with bullets and others torn apart by explosions. Hearing what sounded like a stampede of bulls rapidly approaching, Soren ducked down as he stared upward. Above him, a horde of Ogres leapt over the trench and charged forward — each donning armor that mostly resembled a tank and other military vehicles. Waiting for them to pass, Soren looked around and rummaged through his fallen allies with teary eyes. Grabbing a rifle and ammunition, he prepared himself to resurface onto the battlefield.

With a hand pressed against the sandbag walls in front of him, Soren slammed his forehead against it and took several breaths in and out in an attempt to calm himself. While gritting his teeth he screamed out in resolve and climbed up from the trench, reentering the war.

In front of him was a massive concrete fort, it had layers of defenses which stacked atop each other like a sandcastle. From the hundreds of thin windows came bullets which rained upon the Ogres that sprinted ahead of Soren. And though the lead bounced against their metal armor, many of them still found their way toward Fort Tarasova. Without thinking, Soren just ran as fast as he could. Even as a bullet pierced into his bicep, he continued to run — barely flinching at the impact. Diving forward into another trench, Soren frantically searched around for something.

"Where is it. . ." He said with rushed words. Moving body after body, he eventually found the Commander which led the charge. Rummaging through his corpse, Soren angrily screamed out once he noticed it wasn't there. Explosions then went off around him as two other soldiers ran through the trench, finding Soren sitting against one of the walls defeated.

"Get the hell up." Said Cypher as he held onto a small black container. The box couldn't have been bigger than one made for a ring. The sandy blonde man to his side then spoke out next. "You ain't give up yet right? Or do you wanna go back home where you're supposed to be?" He said jokingly, putting a hand out for Soren to grab knowing that was far from the truth. With fervor wrapping around the Hero, he stood with his help. "Course not, I was just waitin for y'all to catch up."

"We were here first, dumbass." Cypher said while tossing the box to Soren. "Hold onto this, you're the fastest of us — you'll have to be the one to drop it off."

Steeling his nerves, Soren nodded his head in agreement. But as Cypher and Daire got ready to jump out of the trench, counting down the seconds till they did so, Soren stared at the box he held between his fingers. He felt a strange presence radiating from within it. Scratching at the inside of the container, whatever was inside desperately wanted out. Soren was then snapped out of this trance as they yelled out to run. Looking back down at the box for a moment, it appeared completely mundane — confused, he elected to ignore it and sprinted with them.

Charging forward, most of the gunfire had ceased. The Ogres of the 9th Division had already entered Fort Tarasova, drawing most of the attention to inside the base. Reaching their front gate, the three soldiers looked around to see the flames of chaos that danced in the courtyard. Standing there, staring at everything unfold, Soren looked down to the box again. His mind was split in two halves.

'These soldiers fight for a war they themselves had no part in starting. Yet here they are, dying for the cause. So do I unleash the horrors stuck within this box? Let it fester and ravage everything around? I have no fuckin clue what's in here, but it's dangerous. Instead of anything else, we chose **this**. It oughta be worse than what I can imagine, so is it right for me to use it?'

Rotten hands and ripped uniforms then rose from the ground, grabbing onto Soren's legs and dragging him into the red soil beneath him. Everything shifted into a tint of crimson as the ground turned to corpses from both sides.

'My fellow soldiers, my *allies*, my **friends** I came here for have long died. With my own eyes I saw what made them live, as did I see what caused them to die. My pockets are filled with dog tags and pictures I ripped from their corpses and scattered remains – I have more **hate** in my heart than *blood that soaks this field*, so **WHY?** Why am I hesitating? Run forward, kill your enemies and stop at nothing to do it-'

"You alright?" Said Daire as Soren turned to look at him, everything returning to normal as he blankly stared. "I can take the box if you need me to."

3.1 | A Clash of Heart & Mind

"You alright?" Said Huruk as Soren turned to look at him, everything returned to normal as he blankly stared. He then looked down to the campfire as the wind brushed through the forest they staked out in. "Yeah, just — remembering some stuff. . ." Turning up toward the night sky, it still drizzled faintly, but the moon was full and bright. It was many hours later, most of Destiny's Call was here.

Cypher was off hunting while Aurelia and Uval rested. It seemed Uval's wounds were somewhat healed, even if just a bit. Bandages were wrapped around most of his body as Huruk looked away disappointed, wishing he could do more. "It's fine-" Soren said while looking at him with low eyes. "You did what you could. And though we failed miserably — I don't blame you for the plan. We didn't know what we got ourselves into. Fuck, we don't even know each other. We'll- we'll just figure out how to work together, I think we'll be okay." He then saw Huruk nod slowly, staring down to his hands as they clenched into fists.

Leaning onto his knees, Soren asked the mage if there was something else bothering him. Not responding, Huruk stared up through his brows as the campfire's flame shined brightly upon the side of his face. A tense silence went taught between the two of them. Soren slowly slid his hand toward the pistol at his waist as Huruk sat there, the Mage's eyes glazed over with memories that he couldn't see. Soren couldn't tell what he was hiding, this made him feel immediately wary of the situation. Knowing that Huruk was heavily weakened, tired from the spell he'd cast in Printon, Soren felt confident he could take him out if need be. But he didn't *want* to, he wanted to believe that Huruk was trustworthy. Yet his instincts were taking over, he was starting to see him as an enemy.

"I **need** an answer, Huruk." Soren said sternly. He spoke in a way very few people have ever heard from him. "Don't make me do something I'll regret. . ." But despite his efforts, Huruk simply averted his gaze — staying silent as the words were trapped in his throat. Seeing his unwilling behaviour, Soren suddenly stood and drew his weapon — pointing it at Huruk as he stayed seated. The Mage then looked at him, their eyes meeting while reflecting the unsteady flame next to them.

Slowly Soren approached with his gun aimed at Huruk's head. Getting closer he hesitated to shoot, hands shaking as he suddenly grabbed the Mage — standing him up and slamming him into a nearby tree. With the pistol held to the side of his head, Soren's grip tightened in anger and uncertainty. His mind raced with do's and don'ts.

"His name is *Rakesh Nightingale*." Huruk uttered. "I should've known it was him who led me here. Who else would know so much about Seraphics other than one of them. . ."

Backing up from him, Soren kept the gun aimed at Huruk as his eyes went wide. "How-How do you know him?" He asked shakily.

"Rakesh killed my entire institute, and many more from what I've heard throughout the years. . ." Huruk then took out the pen given to him by the mage from his vision. "He's trying to undo an Undying Vow placed upon him generations ago. It's kept him trapped in Mystcall for years, preventing him from ever crossing its border. But he's found ways around it, all except for his physical body. I think that's why he stole the Linking Chalice, it must have something to do with that vow."

"**What**?" Said Orwin as he walked back into the campsite. He looked utterly baffled as he leaned against a tree, seemingly weak in the knees. "Th-that's why he wanted that cup?" Starting to hyperventilate, Orwin fell to the ground and clutched his chest. "I knew it-" He whispered. Huruk and Soren then quickly put aside their situation, rushing to Orwin and helping him calm down. The Rogue then explained that he's the one who stole the Chalice. "Rakesh promised that he'd help me. . .that he'd help find a cure for my wife."

4.0 | Escapade of Escape

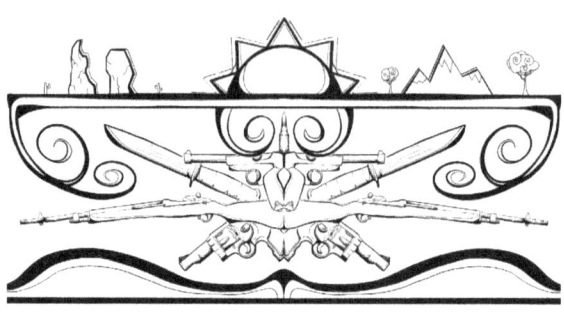

A bit forward in time, the three of them managed to work things out. Mostly in an awkward way. None of them felt the need to outright blame anyone more than the other, even despite Orwin insisting that this was his fault. "If I didn't give him the cup, he would've never been able to start any of this shit. I'm. . .I'm so sorry. . ."

"We all got tricked, there's no point in trying to cut the pie into the right size for each person. We take the same share – no more, no less." Huruk spoke with a relaxed tone. Soren then followed him up afterward. "What? And also, a chalice is a cup? Oh by the way, Huruk I'm sorry for earlier. I didn't know if. . ."

"It's fine, I understand. I would've been just as careful."

As Orwin laughed at the awkwardness the other two chuckled to themselves and decided to move on. At least until everybody else was there to talk. "Okay, okay. Seriously though." Soren said while looking out into the distance. "What did you find out in Printon?" He and Huruk then turned to Orwin as he leaned back onto the tree he sat beside.

"There's **a lot** going on, but here's a general rundown."

With the havoc which stormed through the northernmost part of the city, the majority of the citizens are being moved to the capital of Mystcall – Luminel, The Gates of the Moon. The mass exodus was transported through trains and blimps in hopes to move thirty percent of their entire population within a month's time. Additionally, valuables and memorabilia were stowed within these transports — entire museums, vaults both personal and public, and even niche items of physical value were taken away. This may very well include Uval's armor.

As everyone regrouped, they each had their own reasons to go after Rakesh. Whether it be for revenge, love, or even the need of a tangible goal — Destiny's Call would give in to what he wanted, to be chased.

Traveling through Mystcall they planned to meet *everything* and *everyone* that was being moved from Printon to Luminel. Huruk explained that as part of his deal with Rakesh, he was promised a book of information about the Seraphics, but more important to the mission at hand, he was promised a *collection* of books on ancient objects that tie to the history of this country. Huruk strongly believed that there had to be something about the Chalice in those archives. They simply had to find it.

With each passing day, the group slowly became a bit closer despite the lingering ambiguity between some of them. Most of the members got along swimmingly, but they lacked information on who they truly were. This made the trust between them thin and fragile. However, they were able to joke and laugh perfectly fine as they drove through forests and open plains. Traveling through Mystcall, huge blimps soared above them frequently as trains shot past them time and time again. But eventually, after several days and nights, Luminel was on the horizon.

The Moon hung like a light above its white walls. The towers affixed to these quartz shields reached up to it — appearing like a flower or hand which tried to grab the stars. Behind them, huge iron links were reeled into a bundle as the massive gate was lifted. Several train tracks ran through separate entrances made specifically for them, meanwhile the blimps in the sky sailed between the ivory colored towers, soaring down to huge landing bays at the city port. Destiny's Call then entered the brilliant and vast streets with an air of awe and anxiety filling their lungs.

Seeing the armored rangers, the rotating gears, the steam piping, and the thousands of people that roamed about, a pit formed in their stomachs as Soren spoke. "Guys, I think our luck is about to turn around." None of them believed that.

Garden Of The Sky

1.0 | The Flowers in Words

A calming breeze swept through the city. Flags and banners flapped about as the many star shaped flowers danced in the wind. Trailing behind a young man that ran through the city, he

came to a sudden stop in a vast crowd — walking up to the window of a nearby store, he stared at his own reflection. Checking his olive skin for any blemishes, he then straightened up his black beanie. A piece of clothing not widely seen in Mystcall, elegance was certainly favored more than comfort here.

Afterward he checked to see if his clothes were fine too. They were loose fitting and with many draped bits, something you'd see from a seafarer. After tidying himself up, he smiled at his reflection with his sharp canines out for display. Clyde was always treated unfairly from the way he looked, especially by his fang-like teeth. It was a superstition that those with sharper canines were hungrier in a sense, a statement that can be taken many ways but most not good. So on a first glance you'd more likely assume he was a pirate or thug, but that used to not be true — at least until he decided to feed into these ideas placed upon him. Despite becoming what they thought, Clyde still became wary of his appearance, paranoid of it even. And though he doesn't think this himself, he's a bit more gold hearted than most in his line of work.

"Where to?" Clyde asked himself with a pondering look, still staring at the window as he talked. "There *has* been a lot of stuff coming in from Printon — it's been two weeks and an official newspaper hasn't come out, huh? Those rangers wanna hide the good stuff again. Just when I thought something interesting was gonna happen. *sigh* I miss big bro already."

Walking away from the suit store he stood in front of, Clyde did a double take as he looked inside — he saw what he could only describe as a 'mountain of a lad.' Stepping into the store, Clyde approached Uval as he was trying on a new suit — his old one had been ruined in the last battle. Despite the injuries he sustained and the small amount of time that's passed, Uval seemed much better already — mostly thanks to Huruk spending each night healing him before falling asleep. A bandage went across one of his eyes and covered a gash on his forehead, otherwise his other injuries were gone.

Walking up to the Ogre Clyde felt like his luck was turning around. 'Maybe things *will* get interesting.' He said to himself before speaking. "Aye there! I certainly don't remember seeing anything like you in these streets before!" Uval then looked down to him with a straight face, eyebrows slowly scrunching together. "Wait!-" Clyde said while raising both hands. "Didn't mean anything by it, I just wanted to say hello to *The Ogre of the Ninth Division!"*

Uval's face then did a complete flip, he proudly smiled instantly after Clyde mentioned the Ninth Division. "Why didn't you say you were a fan," Uval said while grabbing his shoulder. "You did not come to challenge me did you? I am trying to find a suit, so I am busy. Sorry." Confused, Clyde tilted his head like a curious cat, "Huh? That's not what fans do. Anyway! What brings a guy like you into Mystcalls capital anyway? I assume it's not for fame, your everyday citizens barely know their own heroes nowadays."

Shifting tones again, Uval's eyes lingered upon the store's window — staring into the dense moving crowd that packed the street outside. "They will soon." He said with a bitter taste of melancholy on his tongue. "Oh? You got a plan to make it big do you? Well let me give you a bit of advice, do NOT try any funny business on 27th and 72nd street — those mob members hate anything that isn't serious. You're gonna have to take my word for it, *terrible* idea."

Chuckling a bit, Uval paid for his suit and walked with Clyde as they both went back outside. "You are funny and a fan — walk with me, let us chat for longer." Taking him up on the offer, Clyde unknowingly became friendly with Destiny's Call — the soon to be 'Most Famous Criminal Group in Mystcall'. Almost equally as feared as those 'mobs' he mentioned.

Cutting forward, Uval and Clyde are in a quiet establishment. One that's a mixture of a cafe and library. Earthy decorations filled the tower as wind passed through the wooden barred windows. The first floor down below is a normal cafe, with decor that resembles a beautiful garden. Trailing up the large swirling stairs, books line the bookshelves and fill the rooms indented into the walls. Climbing up to one of the higher floors, staring down to the bottom Clyde turns to Uval as he sits down at a quaint garden table. A gust of wind passes through the open balcony while the young man joins the Ogre for breakfast.

"So, what do you do for work?" Asked Uval as he scanned through the embroidered menu. Looking at one as well, Clyde clenched his teeth and looked away with his eyes. "Well, uh- I happen to move products around for people. Nothing crazy you know, what about you? What does the great Ogre do now that the war is over?"

"Tha products you say. What kind are they?" Uval then turned to the waitress that came up the stairs, giving her his order the Ogre then looked back over to Clyde as he did the same. As she left, Clyde nervously grabbed the glass of water they were left with and took a sip. "Small packages-" He then put up his arm and placed a hand on his bicep. "I might be a lil strong but I could never drag huge crates across the city, ya know? I could if they let me drive some of the trucks they got but eh, that'll never happen."

A howl of wind filled the void that Uval left before speaking.

"So you could say that you know this city pretty well, no?" Clyde's heart beat faster, he then audibly gulped feeling like he was being interrogated. "You could — yeah, you could say that. If- if you wanted to. . ."

"Sorry if I ask too many questions, Luminel is such a big city. I want to know as much as I can — I am not from here as you know."

"Oh yeah, no I fully understand-" Clyde said while staring off toward the skyline. "Is there anything you want to know specifically? I get that many people still don't trust you, even though you fought for our side."

"Yes, it has been a struggle to make friends here. And though it was by very interesting means, I am glad I finally made some. But I would like to know more, who is tha Queen? I am not used to a Matriarchy. It is very peaceful here — well, most of tha time I assume."

"It can be pretty boring around here for sure — in a good way obviously! But sometimes interesting things find their way here. Matter fact-" Clyde then leans forward, pointing toward a massive cathedral. Huge and intricately decorated pillars line the main street which leads to its front, his finger is placed perfectly beside it through his eyes. "You see that big church?"

"Uh huh." Uval replied while squinting to see better. "That's where her majesty lives. It's been renovated to be more like a castle or mansion, but there's still a huge portion of it left for public use. Mainly the Great Hall of Seven Wings. Luminel used to be a Theocracy, if you know what that means."

"Not particularly, no. I only know of two — matriarchy and patriarchy. You can assume why. But from what I remember in the teachings in the army, it had something to do with religion. Is that true?"

"Kind of. When people think of religion, they think of the newer definition that many use now. A faith or belief in divinity, whether that be to one God or an entire pantheon. They used to actually harness that divine energy, but that's apparently frowned on nowadays — for some reason."

"You seem to know a lot about this stuff. Do you take interest in tha subject? History and all those things."

"Yeah, I'd say so. If things hadn't gone so poorly, I could see myself becoming a chronicler. It's a part of the reason why I love hearing stories of you and the other heroes. The Stagnite Brawler, Heartless Cypher, The Youngest Hero, Red Angel, Fracture, I could really go on and on but you get the point. We only managed to put the world war into a ceasefire because of **you guys** — if Fort Tarasova hadn't been a success, a lot of things wouldn't be the same. We all owe you big time, but here we are leaving your deeds unwritten. I just. . . I just don't think that's right."

As their food and drinks were brought up, Uval took a bite out of his croissant and a sip of his tea. Sighing, his mind wandered back to the war. "Should those moments really be cherished? I'm not so sure of that anymore." He then thought for a moment as he continued to speak. "Maybe it would be best to keep your faith in things that you can't meet. At least not face to face. Speaking of which, what religion do you all serve? I know most of them are similar but still."

"Oh, right. Obviously it's a branch of Firmanism, the worship of the sky, but here we praise the Sun and Moon. To us they're twin deities that help hold back the Timeless Whispers of the void, all that lurks in the shadows and all that jazz."

The two then strayed away from the conversation for a bit, fully indulging in their breakfast. A cold breeze swept past them, alleviating the hot sunlight for a moment. The air was sweet and the atmosphere was soothing as the soft mutters of the cafe filled the tower.

"Question," Uval asked abruptly after taking a bite. "Why have you not left tha city? Scour the world for stories and such. A smart young man like you should use your talents. Your love for history shows."

"It's. . .not like I don't want to go. It's just that it costs a lot of money and it's not only me who I have to take."

"I can help you know. Help with money if that is tha problem. I'm sure if what is in my pockets is not enough then my friends would be willing to help."

"It's not just the money, sir. I made the wrong deals and now I'm stuck here as of right now. I'm – I'm working on it, I promise."

As their meal came to an end, Uval asked Clyde what he had planned for the rest of the week.

"I got a couple of jobs to do, but the most important one is tonight — I can push back everything else if need be. Why?"

"My friends and I require a guide, most of us are new to the city. I want *you* to help us. I guarantee it will be worth your time."

Pausing for a moment, Clyde bit his bottom lip and took a deep breath out. Nodding to himself, he looked to Uval afterward. He seemed to be mapping out the decision in his head. "I'll be there then — whenever you need me."

1.1 | A Day free.

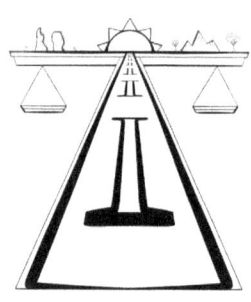

The sun shines, the birds sing, the wind passes, and the city brims with life. Passing down a street decorated with hundreds of colors and thousands of flowers, Aurelia looks over to Soren and Cypher as they all lick at the ice cream they carried.

"Not to be rude, but what the hell are we doing?" Confused by her question, Soren raised a brow. "Eating ice cream. What?" Then, giving her an actual answer, Cypher crunches at his own wafer cone. "Nothing. Uval was sent to get us formal clothes, Huruk is meeting an old friend, and Orwin is gathering intel-" He then looked forward to the giant pillars of stone that ran down the wide street. Vendors and wallstreet stores filled the sides with food and little niche items about their city. At the end of the street stood the massive cathedral Clyde had mentioned to Uval. "Then there's us doing *'reconnaissance'* or better known to the public as — **tourism**."

Raising a squishy toy of a star, Soren shrugged. "This beats real reconnaissance. You remember when we had to become Mastonov citizens for a month? That SUCKED! It was way too cold for me, my eyebrows felt like they were freezing off," Soren then turned to Aurelia with big eyes. "And there wasn't even any snow where we were stationed!"

"Of course I remember," Said Cypher, "That was one of the few times where we weren't getting shot at during the war. It was rather peaceful."

"You must be forgetting the time in that one alley. They shot more bullets at us than when we first landed on the shores."

"I did in fact forget that. . . I retract my previous statement. It was peaceful until then."

Curious about their history, Aurelia asked a question as the three of them got to the front gate which surrounded the cathedral. "Just how long have you two known each other? I heard stories about the two of you for a good while now." They then looked to one another and then back to Aurelia. "Ever since training at least, we were bunkmates. So what, about five years now? Nobody liked this statue of a guy so I took him under my wing." Soren said while putting an arm over Cypher's shoulders.

"Other than the friends you had before the army, nobody liked you either. You were just too ignorant to realize it." Soren then looked to Cypher with a shocked face, turning to Aurelia after. "He's kidding. I think."

"I'm not." Walking with a crowd of hundreds, the group stepped into the cathedral. There were rows of pews in several separate aisles that lined the great hall. The walls held many trophies encased in thick glass. Statues of gold which acted as coffins, crowns of every generation, parchment drenched in a resin-like liquid to retain its writing, and many more items important to this city and country. As Aurelia looked around, she noticed how many heavily armored rangers were scattered about — not to even mention the ones who blended into the crowd. She then leaned over to Soren, whispering into his ear. *"How the hell did Orwin sneak that cup out of here?"* Whispering back, Soren looked over to the empty glass box — merely a velvet pillow was left in its stead, the imprint of the chalice still upon it. *"No idea, why are we here anyway? Cypher still hasn't given me any info."* Aurelia then looked down the great hall. At its end stood a stone obelisk with an angled hole which aimed up toward the huge window above it. The window had seven ornate silver wings around it and a circular cutout in its center. Now speaking normally, Aurelia took Soren back out to the street. "Whatever it is, I don't think it should involve us." She clearly saw a strange look on Cypher's face, a confused blank stare.

Staring through the corner of his eye, Cypher looked at the two of them leaving. Now by himself, he turned back around to see the line of people in front of him. The citizens of Luminel gathered at the obelisk, one at a time they bent the knee. Staring up through the guidelines of the church, the Sun stared back. Basking in the dazzling radiance, Cypher looked to the person in front of him. 'An older gentleman, with a face full of pride casted it aside to lower himself before a God. What purpose does faith serve?' Cypher questioned. Before he knew it, he was next. The clergymen ushered him forward and he did so hesitantly. Bending down, Cypher stared at the Sun which hung within the circular window. The light blinded him so, throwing his vision into a realm of white.

'There's nothing here. No ear to speak into. No mouth to listen to. No hand to hold-' Breathing slowly, Cypher could feel his worries fade and surroundings vanish, his inner voice softened. 'Though, the warmth is nice. . .'

Standing up, Cypher walked away with his mind floating in the clouds. He believed this whole thing to be peculiar, perhaps even silly. But he can't ignore the peace he felt for just a moment. 'A fluke maybe?' He thought. 'I still don't understand.' Looking to a nearby clergyman, he walked over and greeted her. "Priestess-" Cypher said while approaching. At this point many armed rangers stood between him and the ornately dressed woman. She then waved them off with a smile. "Yes?" She said with a voice as soft as silk, as sweet as a berry. "Do you have a question?"

"Yes. . .what — what does it mean?" Cypher said, stumbling on the many thoughts that hopped about in his mind.

"What does what mean?" She asked while gesturing for him to follow, it was clear to her that they needed a bit more space than this great hall allowed. Following, the two went toward the mosaic window as a line of armored rangers separated them from the rest of the crowd.

"Faith. . ." Cypher said as the word pushed itself to the forefront of his mind. "What is it? What do you all see that I don't?"

Leaning forward, the woman's eyes sparkled like the ocean as the sunrise hits it. She appeared pained by his question, worried about the man who she does not know. "We see but the same things, I can assure you of that. It is what we *feel* and *choose* to see that differs."

"So if I choose to see, will that work? Will that help me? Can the unseen be that powerful?" Through the motionless mask which Cypher had always worn, pure emotions slipped through every so often. Sneaking between the cracks that formed with every question, Cypher's eyes seemed alive. The woman softly chuckled before speaking. "No, it won't be that simple I'm afraid. But it is the first step. What is it that you seek anyway?"

Standing completely still, only shifting his head down to the quartz panels, Cypher looked back up while realizing what he needed. "Guidance. . ."

Curious, the woman leaned in closer, being sure their voices could only be heard by themselves. "What in particular do you need help with? The visible can be just as helpful at times. An ear to speak into can work wonders you know."

"Nothing I can say to anything that might understand me. But I am curious, is a Priestess supposed to ask questions like that?"

The woman then backed up with a toothy grin, she stood with a proud stance which betrayed the version of her from just a moment ago — a regal and elegant woman.

"You really don't know who I am, do you?"

Staring at her with a raised brow, Cypher had his mouth agape in confusion. "No, not at all." A silent moment passed as the rangers approached him from behind. "Oh. . . I see."

1.2 | A Night ensnared.

The darkness of the sky swallows the now bitter city. Deep into the crevices where criminals roam, where floral streets turn to bannered halls, Huruk walks around with a hood over his head. Amidst a crowd of figures, split into an even mix of shrouded robes and refined leisure, the mage walked amongst them whilst dressed like the in between of both. Walking through the shadowy streets and alleys as chained lanterns hung faintly above them, Huruk looked around at the two groups that could be seen clearly. His interest peaked in how vastly different they were. One side wore wispy rags, usually a darker color but never purely black. The ends of their cloaks were shredded, shifting like the tips of flame as they moved about. He knew these were the Midnight Candles, a group that's spread across the darkest places in the world. But what Huruk knows isn't what interests him. The other side was far more elegant in their fashion, sporting suits and outfits that could easily blend into the city. These mob members seemed equal in size to the Candles, he wondered how deep their connections go.

'So these are the groups Uval warned us about. Glad to see that I don't know one of them. . .' As Huruk was thinking, he noticed a crudely painted sign. A cloaked man slapped the hanging scribblings of red as he walked by with his friends at his side. Their ramblings and banter swept past Huruk as the Mage made his way to the door — entering the Scarlet Drake. Walking in, he took one look at the once luxurious restaurant and deeply sighed. Chandeliers were replaced by rustic lanterns, ornate table sets by rickety seats, and lavish curtains by draped rags.

Making his way through the staring crowd that lingered amongst the masses, Huruk made his way to the back and held the doorknob to the office room. Pausing, he looked through the thin curtains that hung through the window, it was dark inside with no lights — despite that, there was very clearly someone sitting at the desk. Staring down at the knob, it suddenly turned on its own as Huruk walked in. Sitting down, he placed his hands on the table and waited silently.

"No need to be so tense, speak. A Mage's tongue is their greatest weapon, you're free to use it as you please." Huruk then acted slightly more relaxed, his shoulders lowering though his attention stayed on the person in front of him. "He's stronger than we thought." Huruk said as he looked down at the desk, it was empty except for a single glass of water — filled till it peaked just above its edge. "I think I need your help to kill him." The Shaper looked at Huruk, his eyes looking at him disappointedly.

"You ignore my warnings, march toward the eye of a storm, live and come back — then ask for my help? My, you've truly grown glutinous since we last met."

"It has to be done, if Rakesh is allowed to live then all Mages to come may be in danger. What kind of man would I be to let that scar on us breathe for any second longer?"

"Simple. You'd be a living one."

Huruk then raised his head to the ceiling, closing his eyes while taking a deep breath in. Breathing out, he looked back down to the man. "Just tell me, how many spells do you know? If we compile what we've learned throughout the years maybe there's something there to defeat him. . ."

"I know but one." The Shaper said in response. Confused, Huruk questioned him with a shocked expression and tone. As if he'd been misled by his actions and words leading up to this moment. "And that was enough for you in the war? A single spell?"

"It was more than enough, even the three years since."

Even more curious, Huruk followed up with another question. "Do you think it would be enough to kill *me*? Enough to kill **Rakesh**?"

"You'd give me trouble, there is no doubt in that. But you or any living creature besting me? There are better chances of surviving in the Taltoa highlands with nothing to protect you from its magic. To best me in sheer power is nigh impossible, but in intellect I concede. I can be beaten. Otherwise I am a summit hard to reach, a chasm tough to cross."

"You speak high of yourself, Shaper. Perhaps a bit cocky even. I don't know what role you played in the war, but could it have warranted this much arrogance? You weren't like this when we were younger."

"Do not read my cockiness as is. My pride is a verbal warning to those who **think** they are brave enough to face me, to stand before a peak far greater than themselves. Only perfectly using any tools you have may give you a chance to scale up to my height. So know that the thunder which booms from my lips is but a warning of the lightning that it can summon. I suggest you heed it before I show you a glimpse of the storm."

Huruk then smiled and nodded. "Very well, I won't dare to go against *these* words of yours. But I am curious, what *did* you do in the war? In my travels I didn't hear your name in any of the campsites from Vola to Mystcall. Even in the documents as I searched for Rakesh, you came up empty — I could have sworn you told me that you participated, or am I mistaken?"

"You certainly aren't. However, it appears you've misjudged my words and made an assumption. It was Mastonov that I worked with, though I do regret the side I chose. The little tricks Mystcall had tucked away took me by surprise, I would've loved to dissect the Black Box before it was used."

"Of course. . . I thought it was odd that Mastonov was holding ground so well. After the initial bombing of Northridge and the invasion, there were barely any troops left in their own home. So when Mystcall invaded, I and many others thought that was it. They'd easily secure the capital with nearly ten times the army that Mastonov left in their lands — but no, they were kept at the southern shores. That was you, wasn't it?"

"Me and a handful of others. To give them their flowers, the troops we had left did well to stay alive — without them and their colorful tactics we would have been swarmed. But no doubt, I and the others recruited to maintain Mastonov pitched in more to the pot. That does remind me, one of them was a Seraphic — judging by their love for a certain Titan, they and Rakesh must know each other."

Huruk's curiosity became nearly insatiable. The mere mention of these other people sent fireworks blasting in his mind as the thought of it made him smile crazily. "If you don't mind me asking, how many others were there? And what are their names?"

"I do mind. Secrecy was a fickle bond that kept us tied, severing it would undo what we had made together. But I *can* tell you one thing. Though war has ended its greatest practitioners still roam. And unlike us mages, they were made for it. Thus, they will continue it. So please watch yourself, Huruk. Your next question you need answered may kill you."

2.0 | The Stars Struggle

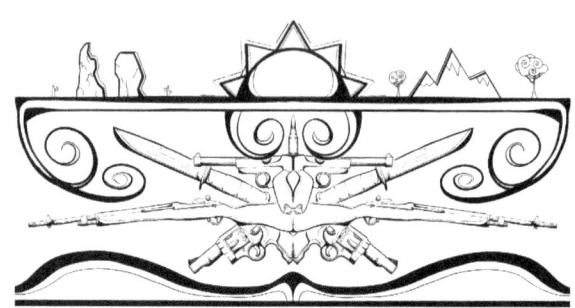

In a tired amble back home, Clyde stretches to relieve the stress built in his muscles. His eyes stare up to the stars which fly across the sky, a swarm of them like fireflies zooming from one horizon to the next. Stopping at a nearby window, he taps on the wooden shutter in a short rhythmic pattern. Opening it up excitedly, his younger sister smiles with glee. She sits up on the seat that is leaned against the window as she sticks out her head. Putting his hands up and signing to the young woman, Clyde asks if she's hungry. Signing back, she lets him know that she already ate. "Have you eaten?" She wonders. "Yeah–" Clyde says, knowing he hasn't actually done so. Feeling his stomach rumble, he reaches into his pocket and takes out a napkin — on it is an address which she longingly stares at.

"Will you be fine if I leave out for something? I'll try and be back before you sleep." Clyde leans against the window, putting on a silly face to try and persuade her. The younger sister playfully pouts as she stares plastic daggers into him, smiling after — she nods. "Just bring back some coffee for me!" Looking at her with a smirk, Clyde responds by rubbing her head.

"I told you you're too young for that! I'll get you something sweet instead, how does that sound?" Seeing her gleefully nodding, Clyde makes his way down the street, the window shuts as he begins to jog. 'I wonder if Uval is even awake at this time of the night. Actually, do legends like that even sleep?'

Laughing a bit to himself, Clyde went into a full on sprint — dust was kicked up with each step. Racing through the back streets of Luminel, newspapers were tossed into the air and flowers were ruffled about as he sprinted past.

Clyde was filled with an excitement he'd never felt before. Feeling his heart beat rapidly, he couldn't help but smile wildly — his sharpened fangs glistening just like his eyes did. The young man then recalled a memory from his late mother, when she told him a story of Fate. How it can turn and shift, but more than that — you can be aware of it. The sudden pit that formed in his stomach was proof enough for her story. He knew he had to chase this feeling, this turn of fate that was before him. "I sure hope this is good. . ." The young man whispered to himself. He'd heard many tales of these 'turns', all drastic but all varied. Nobody knows what will happen, only that the change will be radical.

As he ran while staring at the moving lights in the sky, Clyde could feel something resonating in himself. A strength that was being given to him. For what reason? He's unsure, 'but it can't be a coincidence' he thinks. Adrenaline pumped through the man, feeling the rush of the moment, the excitement of being chosen for something, it led him to try something irrational. At least for the version of Clyde he was before. Seeing an upcoming building at the end of the alley, he planted his lead foot forward, the newfound strength flowed to his legs as he crouched into a squatted position. A rush of energy consumed his mind and body as he then sprung upward, leaping over the two story building while flailing his arms around.

"HOLY SHIT!" He yelled with excitement, landing on a rooftop and skidding to a stop. "O-o-okay. . ." Clyde said to himself several times, trying to calm himself down from the high he's feeling. Pacing around and constantly shaking his hands, Clyde looked back up to the night to see that the shooting stars were gone. "Did – did you give me this?" He asked the Sky, but none of them replied.

Hearing commotion beneath him, Clyde suddenly looked down to a nearby street with a shocked expression. "Big Bro?!" He said while looking over to Orwin as the Showman walked out the backdoor of a nearby museum. About to jump down to meet with him, a voice suddenly spoke out from his side. Clyde's head then slowly turned to the man with a rifle in hand.

"So *that*'s the Greatest Showman, my guess was right then. Destiny's Call **is** here." Dario the Bountyhunter then turned to Clyde as he spoke. "The what? I don't know who you are, but I hope you don't plan on using that rifle right about now."

Dario then took out a rolled up piece of paper and tossed it to him. "News came early, this'll be shipped out to everybody tomorrow morning." Clyde caught the paper and opened up the newspaper, scanning through the articles afterward. Nodding his head, he looked back to Dario while tossing the paper to the wind. "Okay so you're a bounty hunter. Alright then. Listen, I can't let them get caught. Mainly because they're my heroes, but also I got a good feeling that everything in that article was a lie. They'd never work with that Abbot fella." Clyde then started walking side to side, reaching up to the beanie on his head and pulling it down. Staring through the cutout holes, his eyes filled with excitement after seeing who was in the group. "I'ma fix all that soon enough though, but you and me? We got a **now** problem."

Quickly turning and scoping onto Orwin as he walks down the street, Dario replies to Clyde as his finger rests on the trigger. "Not interested." The bullet then shoots out as it lands to the side of the Showman, his head whipped back to see two silhouettes on a rooftop behind him — their outlines traced by moonlight. Orwin then immediately took off in a sprint. With gritted teeth, Dario looked to Clyde as his foot was on the Hunters gun. "What's wrong? Did I mess up your aim?" Pushing him off his rifle, Dario slung it over his back as he took off and sprinted in Orwin's direction.

"Ignoring me? Let's see how long that lasts." Clyde then sprinted after the Hunter as they jumped from rooftop to rooftop. Reaching into his pockets, he put on two knuckle dusters that covered his hands like gauntlets. Chasing Dario as fast as he could, Clyde soon realized that he couldn't catch up despite the gift he was given, they moved at similar speeds which was puzzling to him. 'Fuck, did this guy get blessed too?'

Knowing he'd have to do something to slow him down, Clyde reeled back his fist and smashed the knuckleduster into a nearby metal pole, sending it flying at Dario. Slamming into his back, the Hunter turned around with a vexed expression — pulling out a curved blade he aimed to cut down the idiotic fool that lingers on his trail. However, he turns to see wildly twisting lines with clothes attached to them. The metal pole had been holding up someone's laundry. Between the thrown articles of clothing, Clyde raced forward and gained distance. Seeing him push through, Dario horizontally swiped. Ducking the slash, Clyde planted an upward punch directly under the Hunter's chin causing his head to jolt up. Following up, he did a straight punch into his stomach — however, Clyde didn't feel the stopping sensation of his body. Looking up to Dario confused, he saw a hole in the Hunter's stomach — his insides looked like sand and it dripped down like an hourglass. Shifting his head to look around Dario, Clyde saw the chunk of his body he had punched — it was a clump of sand and a rooftop over. Stunned by his confusion, Clyde was hit on the back of the head. Stumbling backward, Dario continued to run after Orwin while he recovered.

Jumping over to the next rooftop and continuing the chase, Clyde took notice of the clump of sand in front of him. He saw a couple of grains falling down from the pile as an arm suddenly sprung up from it. It then shot at him with the pistol as Clyde was jumping over it. The bullet grazed his cheek as he reacted just fast enough to dodge.

"Just what the hell are you? I've seen some crazy shit from people that use artifacts, but I've never seen this — you a mage or something?." Clyde yelled over to the Hunter. Dario then scoped in while responding. "I don't know all the classifications for Magic Users, but I know I'm not a Mage." Pulling the trigger, the bullet could be heard hitting something metal as he pulled the bolt handle to fire again.

Down below, Orwin held his chained knife to the side of his head as he stared into a nearby noisy cafe with longing eyes. His hurried steps slowed to a hypnotic glide. The bullet Dario had shot slid down Orwin's dagger as he walked to the cafe, staring at a woman who sat at its window.

Back up top, Clyde had punched the side of Dario's rifle, completely dismantling the gun one he caught up. Taking his blade back out, the two entered a stand still, each trying to gauge the distance from one another. Leading forward with a sweeping slash, Dario waved his sword like ribbon and aimed for his arm.

Turning his body, Clyde used the metal part on his palm to block the attack and then grabbed it — punching at Dario's arm with his free fist. As it made contact, his arm exploded into sand along with the blade. "So were you born like this or what?" Clyde asked as he jabbed at his face. Hitting him square in the mouth, Dario backed up, showing a bit of a smile.

"Magic Users aren't born dumbass, they're made or chosen." Spitting out blood onto the floor, an arm poked out from the sand beneath Clyde and jammed a knife into his thigh. Wincing in pain he kicked at the arm and ripped out the knife. "Who the fuck chose us? I gotta assume the Gods." Clyde asked as he slammed his foot into the floor, trying to make sure his leg was awake.

Dario then stood there as all the sand he lost began to lift up and fly toward him rapidly, regrouping and forming back into his body. "How the fuck am I supposed to know?" He said with a big grin on his face, the Hunter himself was a bit confused on why he was being somewhat friendly with this stranger. It was as if he'd forgotten what he originally came here for, Dario began to grow excited by the fight — thrilled by the battle between them rather than his goal. Meeting his enthusiasm, Clyde slammed his knuckle dusters together causing sparks to fly out on impact. "I'm thinking we figure out what exactly we were given. I gotta know what super power bullshit I got. I bet it's better than sand." He said while getting into an infighter boxing stance, leaning forward ready to burst into a sprint.

"I was thinking something similar. *Bring it on you sorry fuck.*" Dario replied and reached into his own chest, pulling out a knife and sword from the sand he'd become.

The two would exchange nearly a hundred blows as Orwin talked to the woman in the cafe. Each trying to best the other in a battle of self understanding, an effort made to utilize their newfound abilities better than their opponent.

Inside the cafe beneath them, Orwin sat with a woman with dark skin and brown fluffy hair. 'A honey dandelion' he describes in his head. Confused by his appearance in this cafe despite the introductions they'd just shared, the woman asks a simple question that clenches at the Showman's heart. "Sorry, but do you know me?" Her words were spoken with a level of sincerity that both warmed and shattered Orwin. He knew the answer was yes, it's what his soul screamed out to her, but he couldn't say it. "No. . . I don't. I just happened to see the book you were reading."

"Oh!- do you like it too?" She said while holding it up. Seeing the title, Orwin remembered the many times she would ramble on and on about its story — 'never ending were her words, yet I found paradise in her company.'

"Yeah, I've heard so many good things about it. But admittedly, my memory of it is a bit foggy." With a bright and dazzling smile, innocent and pure, she opened it back up and asked, "Then do you care for a refresher? This is a classic afterall! Poetry at its finest, can't go wrong with another read through." Orwin then leaned onto the table, placing his chin on his hand as he stared at her.

"I'd love that."

2.1 | The Flowers in Words

Back on the rooftop we find Clyde tackling Dario as they descend into a back alley. Crashing into the tiled floor, the Hunter explodes into several clumps of sand that scatter about. "Not this again. . ." Clyde says with a heaping ton of annoyance. Punching out toward the clumps, gusts of wind  are shot out with each strike. These air cannon-like shots blast away the sand as Dario recollects all of it to form himself again. "That just had to be your power, huh?" Dario says while stretching his shoulders. "Not a fan? How bout you come closer then." Leaning into the fight even more, Dario begins to sprint forward as he scrapes his sword and dagger across the floor. "MAYBE I WILL!" He yells out with excitement.

As he approaches, Clyde slams his foot down onto the floor causing a stone slab to fly up. Punching a gust of wind toward it, the slab is launched at Dario. Dodging the attack, several more come at the Hunter as he approaches swiftly. Maneuvering between them like a dragonfly, he closes the distance and swings his sword. As it's met with knuckle dusters, sparks fly while Dario parries the punch with his dagger — swiping with his sword after. In order to dodge the attack Clyde leaps backward and launches several rapid punches down at him — blasts of wind crash onto Dario as he underhand flings his sword. The blade spins to a blur while Dario tanks the explosions of air. It then slices across Clyde's cheek and ear as he tilts his head, just narrowly avoiding it. "You cheeky fucking bastard." He says with a clenched smile. Then, Dario suddenly bursts into sand as all of it swarms around Clyde. The Hunter reforms behind him and swings at his back.

Turning around as they land, Clyde sends a haymaker into reforming sand. The strike lands upon the side of a sword as Dario is pushed across the street, entering a different alley. Walking toward one another, they meet where cars cross and come to stop. Clyde then turns his head toward the cafe Orwin is at.

"I really hope that's going well for him." He says while looking back to Dario, prepared to fight more. Curious however, Dario looks into the cafe too.

"Who is that anyway?" He asks while flourishing the blade in his hand, spinning it around rapidly.

"The love of his life. The whole reason he's a thief in the first place. Once she started losing memories, Orwin went into a spiral trying to save her. But no doctors or Mages could help. I'm starting to think that's where the Abbot came into play."

111

"You really don't think they're in kahoots? A lot of faith coming from someone who doesn't even know them." As Dario finishes his sentence, Clyde looks at him with an annoyed glare. "We don't even know what **we** are, it ain't a Mage or a Wizard. All I know is that we're the same thing."

"What the hell does that have to do with what I said? Are you idiotic?"

"Ugh, the point is that we don't know what's going on. A lot of stuff in this world can't be explained, but those guys have the answer to what Destiny's Call is. Whether you have faith in them or not doesn't matter, they know what they are. . .why am I even talking to you? Put your fucking weapons up, bitch."

"Hold on–" Dario says while putting up a hand. "Why don't we just stop here. I don't care if they're evil or not. I just want to kill Soren, that's it. I was hoping getting Orwin would drag him to me but obviously you have some ties with him. I'll figure out another way to get to that False Hero."

"We could. . . we definitely could stop here — but nah." Clyde then rushed forward and clocked Dario in the face, sending him flying into an alley and crashing into random wooden objects. "Now we can stop. That was for cutting my face, people are gonna think worse of me now. *sigh* I just hope it looks cool when it scars."

Getting up, Dario stretches his neck as blood rolls down from his nose. "You know I'm gonna have to cut you again for that right?" He asks while stowing his weapons.

"Yeah, I figured, but that'll be some other time — right?" Looking at him, then to Orwin who sat in the cafe, Dario responded. "Yeah, some other time." The Hunter lowered his head a bit, wiping the blood from his nose as he walked away into the alley.

Giving him a nod, Clyde walked over to the cafe while a crowd came out — the loud music booming from the stage seemingly came to a stop. With the show over Orwin made his way to him and continued to go down the street as Clyde followed. "So, how'd it go?" He asked the Showman hesitantly. "It was. . .nice to see her again." Pulling up his beanie so it no longer covered his face, Clyde slung an arm over his shoulder. "Care to talk about it?"

"I don't think. . .I can."

"That's alright then, Big bro. Let's just go for a walk."

3.0 | The Party Gathers

At the edge of Mystcall, where waves move from horizon to concrete shores, several warehouses sit empty on Luminels harbor. In one of them, Uval, Soren and Aurelia sit at a poker table on the open 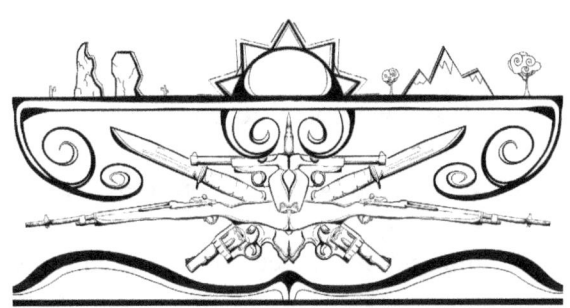 floor. In the middle of their game, Orwin and Clyde enter in from a nearby door. With big waves they greet each other. But more presently, the young man smiles from ear to ear as he sees Soren. Fanboying a bit, he rushes over to specifically greet him — shaking his hand frantically. Almost feeling Clyde's energy rub off on him, a young man nearly the same age as himself, Soren smiles and starts to jump up and down with him. "WHY ARE WE JUMPING!" He asks Clyde as he continues to squeal. A moment later they both calm themselves and sit like civilized and mature men. "Anyway." Clyde coughs out while looking at the others. "My brother and I have some things to share with the class."

"Brother?" Aurelia asks while pondering the story in front of her. "You guys look nothing alike, Orwin, are you adopted? But I thought you were from Vola. . . something tragic must've happened."

Uval and Soren then joined Aurelia as they all looked to Orwin with listening ears and focused eyes. With disappointment Orwin looked away, only to see Clyde doing the same thing as them. "Why are you looking at me like that?! YOU KNOW THE ANSWER!" The Showman then looks at the others. "He helped with stealing the Linking Chalice and has grown to be on my hip ever since. Anyway, we have to get him up to speed. Apparently he wants to help again."

Clyde then stared at everybody intently, patiently waiting with a bit of visible eagerness. "Well, I've been waiting for this anyhow. How bad could it be?"

Cutting forward to when it was all explained, Clyde was found staring off into the vast ocean on his lonesome — confused on how answers gave him more questions. Turning away from him, Soren looked to Orwin and asked, "Is he- is he gonna be okay?" Looking at him, Orwin shrugged and went back to being serious. "Besides him, I found some interesting stuff. But where the hell is Cy and Ruk? I'd hate to repeat the meeting. Weren't they informed to return around this time of night?"

"Tha Mage is talking to his friend, the uh–" Uval says, struggling to remember the name. "The Shaper" Aurelia states, helping him out. "Yes, that one. Why does no one have real name no more? Always title. So weird — I am proud to be a Lotrensky."

"Okay well, that takes care of one of them. What about Cy?" Orwin turns to Soren, assuming he knows where he's at. Doing a double take toward him, realizing he's asking him specifically, Soren sits up straight.

"Oh– yeah, um. I have no idea. . .sorry. Last I saw him was in the main church. He never left from what I'm aware, unless you–" He says while turning to Aurelia. "–know something different."

"I know. . .that those visions hit Cypher a bit hard. Something in his head was jossled and it has him rethinking a lot about himself. I can only assume he's off thinking about it. Fuck, how does Huruk deal with these all the time?"

Uval leans back in his chair and stares off to the rising sun as Clyde sits in front of it. "I do not know, but surely you eventually become numb to it right? Like working out, enough reps will make you stronger."

Pondering the thought, Aurelia seems to dig into the idea of 'making your brain stronger' a bit too much. "No. . . he might be onto something. Maybe he has a resistance to it now, like how drinking poison will eventually make you immune to it. Antibodies and all that jazz, I never went to real school — I wouldn't know the science behind it."

"What is tha school? They did not have that in my village" Uval asks. Right after Soren and Aurelia start explaining it as Orwin yells out to get their attention. "GUYS **PLEASE**!! We need to find these two so we can start going forward with the plan. I know generally where the archives are going to end up but the main problem is getting into it. We just need to brainstorm a strategy together."

Soren then raises his hand, and though reluctantly, Orwin points to him like a teacher. "Well, while they're not here we could continue discussing Huruk's magic. What if we all were able to use it? Wouldn't that make everything go so much smoother?"

Aurelia then plays along, raising her hand as well. "Additionally, Mr.Trinket, we wouldn't have to rely on him as much in certain situations — as a group we would become that much more versatile."

And not knowing what's going on, Uval raises his hand and just speaks without being called upon. "Tha magic he has is very strong and cool too — I would gladly have some if I could take it. Imagine tha power I could have with that stuff."

Soren then looks at the Ogre confused. "Don't you have powers already? I thought that welding ability was a part of your armor but it isn't."

Overhearing the nonsense, Huruk walks in with a disappointed expression. "Please don't romanticize magic." He says while sitting down at the table, throwing his bag over his shoulder and onto the table. A bunch of snacks pour out from it as everyone takes something.

Confused by his demeanor towards their enthusiasm, Uval speaks while scarfing down some sweet bread. "Do you not love what you seek, Mage? Is that not your purpose to wander tha lands? Other than to kill this Devil of course."

"No, not really. Magic is unruly, wild, chaotic, and ever changing. What I seek is the Arcane."

"What- *munch* is tha difference anyway? Magic, arcane, they are the same, no?"

Thinking to himself for a moment, Huruk snags a loaf for himself and takes a bite. "What's the best way to say this–" Leaning forward, he whispered and waved his hand. Flourishes of blue lights sparkled above the table in chaotic yet beautiful ways. Restless like fire, but flowing like water.

"**Magic**; Primordial chaotic energy. Everything you can and cannot imagine exists within it, flowing until it reaches our world to explode into anything. It is a force that, on its own, would ravage our land into a fantastical state. Many places in our current day and age reflect that possibility. The northernmost part of Mystcall, past the Dratari Isthmus lies Taltoa. An environment with raw and wild magic. It's why no major cities or towns are there. Nothing tamed is born on that land."

Waving his hand again, the swooshes of magic formed together to display natural disasters. Lightning storms, earthquakes, eruptions, hurricanes, and more.

"**Arcane**; Subdued Magic. Some people are naturally born with the ability to harness the chaotic energy, fold and bend it to their will. Through this, spells can be created. For Mages we use Ancient Tongue directly, but usually all the other Magic Users filter it through their structure. For example, Witches will use brews and potions, Wizards will use staffs and wands, and Paladins will use their faith and Gods. Regardless of the power system you abide by, Ancient Tongue is always prevalent. It usually is what causes them to gain their unique abilities. But Mages are different. We are not given those whispers, so instead we seek the words given out."

During this, Clyde makes his way over after hearing most of it. Confused, he asks Huruk a question. "Wait. I was recently able to do a bit of magic, but my body specifically feels a lot more powerful. Before it happened, I remember seeing the shooting stars above me. I thought it was weird but I think I heard those whispers, I'm not sure though. I– I don't know what I am."

Taking a moment to ponder it, Huruk replied. "During my travels across the world, I've seen many like you. Ever since the start of the last war, many people have been chosen by the Gods — given powers and boosts in strength. For what reason? I'm not certain, but it can't be for nothing I'm afraid. They may be preparing for something. As for what you are, however, I believe I know what it is. Among all the types of Magic Users in the world, one remains the pinnacle for battle. A Magist."

Soren then leans back, memories flash across his eyes. Breaking from their grasp, he speaks. "So these whispers, the ones from these Gods. They- they change you don't they?" Huruk nods in acknowledgement. "More than Ancient Tongue when spoken through mortal lips." A drained expression then goes across Soren's pale face.

Aurelia then speaks her mind. "Is there a way to gain these whispers then? Or is it the luck of the draw? As much as it was a joke earlier, I'm a bit serious now. Becoming a Magist or whatever could be what sets us apart from the main players in what's going on in the world. At least in what the future holds."

"I'm not sure," Huruk says while staring out into the sea. "Most times it can be stress or shifts in your life, great ones at that. Anything that may gain the attention of the Gods. That's why many soldiers are chosen by them, at least as of recently. In each generation or so, the most relevant type of Magic Users changes. In the last hundred years it was Witches, that was when most conflict in the world happened in the far reaches of nature. Now it seems to be Magists."

Orwin then sighs before speaking up. "Maybe we'll get those whispers on the way then, but can we get back on track now that the majority of us are here? I haven't even talked about Uval's armor yet." The Ogre then rose from his seat. **"My what?"**

4.0 | Painted History

The next morning when they planned to proceed with their mission, Cypher never turned up. Forced to move without him, Destiny's Call made their way to the museum Orwin had been seen

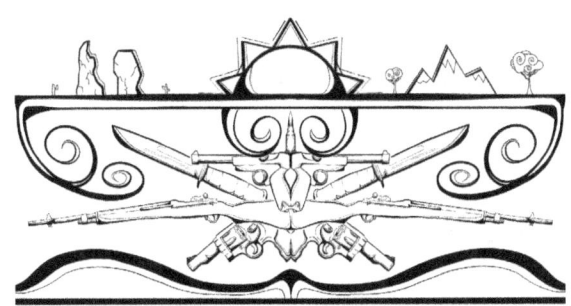

scouting out. However, one thing they didn't notice was Dario. He'd been trailing behind Clyde ever since they split up, knowing he'd be led straight to Soren. So as they gather round the luxurious museum, the Hunter trails behind them as they slowly enter the historic halls.

The rooms were lavish and taller than needed. Each exhibit was strung up with wires or placed upon a podium, meant to feel momentous before a visitor of the arts. Strolling through the exquisite displays, they'd feel almost rudimentary in their sections. There was a hall dedicated to bones. Curious creatures that somewhat resemble what we have today, but most visitors would see their physical nature as far more outlandish. Huge beasts with hollow bones, still dense enough to withstand strikes from a bat or mace, yet light enough to fly — not unlike the raven which befell Printon. But this skeleton had no wings, only propellor-like spines at its end, huge hulking arms that draped down from its body like curtains and a stubby face with three-sets of eyes on each side. "Or at the very least, that's what the researchers believe." Said the tour guide. Staring through his circular glasses, the older man twisted the ends of his mustache as he waited for his following visitors to be struck with awe — unfortunately for him, Destiny's Call was on a mission. They didn't give a single fuck.

Each member, especially Uval, darted around with their eyes in search of his armor. They already knew the location of the archives were in the queen's cathedral, tucked away in a large vault underneath it all — though they didn't know how to get in, Uval assured them that with his armor, no wall could stop him.

Seeing their lack of care for his words, the tour guide cleared his throat and hurried along to the next exhibit. The golden hall was decorated with elaborate paintings. They depicted great wars of the past, each with their own reasons and locations. These images seemed almost picturesque in their detail, yet fantastical as if ripped out from an old storybook. "In my humble opinion as one of the head curators of the Sistario Museum, these fine works of art are without a doubt thee most striking pieces we have. There is beauty in history, and wonderful artists like Pintacho Muisili, Irtaro Regaro, and Unel Quaves have truly captivated such."

The tour guide pranced around the hall, waving his arms while trying to display the wonders before them — but as he turned around, only Huruk was looking. Soren and Orwin had completely disappeared, likely pushing forward the mission at hand. Meanwhile, Uval and Aurelia stayed behind with the Mage begrudgingly — they desperately wanted to go help with the mission.

"Why am I staying? It is *my* armor. . ." Uval asked as he leaned down to Aurelia. She then glanced at him and went back to staring at the fine works around her — she actually did enjoy the paintings, but her mind was solely on the goal ahead of her. "C'mon, you know you can get a little silly when it comes to fighting. Though I do wish I got to go, it's been a whole lot of nothing for a bit."

"Oh I know how I can get, but Soren? He is much scarier than me on tha battlefield, but I suppose he is quieter."

"Hm? Soren being scarier? Yeah, I don't know about that. Have you seen him?"

"Of course I've seen him. Those Magic Whispers Huruk mentioned, I got them long ago in my village while hunting. I'm sure something similar happened to Soren, probably during tha war. And he may be bubbly now, but there's something else in there. Something more dangerous than an Ogre."

The two then continued to follow the tour guide as Huruk stopped to look at the paintings. He noticed a small detail hidden behind each depicted battlefield, a mountain which pierced the clouds, high and mighty with a view to see the world. His home.

'**My** home. Every painting of each war had it — tiny it was, etched into the background of warfare. But that means this order was wrong, the labels given to these pictures were **wrong**. In my mind I began to throw the paintings around, rearranging them in a specific order only I'd know. We were taught the history of Terox Academia thoroughly, shown the way each brick was placed through a spell they'd taught us — it let us see its history through our own eyes.

I've done it myself a hundred times. No — a thousand. I know what my home was like, how it was built within every year because I'd seen it myself every night that I lived there. So when others visited their families from off the mountain I stayed, learning of every building and every mage that has ever been. Because that was **my** home. So before me now, only through my eyes I see the real order. I still don't know what these pictures are trying to tell me, they aren't as clear as the visions. But I can feel the arcane warmth of other mages, reaching out with gentle hands trying to warn me of something. But what is it? I can't tell, all I see is the decline of our kind — each war taking more and more of us away from the canvas until we are but a handful of brushstrokes that fills the ocean of color. So to me, the only thing that is clear is how rotten our involvement has been. Because as we wither away, war has only grown more hungry — is it not satisfied with how many of us its eaten? Maybe we should have never helped. **Maybe** my masters were wrong. It was never our turn to guide the world with magic, it was our turn to fall victim to it.'

"Huruk!" Uval yelled over to him, the Ogre then gestured for the Mage to follow. "Tha boring guide is leaving us, c'mon my friend!" Looking over to Uval and Aurelia, Huruk simply nodded his head and followed along. Shifting his gaze back, he stared at the painting which rightfully belonged to be first — it had the most mages and the academy was immature, not yet grown. His eyes suddenly opened wide as he saw something hidden in the brushstrokes of the mountain — *Ferano*. An ancient word derived from the people of Northridge meaning fire or spark. Staring at it for but a glance, Huruk turned away and continued on with the guide. Thinking about what it meant.

"Still no info on Cypher?" Soren asks Orwin as they wander the maze-like halls. Looking around, the Showman spotted a sign saying, 'Modern Relics'.

"No, I got nothin on Cy. But that ain't our problem, he walked away on his own — he probably just chose to leave. Might even be better that he does." Soren then came to a sudden stop. "He wouldn't. I think it's pretty obvious that all of us are too involved to just walk away."

"You say that, but where is he now? He left without saying anything. We all faced our own vision during our brawl with the Abbot. I don't think it'd be wrong for him to leave." Orwin stopped and turned slightly to look at him. "Still, I know him. Cypher will come back. Maybe just not when we expect it." Orwin turned away from him as Soren spoke, sighing as he replied. "Listen, I don't really care if he comes back or not. But a lot of us have something to fight for, I just can't see that with him. Let's just get this mission done and get one step closer to our goals."

The entrance to the Modern Relics section was taped off, peeking through the windows there were several workers hauling in a huge wooden crate. They struggled to heave it onto the metal podium specifically built for whatever was inside. Looking at Soren, Orwin simply nodded to let him know that this was it.

"How does the Greatest Showman wanna do this?" Soren says as he bows to him. Looking at him with a slight smirk, Orwin grabbed the doorknob. "No need for anything elaborate. We knock out those guys who are pretending to be workers and we take the armor before they can switch it out, easy peasy."

"Lemon squeezy. I'm ready when you are."

The doors burst open and Orwin unleashed his chains outward. The links poured out from his sleeves as they landed on some of the indoor scaffolding that was set up for the hanging lights. As the workers looked to him in shock, Soren placed his hand in front of Orwin as he was about to pull it all down atop them. "WAIT! Are we sure these aren't normal guys?"

"If you wanna figure that out yourself, be my guest Unluckiest Hero." Orwin refrained from pulling all the scaffolding down, though he didn't move away from *not* doing it. This made the workers stay still, unsure if he was going to crush them with it or not.

"Alright. . ." Soren said, trying to hype himself up. The nerves of the situation were getting to him a bit. He shook his hands and slowly walked toward them. "Fellas. My lads. My friends — why don't you guys just walk away? Oh wait, you'll probably call somebody. Okay, why don't you guys sit in that corner over there–" Soren then turned to point at said corner, in that moment a bullet suddenly whizzed past his head and he frantically ducked in fear.

"FUCK!" He screamed while turning around. Some of the workers pulled out guns as the others sprinted forward — a shroud of darkness surrounded their uniforms as it was replaced with clocks, each one dark but never black. Reacting to everything, Orwin yanked at the chains causing the scaffolding to fall upon the criminals in disguise. Wrapping the links around Soren's torso, Orwin spun the Hero around as he then tossed him at the criminals. "Hold on, WAIT, WAIT GOD DAMN IT!" Screaming out Soren slammed into the cloaked figures like a bowling ball. As all five of them were getting up, he stared at them while they pulled out knives made of bones. "Please. . . rethink this. I really don't want to fight any of you. This time I can't just run." Ignoring his plea for a peaceful ending, the rogues charged at him.

The first stabbed at his chest. Seeing it come at him, Soren shifted his stance and easily disarmed them — sweeping them to the ground with his leg and sending a downward punch into their face. After knocking them out, he looked to the next one. "Please, just stand down." Soren pleaded, there was clear desperation in his voice.

The next rogue approached and slashed down at his shoulder, raising the blade he'd taken, Soren blocked it. Headbutting them, he then used an elbow to chin check the rogue as they were dazed. The flow of battle seeped into the Hero, his eyes became focused and his words silenced.

Seeing the rogue approach Soren tossed the knife at their right foot. It went clean through and stopped their momentum. During this the last two rushed him with a flurry of strikes from his sides. Dodging and blocking most of them, Soren lifted his leg and delivered a front kick to the one on the left — pushing them back. Before his leg was retracted however, the other rogue stabbed his thigh. Soren didn't wince at the pain and instead used it to his advantage. While they pulled out their knife to attack him again, the Hero lifted his planted foot and swung it around — that leg whipped around to strike the rogue in the stomach. Soren then fell to the ground as they dropped to their knees from the pain, it sounded like a gunshot when it made contact.

Seeing the Hero on the floor, the staggered rogue that was pushed back ran at him. Jumping up they stabbed down at Soren, but seeing it come from so far away he was prepared. He planted his feet on their chest, stopping them from landing on him, he kicked them away causing them to crash into a large glass container. While they were stunned by the attack, Soren stood and approached. The rogue put their arms up to protect themself but the Hero rained an onslaught of strikes upon them — relentlessly he attacked. It was to the point where the rogue's arms began to give out from the pain, once they lowered a fist landed directly in their chest. The impact cracked the glass the rogue leaned on. Though their eyes were hazy, clearly out of the fight already, Soren continued to strike the rogue — each punch cracked the glass even more. This continued until it shattered.

Breathing heavily, Soren backed up with bloody knuckles. Looking down to the knife in his thigh, he ripped it out and looked over to Orwin. The Showman had already gone over and dealt with the gunman but as he looked back at the Hero, he seemed a bit different. Soren had angry yet focused eyes, his rage was not blind but perceptive. Worried, Orwin asked if he was okay. "You good?"

"Yeah, I've been dealt worse wounds. This is nothing."

"That's not what I- nevermind. Let's get the armor, all that commotion had to have alarmed everybody."

Sprinting to the box, they grabbed a nearby crowbar and forced it open. In shock they both stared at what was inside — "They swapped it out already. . .." Orwin said as he turned around with his hands on his head. He then frantically began to talk to himself. "There's gotta be a truck or something outside — they couldn't have gotten far. These guys were supposed to come back — fuck, they're leaving **now**."

The purring sound of a motor being turned on echoes out from a nearby doorway, it leads directly into a large garage where trucks bring in the items. Hearing that noise, Orwin turns to Soren and gestures with his head that they need to go. Nodding back, they make their way out.

4.1 | Masks Burn

Bullets fire out as screams echo from deeper halls. The entire museum goes into a panic as Uval immediately sprints toward the chaos, knocking over nearby rangers that were rushing over first. "OUT THA WAY!" He yells. Aurelia then follows the Ogre in a hurry, yelling out to Huruk that they need to catch up. But in the heat of the moment, he turns to look back into the hall of paintings — his curiosity beginning to guide him.

Entering the Modern Relics room, Uval and Aurelia look around as they see several people already unconscious — but more importantly, the armor and their friends are nowhere to be seen. Right after, the rangers rushed in behind them to say that they couldn't be in here. But after seeing Uval's face, they stayed silent. He was furious.

"If one more thing goes wrong. I may very well lose it — but I have faith in them. Those two will be fine." Looking up to him, Aurelia placed a hand on his shoulder. "As long as you know." Heading to the back doors that were seemingly slammed open, she gestured for them to go.

"We'll have to play catch up." Running out into the loading dock of the museum, two garage doors were already fully open — while sprinting out they could see two trucks fleeing the scene. Aurelia then jumped up onto Uval's back as he began to sprint forward, ripping a chunk of metal from a garage door and creating a shield with it.

The halls became quiet as everyone fled, Destiny's Call, the Midnight Candles, and even the staff members. But Huruk was still there, staring at the paintings. Behind him, footsteps clattered out and approached him. The Shaper appeared and spoke out to him.

"Is this the question you wish you to risk your life on? Are you really prepared to cross a boundary all mages fear and adore?"

Without turning, Huruk responded. His eyes still trained on the paintings. "Is that not the path a mage walks? To figure out the answers to their questions, to know the unknowable. We are not chosen by the Gods, not bestowed their words and given power — yet we seek it. In a way, is that not sin? Is it not greed that fuels us to learn? Personally, I don't think it's wrong but many of us mortals say it is so. I see it as a natural reaction to the unknown."

The Shaper took a step forward to him. "Yes, the Gods may not have chosen us. But there are worse things out there that will. The Titans, they'll find space for you among their thoughts. The Sun, Moon, and Void do not wish well for us — they do not wish at all. In truth they are hollow, the first children of Magic. Those three are merely cogs that will eternally rotate, and in that cycle we will fall victim."

"I believe our kind has already **been** victims. You make ill comments about those three Titans, but our world views them as the pinnacle for the Gods. What does that say about them? Perhaps we simply lack the truth, or maybe there is truth in what we already know. The fact that we don't understand it makes wanting it human. If not I — someone else will walk this path to its end. Let it be me."

The Shaper took another step forward. "You know I can't let you do that. I've seen too much loss come from ambition like yours. It almost took me as well. Others have already reached the end of this path, and they realized we were **wrong** about the Gods. The Hollow Titans do not think as the others do. They are embodiments of Magic itself, chaos and order wrapped into a force beyond our comprehension. These Titans don't share the kind of mind the Gods do — they are Magic incarnate. Not representations of disasters and phenomenons."

"And where are those findings now? Burnt to a crisp and lost to history because of our involvement in the wars. We were too kind to realize that our endeavor for knowledge needs to be sought alone. By the very nature of Ancient Tongue, sharing what we learned should have been forbidden. So now as you reference information that no longer belongs to us, I have to stand here and question it. Because it has to be refound, relearned, and retaught. And if you should still disagree with my philosophy, strike me down now — you were confident last we met. It shouldn't be a problem since I'm reaching for something I shouldn't."

"You don't know what you've fallen in love with, Huruk — I stand here not as the Shaper, but as the friend you once knew. I beg you, don't follow a trail that leads off a cliff. Think this over, I still remember enough. Instead of learning it like this, I can teach you."

"Think it over. . ." Huruk said as he started to pace around, the paintings blurred behind him as he shook his head — a scornful look appeared on his face as his eyebrows scrunched together. "I **have** thought it over. Again and again, I think of it. The moments where ash filled my lungs as our home burned. We are the last two of our Academy, and yet you stand here and believe I am wrong?" Huruk looked at the Shaper, grabbing at his own shirt tightly as he spoke.

"That **I** am wrong?! I am trying to finish what our kind has started, they may have reached the end but what is beyond it? With all traces of our history gone. . .I HAVE TO START AGAIN. I HAVE TO WALK THEIR PATH **AGAIN**." After yelling out, he paused. Calming himself and looking at the paintings. "But I won't make the same mistakes they did, I'll be better. Stronger, so I can carry the weight of all of us. I was a fool for hoping you'd think the same."

"Huruk, please just give me time to explain. I know you can feel something behind those paintings. I know that there's a pit in your stomach right now, telling you to find out what it is. And I'm here to tell you that I feel that pit too — but it's telling me to stop you. Just give me more time to explain. You may not be able to climb back up this cliff if you fall."

"That's enough, Zevyn. Nothing you say will sway me. We know that already. So how do you want to do this? Shall we do it like the old days, how we used to duel as kids?"

"We're not kids anymore, if we fight it won't be pretend."

"And I wouldn't have it any other way. Ready yourself."

Struggling to find the words to say to what used to be his little brother. The Shaper clenches his raised hand, and at the same time — they spoke aloud.

The Shaper | Huruk Rem

"Vectis" | **"Ferano"**

Hearing the opposing words for the first time, visions passed them by. However, with the mental fortitude they've built up throughout the years these images shutter between reality and memory. The effects of their spells cause the hall to burst with flame as segments of the floor are crushed and lifted slowly into the air. Looking at one another their visions force them to see the past for moments at a time, trying to tell them not to fight. So before them they see the man that stands today, and the innocence that once was.

Huruk, a child with a bright smile, points his hand forward as bubbles of water shoot out. Now stricken with grief and pained by revenge, that smile flickers to a regretful grimace and scornful eyes filled with deep loss that he cannot forget.

Zevyn, a young boy with a proud look, points his hand as he lifts small pebbles to send forward. Now pained with the failure of saving his friends and family, that proud look flickers to a pride only found in the power he now possesses — yet still he feels empty.

The flames then begin to tear at the paintings as the lifted objects are thrown at Huruk, but the fire surrounding him burns brighter — shooting up, pillars of his anger shield the Mage from the flurry of attacks the Shaper throws. Yelling out to Huruk, Zevyn reaches toward the glass wall behind him — with open hands he clenches and the windows shatter while staying aloft.

"NOT **EVERYTHING** IS MEANT TO BE LEARNED, HURUK!" Zeyvn screams out as chaos sputters out of control in the museum.

"HOW DO WE KNOW THAT? I CAN'T CALL BACK TO PAST MISTAKES BECAUSE IT'S BEEN BURNED! IF I NEED TO PAVE THE PATH AGAIN, TO BECOME THE MARTYR FOR FUTURE MAGES TO LEARN FROM — THEN I'D GLADLY FAIL KNOWING I'VE DONE THE RIGHT THING!"

"STOP WASTING TIME ON A LIFE THAT'S ALREADY BEEN LIVED! WE MUST MOVE ON, IT'S WHAT THEY WOULD'VE WANTED, HURUK! YOUR AMBITION IS GOING TO BE THE DEATH OF YOU!"

"YOU DON'T THINK I KNOW THAT ALREADY? I'VE FELT DEAD EVER SINCE **WE LIVED!**"

The flames twisted and pranced around them like dancers, stirring up a wind which flew throughout the room like a bird. Between the dancing fire, Zevyn and Huruk stared at one another. Their faces lit by the anger that swelled up from the Mage. "Please-" Zevyn pleaded, putting his ego to the side and lowering the glass behind him. "Let me show you a better way. We can figure out the future of Mages together. There's no need for us to be tortured, I beg you brother. Don't fall victim to a trap set years ago. . ."

Zevyn reached out through the flame. Staring at it, Huruk pondered. The fire began to die down as he thought to himself. Looking into his eyes, his own seemed to calm. Reaching back, Huruk grabbed his hand. Speaking softly to him though the flames around still lingered.

"Maybe that *is* something we can do. But I can't ignore the weight of the past. I can't let their efforts be wasted, so I'm sorry. . . *Tesaso Irbum Unvas*." Whispering to him, Zevyn suddenly vanished into smoke as his screamed plea quickly faded "**HURUK NO–**"

Teleported away, Huruk now stood alone in the burning hall. The flames rose once more but not through rage, and as they grew, Huruk walked to the paintings. They burned at their corners and beneath it was another image, raising his hand Huruk whispered. Swiping his palm slowly across them, the flame moved along with it — consuming the artwork and unveiling what was beneath. He saw something that struck him with confusion and fear. "That's it? That's what we've been fighting for?" Huruk chuckled to himself out of surprise. His eyes were wide and his heart sank.

"The questions only go deeper, don't they?"

In the far distance, a loud crushing noise can be heard. Standing at the crash site of two large trucks, Soren turns his head to see this pillar of grey rising to the clouds. His gaze shifted down to see the rooftop of the museum, flames covering it completely. "What the hell?" He then turned to Aurelia, but she couldn't look away from the fire. "I- I don't know. . ."

4.2 | Truth Rises

Soren and Aurelia race back to the burning museum while Uval and Orwin open up the truck. Inside stood a large tan colored suit of armor with a massive mechanical pack strapped to its back. Long thin barrels overlooked the shoulders and the emerald mono eyed Ogre suit stared at its wearer — completely unpowered in the darkness of the truck. Walking up to it, Uval rested a hand on its shoulder as if it was himself. Staring into the green glass of the helmet, he spoke out to his own reflection. "Are you still there? Though you are finally in front of me, I cannot hear your voice, I cannot feel the love for war we once had." Placing his other hand on the angled breastplate, the armor opened up as gears and wiring purred aloud. Stepping inside, feeling it clasp down onto his body, Uval thought to himself. "Was it you that made me whole? I do not feel tha same as I was, will I ever feel that way again?" Though the suit remained unpowered, Uval raised his arms to stare at the tank-like armor that plated his skin. "At tha very least — I feel at home."

"Hey uh, Val?" Orwin says from outside the truck. He can be seen looking up and down the street they were on. "We got trouble. I know that thing is dead, but can you still move in it?" Hearing the rapid approach of criminals, some holding guns and others cloaked with blades, Uval steps out and onto the street — the ground shaking with each one he takes.

Turning his head to the left, there are a horde of cloaked figures racing forward with bone weapons. And turning his head to the right, there's a mob with a variety of guns toted in their hands. "I will be fine."

Taking out his chains, Orwin watched Uval jump high into the air — slamming down upon the gunman that approached. Spinning his weapons around, the Showman looked the other direction as he saw all of the rogues sprinting down the street. "Yeah, I'm gonna need some help this time around. . .**CLYDE!**" He yelled, but after being met with silence he realized that Clyde wasn't coming. "Okay then, well — fuck."

Throwing his arcane chains outward, they slammed against a nearby door and the shockwave broke it down. Entering a random home, he looked around and yelled out for anybody that may have been inside. "ANYBODY IN HERE? IF THERE IS, I SUGGEST YOU LEAVE — *RIGHT NOW*!" Turning back to the front door, several rogues stormed inside and chased after him. Using his chains as a deterrent, he kept the first couple away from him as he spun them around — but growing antsy, one of the rogues sprinted forward. With one of the outstretched chains, Orwin kicked down at the links and caused the knife at its end to shoot backward. It stabbed into the rogue's leg as he then punched them in the mouth.

"C'mon then, I know how you rogues operate. *Let's keep going.*" Orwin spoke to egg them on. The others then raced forward as more swarmed the building he was in. They were like bugs with the way they amassed around the home.

Wrapping the chains around the legs of a table, Orwin chucked it toward the closest rogues and cleared a path toward the stairs. Racing up while being chased, he looked outside to see the rogues scaling the walls — slamming their bone knives into the windows, the glass shattered as they let themselves in.

Getting to the top of the stairs, Orwin came to a sudden stop. Reaching the corner he leapt into the hall as knives stabbed into the wall he was just pressed against. Now running through the second story of the building, he looked in front of him to see a window at the end of the hallway — it shattered as the rogues swarmed in like flies. Trapped on both sides, he placed his back on a door and constantly looked to his left and right. Sweat dripped down onto his feet, nervous while they slowly walked to him. Both sides were cautious of the weapons he spun. The chains began to glow blue and Orwin gained a bit more confidence. He watched the two rogues closest to him on both sides look to one another, signaling the other with the slightest nod as they reached out with their knives to try and stab him. But seeing this happen, his chains wrapped around their lead arm as he crossed his own. This sent both of them stumbling into one another as a large shockwave shot out from the impact. Everybody was pushed backward and Orwin broke through the door behind him, shutting it and placing a large desk behind it.

Breathing heavily, the Showman searched the room for anything that could help. A window not broken or blocked, a closet with an eye peeking through, the main door rumbled by the rogues trying to break in, and a — 'Hold on.' Orwin walked over to the closet and found a young girl hiding in her own clothes, a pained expression went across his face as he stared into the glasses she wore. "Sorry bout all of this. . . are you– are you okay?" But before she could answer, the young girl pointed out to the door in fear. The hinges broke off as a group of rogues let themselves in.

She then saw Orwin race forward to meet them, standing his ground in front of the closet as he used his foot to close it a bit more. His chains swung around beautifully, wrapping around legs and arms to sweep the rogues onto the floor or to throw them into the others. As more approached, the man's movements became faster — more blurry yet somehow elegant. He danced around like the artists she'd looked up to, that she dreamed of becoming. In awe she watched the hero before her as he fought against one of the forces that plagued the city she'd known her whole life. But slowly Orwin was overwhelmed, a sudden gash went across his lead leg from the stroke of a blade he couldn't see. Pushed back closer to the closet, he looked over to the window knowing he would be able to escape. If he died here and now, there would no longer be a chance for him to ever be with his wife again. But Orwin knew that if he abandoned this child, he would also no longer be the man she loved. Hearing the little girl's soft cries behind him, Orwin spoke aloud while standing his ground. "Don't worry, these tiny scratches ain't even hurt. And besides, I've dealt with these guys before — I got this."

Another knife slices across his skin as he grapples a different rogue with his chains. Barely able to fend back the criminals, they start to overwhelm him with attacks — though he disarms and evades the ones that may be lethal, Orwin has no choice but to take the attacks that leak through his defense. Three knives then slash down upon him, raising his chains he has no choice but to bring his own hands up to shield himself. While blocking the attack a knife plunges toward his stomach from down below.

Looking toward the window to his side, Orwin smirks as the knife stabs into his stomach. However, it isn't deep enough to be fatal. At this point Orwin's back was pressed against the closets door. His arms were held up as he used his chains to push against three knives that stabbed down to him and his right leg was extended out — pushing against the chest of the rogue that stabbed into his stomach, preventing it from going any deeper. With no options left, the other rogues sprinted to his sides, ready to finish him for good.

But as they did, a blast of wind crashed through the window — knocking over all the rogues in front of Orwin. Jumping in from the broken glass, Clyde landed and sent another punch toward the door pushing all the rogues in the hallway back. Holding his stomach, Orwin smirked as he kicked Clyde in the back. "One helluva power, kid. How bout you keep using it?" Turning his head to look at him through the corner of his eyes, Clyde pulled down his beanie. Despite that you could tell he was smiling. "I think that's a pretty damn good idea. "

"By the way, we got a bit of an audience." Orwin gestured to the closet as it slowly opened, the young lady peeked her head out and her bright brown hair shone in the light.

"Oh– well don't you worry lil lady, you're in good hands now. Even though I'm pretty sure this is all Big Bro's fault anyhow."

"Well. . . it is but, actually – shut up." Orwin then turned to the young girl. "I'll pay for all the damages, and I'm real sorry bout your toys."

Admiring the heroes she saw in front of her, the two continue to brawl with the rogues that swarm around the house. During this, outside you can hear Uval the Ogre steamrolling the mob members on the street. The gunfire slowly lessons with each stomp and attack that crashes down upon them.

Pushing even farther outward, Aurelia and Soren sprint down the street toward the museum. The two of them speak aloud to one another as Soren's attention is turned to a nearby alley. "Go on without me." The Hero says.

"What? Stop playing around, let's go." Aurelia seemed confused by his words. But the glare in his eyes was different — she slowly realized what Uval had meant. And with the silence Soren had left as a response, Aurelia decided to just continue.

As she sprints away, Soren looks to the silhouette that walks out from the alley. Looking at him with a serious expression, the Hero speaks aloud to him. "Dario, I'm sorry I couldn't bring your brother back to you. And I won't try to say it wasn't me who got him killed, in that way we feel the same. But I can't just let you kill me, there's too much I have to make up for."

The Hunter then walked toward him. Reaching into his chest and pulling out two identical blades. Throwing one of them over to Soren's feet, he walked forward while flourishing the one in his hand. "No more running, you die **today**."

"Please, if we can, I'd rather not fight. And I don't say this to provoke you — but you won't be able to kill me. Many have tried, and yet I'm the one standing here."

Scoffing at his claim, the Hunter smiled. "Let's see what the war has made of you." Dario then raced forward and swung down at him. "I promise it's far uglier than you think." Soren says while bracing his sword to block the attack. They then pushed against one another while in a bind. "I'm sure someone named 'Hero' can't be as monstrous as you claim." Pushing Dario away and taking a stance with his blade held forward, Soren took a deep breath in and out to focus. "You don't know what our enemies called me, do you?"

With the sound of clashing metal behind her, Aurelia comes to a sudden stop. In front of her stood the garage doors and docking bay, all filled with flame. "Huruk, you can't be in here can you? There are so many ways for you to escape. . ." Clenching her hands, Aurelia listened to her gut as she sprinted forward — jumping over the sprawling fire that began to stand up.

Racing from Modern Relics to Paintings of War, Aurelia pushed through the creeping flames and saw Huruk knelt down. He stared at the portraits in front of him with an odd look in his eyes, it was as if he was possessed. About to enter the hall, all the flames suddenly turned black. Looking around confused, The Abbot rose from a shadow in front of her — blocking her path to Huruk. His eyes were pure black, this was a Husk. "Hold on, Aurelia. We may be witnessing something great here — *the birth of a Seraphic*. He's currently falling to my Lords domain, let us show some etiquette and let him."

Taking out her pistol and a knife, she looked at him while stretching her neck. She could see that there were shadows protecting Huruk. "Looks like you've made sure he won't die in here anyhow, which was the only thing I was worried about. So sure, I guess I can kick your ass then get to him after. This is a Husk ain't it? I got this." Aurelia then looked to Huruk, her mind thinking of different things in the moment. 'You're out of energy already?! Just what the hell did you do?' Pointing her gun at the Husk, she asked it a question. "What's a Seraphic anyway? You must be a dying breed if you want your enemy to become one too."

"We are the ones closest to the–" A bullet shot through the Husks jaw, causing it to swing by the fleshy strings that barely held it up. As it healed Aurelia shot several more times, each one landing in its chest — pushing up as she was shooting. Once she had to reload, the Husk reached out to her. Several black tendrils sprung forth from its sleeves and in reaction to this, Aurelia leaned away from the attack while lunging forward. Jamming her knife in the Husks neck, she leaned in even more to plant several elbows onto its face. In the middle of this barrage, Aurelia was struck on the side of her body with the tendrils, sending her flying toward nearby flames. Digging her heels into the ground as best she could, Aurelia barely came to a stop as she felt the fire tickle her back. Not giving her any time to breathe, the Husk shot the tendrils at her again. This time however, the black mass twisted to resemble a toothy maw which opened widely. As it chomped down upon her, she took the moment to reload instead of running away.

The teeth then sank in her forearm and foot as she tried her best to wedge the mouth open with her body. Using her pant leg to rack the pistol, Aurelia yelled out to the Husk. "Why the hell are you here anyway? Don't you got better shit to do than fuck around with us?"

"You all are a part of my business, and seeing that Huruk may grow stronger should prove useful in the future. For **everyone** involved. This is good, no?"

Struggling to keep the teeth from crushing her, Aurelia lifted her pistol and shot the Husk in the head several times. This caused its entire body to go limp for a moment as it regenerated. In that time Aurelia ran out from the mouth and charged at the Husk. Raising the knife up, she stabbed directly into the body's heart. But it twitch as if alive, she continued to push forward — shoving the Husk backward as she sprinted through the flames, screaming out as she steels her nerves. Slamming it into a wall, the blade dug even deeper into its heart. Breathing heavily, Aurelia backed away slowly while leaving the knife in its chest. But before she could take another step, the Husk reached up and grabbed her arm. Its healing was much slower than usual, but as soon as the mouth was recreated, it spoke. "Did you *really* think this body lives through a mind and heart?" The Husk then cackled aloud as it lifted Aurelia up into the air by her arm. "*IT DOESN'T EVEN HAVE A **SOUL**! HA HA HA HA!*" Its wicked laughter exploded out into the museum as it threw Aurelia further down the hall. Her body crashed into the tiles until she ended up toward the front of the building. Grabbing at her own arm, she saw that it was purple and bruised — otherwise, the adrenaline she was feeling helped her ignore the other injuries. Standing up, surrounded by onyx flames as the Husk approached — a cocky smirk appeared on Aurelia's face. "You know, Rakesh. . ." A single brow raised upon the Husk as it slowly walked toward her. "So Huruk told you all, *how interesting.*"

"You're one smug bastard–" Aurelia continued as the Husk charged forward. "You don't even know that **one** of these days, *we're gonna kill you*." She slowly took a step back, blindly reaching to one of the stanchions that outlined the lines for people to get into. Gripping the heavy metal pole, she instantly felt that its weight was like a bat. As the Husk sprinted forward, the black mass formed a spear onto its arm — jabbing it at Aurelia once it got close enough. Her focus was so intense in this moment, that she leaned back such a tiny distance. Perfectly spacing the end of the black spear from her stomach. Twisting her body around, she held the stanchion in her hand and she swung it at the Husk. The flared base of the metal pole then sank right into its skull. Dazing the Husk for a moment, Aurelia jumped at it — planting a knee onto its chest they both fell to the ground.

The Husk then began to regenerate and regain consciousness. Knowing what was happening, Aurelia took out the knife from its chest and sank the blade into the arm which had the black mass, pinning it to the ground even if temporarily. Reloading her gun, she jammed the barrel through its teeth and continuously shot. Once it emptied, she used the time it took to regenerate to reload again. Placing the barrel on random places on its body and shooting. 'This fucking things gotta have a weakness right?!' But as she ran out bullets, she stood there shocked to see the shredded body begin to reform. Waking up, The Husk slammed its arm into Aurelia, sending her flying into the strung up structure of bones. Crashing into the skeletal remains, she and the exhibit fell to the ground.

"You've done **quite** the number on this body, haven't you?" The Husk reached out to send tendrils toward her but nothing reached. Along with its healing being much slower, it appeared like the body was losing energy.

Planting her fist into the ground, blood leaked onto the floor as Aurelia stood. "Just you fucking wait buddy. . ." She said while squinting through one eye, her other was bruised and purple. She had a limp in one leg and her ribs felt like they exploded. Despite everything, Aurelia still had a smirk on her face. "Come on then, you gonna keep a lady waitin?" She gestured for the Husk to attack. Her legs wobbling as she taunted it. Though everything was in the Husks favor, it looked oddly hesitant to approach her in the sea of bones.

"How unlike you, Rakesh. I thought you had more manners than that. C'mon, **dance with me**." The Husk then did just that. Approaching fast, Aurelia seemed completely shaky. But as it got closer, her unfocused eye sharpened and her wobbly legs became steady. Slipping the knife hand which the Husk threw out, a left hook was planted onto its chin. The Husk then swiped horizontally to try and behead Aurelia, but she'd already shot down low for a takedown. Wrapping her arms around its legs, Aurelia pushed with her shoulders and head — slamming the Husk onto the floor. Grabbing a huge sharpened fang with both her hands, she sat on its stomach and slammed the tooth down toward its chest. Reacting to everything late, the Husk barely managed to put its arms up — a black mass wrapping around them as the fang pierced through everything with ease. The tip of the tooth tickled the base of the Husks neck as they pushed against one another. Aurelia screamed out as she used all her strength to shove the tooth down. Seeing that this tooth was starting to erode the black mass, a fire stirred within her.

"SO THIS IS IT HUH?! THAT'S WHY YOU WERE SCARED TO APPROACH? BONES IS IT?! THIS IS HOW WE KILL YOU IN THE FUTURE, **FEAR THAT DAY!**"

Pushing harder, the tooth pierced the chest of the Husk — all its injuries seemingly halted in the middle of its healing process. "So much *hate* but for what? **I** am the one who gave you lost souls a goal to chase. Without me you all would be wandering this world meaninglessly. . ."

"SHUT UP! NOTHING YOU SAY IS GONNA STOP ME!"

"Who do you think made that **Showman** bring his talent back out to the world? Without me his skills would've gone to waste."

"*STOP TALKING!*"

"Who do you think gave those **soldiers** a mission? They roamed the country as a *shell* of their former self after the war. **I** gave them *purpose*."

"**THAT'S ENOUGH!**"

"Who do you think woke **you** up from your eternal slumber? Your tortuous days as your fathers puppet? **I** gave you the freedom to be yourself. . . you all think everything was fate leading you to one another — that I was lucky to bring you together as my band of scapegoats. **No**. I've known you all for years, *I made you*."

"*YOU'RE LYING!*" Aurelia screamed, shoving the tooth down as her energy permeated in the air. Hearing the whispers of something in her ear, strength filled her muscles as she plunged the fang into the Husks chest and as the tip of it hit the floor. The body then went limp and slowly sank into its own shadow, dispersing into a black goo-like substance. Breathing heavily, Aurelia backed up while holding the fang in her hand. The fire around her crackled while returning to its normal state. Suddenly some of it was blown away by a strong wind. Huruk, stumbling into the room she was in, fell to his knees. His eyes were completely bloodshot and he struggled to breath. He no longer had any energy left in him.

"You dumb fuck. . ." She said while making her way over. Getting under his armpit, she started to drag Huruk to the front of the museum. However, as she peered through the flames there were rangers and firemen waiting. Turning her head to the opposite way, Aurelia tried her best to exit through the back.

Dragging Huruk in her weakened state, they slowly made it to the docking bay. As she ran out of strength, the rest of Destiny's Call made their way to her. Orwin and Clyde raced inside to drag both of them out while Soren looked over to Uval. The youngest hero had many gashes and cuts all across his body but none of the injuries seemed to bother him at all. He stared at the Ogre because he held onto Dario like a child would do to a teddy bear. Uval then spoke to the Hunter, his voice muffled by the unpowered helmet he wore.

"Try your little magic tricks and I will crush whatever there is in my hands." Not wanting to take that risk, Dario simply hung there in his arms while seething. "I admit that I can't kill you now, Soren. But just you wait — I'll figure out a way." The Hunter spoke while looking down to him.

"I doubt it. Stronger foes promised me the same thing, and I'm still waiting for them to return." Soren then turned away from him, looking over to Clyde and Orwin as they grabbed the injured members.

"Just what kind of Hero are you?" Dario asked, the hatred in his heart slowly fading. Anyone around could feel the somberness emanating from Soren.

"One born from war."

As Huruk and Aurelia were loaded onto a car they'd stolen, Orwin looked over to Uval and Soren as he sat in the driver's seat. "Listen, Clyde and I are gonna head back to the warehouse. But I think it's better if we go for the archives today, with all this chaos going on we should be able to get it done — even with them out of commision."

Soren then raised his hand. "What are we gonna do about this guy though?" He said while pointing to Dario.

"I- I don't know, throw him in the ocean for all I care. Just get yourself and Val to the cathedral, we need somebody to break through the vault door."

While Clyde and Orwin rushed off to the warehouse, Uval and Soren looked at one another then to Dario. "Listen-" The Ogre said while looking down at the Hunter. "You have two options. You can try and kill my friend now, then die — or you can just leave and come back to die later. What do you choose?"

With angry eyes, knowing there's nothing he can do, Dario chose to leave. However, he then thought about something. Looking to Soren, the Hunter took a deep breath in and out. "I need to know more about my brother. As it stands, I can't kill you. But it looks like you don't plan on killing me either, so fuck it. Just tell me the truth. What happened to Daire?"

Hearing his words, Soren started to walk away. "I don't think I can talk about that right now. There's too much going on, and hearing all that chaos in the distance — it-it's reminding me everything. If the mission goes well, I'll try and tell you."

". . . Fine, but I'm helping then. You can't die unless **I** kill you or you give me the truth. That's the only way I'll be able to sleep at night."

"Let's make it out of this alive then." Soren put out a hand for Dario to shake as Uval let him go, and while looking at him there was a split second where he could see his comrade staring back at him. Soren could remember when he gave the Black Box to Daire. Shaking hands with Dario, the sound of gunfire in the distance refocused his mind.

5.0 | Who am I?

Several blocks away, the Sistario Museum burns as gray smoke trails up to the clouds. Several trucks clutter around the building as firemen spew water from the hoses they hauled around. During

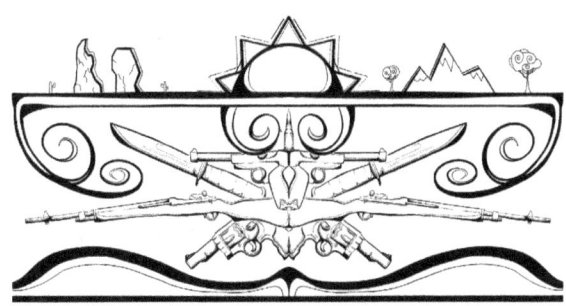

this, the rangers fought fiercely against the criminal underworld — bullets and blades were used in tandem in the nearby streets. Observing it all, Cypher sat in the tallest tower of the cathedral. Hands pressed against the iron bars affixed to the windows. Behind him rang the huge brass bell tower, marking the top of the hour. The noise was so deafening that it caused him to cover his ears. Looking up, a large ornate glass ceiling could be seen as the bell swung back and forth — shining a bright and concentrated light into his cell.

On the opposite side of the bars, the Priestess sat in a wooden chair just at the top of a set of stairs. She held the latest newspaper in her hands and a change of outfits. It was far less elegant than the regal outfit she wore in the church. It looked almost too normal of a dress, still higher fashion but streetwear nonetheless.

"Is a queen supposed to be dressed like that?" Cypher asked as the ringing came to a stop. Looking up from the newspaper, she looked at him with just her eyes before going back to reading. "Is a criminal supposed to be wandering around in my city?" Cypher didn't respond, instead he walked away and paced his cell. "Didn't think so." She said while putting it down.

The Archer then stared up to the bell and ceiling, looking to the iron bars afterward. "Which came first, the annoying thing above me or the jail cell?" Cypher then walked to the locked door, pressing himself against the bars as he scanned Queen Eldora with her eyes.

He could see the keys on her hip and a handgun on her lap. "The bell. It's an object that's seen its share of bloodshed, and now it can be used against corrupted forces. So I ask, are your ears in pain because they're sensitive, or have you gone heretical?"

Confused about the question, whether it be real or not, Cypher had a bewildered face. "I don't understand what you mean, is this a religious question? I thought your faith was just that, something to believe in."

Eldora then stood and walked up to him — the iron bars were the only thing separating them. "Yes, not all things we believe in may be true. Our faith is that we believe it is so, but all of it originates in something undeniable. We may not feel the same things, but we see the same Sky. I can't tell what's going on in your head, so please answer — what kind of man are you?"

"How am I supposed to know the answer to that? I barely even know myself. I used to squeeze the trigger of my gun without feeling a thing, now I found myself hesitating at every press. Though that pause may not be visible to others, it feels like a lifetime to me. I'd do anything to make this torture end. . ." As Cypher spoke, though neither of them noticed, his shadow seemed to grow darker. But with the concentrated light shining down so brightly, the darkness was maintained. The two then looked each other in the eyes. He then tilted his head to see the chaos and havoc in the distance, all of it just behind the queen's head through the window.

"Shouldn't you be doing something about that?" Cypher asked, and without even turning, Eldora responded. "I've already contacted all the ranger departments and issued a high alert to my citizens. Though the streets of Luminel look grim, they will soon shine again. Even in dark moments, light is there. I assure you that everything is being taken care of." Holding the pistol with one hand, her other ran across the iron bars as she paced up and down the room — following with his gaze, Cypher watched Eldora as she looked at him with altruistic eyes. They gleamed with hope for him, and he hated it. "Even still, your majesty. Surely there are things more worth your time than sitting here and chatting with me." Though his face remained collected, Cypher gripped at the bars in frustration.

"The Moon warned me about you. Long before you arrived in that cathedral. Though I didn't know your name, as soon as I saw your face I knew you were the one they spoke of in my dreams."

"And just what did that thing say to you?" Cypher spoke with a mask of sarcasm which hid his genuine curiosity.

"Their whispers told me that you would bring about a *turn of fate* for all of Mystcall. Of course your friends would be involved in this as well, but not all of them."

"I'm not familiar with the term, but are you suggesting that I'm fated to do something good for this country? The only **good** I've ever done is serve in the war, even then that was for my own gain. Your Gods may have mistaken me for someone else." His shadow darkened just a bit more, enough for the light of the sun to sizzle at its growth. The steam that rose from the stone was small, unnoticeable unless you were looking for it.

"The conclusion of this drastic change is still up in the air, undetermined until *you* find yourself at its choices. So your involvement being bad may very well be the case." Cyphers shadow grew darker. "However, I don't believe that's how this ends."

The two then met the iron bars, leaning onto them as they stared at one another. Cypher then spoke, a slight smirk appearing on his face as his eyes narrowed. "That doesn't seem like something they said to you."

"Does it not?" Eldora said while reciprocating his expression. She leaned in more, becoming very interested in his thoughts — the queen became more and more infatuated with understanding the puzzling man before her.

"Seems more like a personal thought." Cypher said while reaching out through the iron bars, grabbing hold of Eldora. Before she knew it her back was pressed against the cell. With a hand at her neck and the pistol taken, Cypher whispered into her ear.

"Throw the keys onto the ground and slide them into the cell with your foot. Don't make any other movements or any noise." Despite the situation, the queen seemingly didn't listen.

"Do you plan on killing me if you don't get your way?" Placing the barrel of the gun to the side of her head, Cypher coldly responded. "That would be easier, wouldn't it?"

"Then do it. Prove me wrong, be the man you think you are. Be as heartless as the stories say." His grip tightened on her neck. "You gamble your throne? For something as insignificant as me? A poor choice, Queen Eldora." In response, she said nothing. Closing her eyes Eldora grabbed the keys on her hip and threw it toward the door — it was easily in reach from inside the cell. This single moment between them lasted long. Neither of them moved despite the slight twitches in their fingers. The world continued to move though they stayed paused.

In the distance you can hear the echoes of battle as flames erupt onto buildings. The Midnight Candles, rogues in wispy cloaks, tear through the city as Soren, Uval, and Dario fend them off — seemingly putting a hold on the original mission. These three can be seen sprinting through Luminel as they rescue as many citizens as they can. Bringing them to the rangers they're looked at with an odd stare, guns point at them almost immediately. However, as the rangers realize who they're fighting for, the guns lower.

Through the windows of the bell tower behind the estranged two, gunfire blares out as the Vinciano Mob marches down several streets. Finding themselves in the crossfire between the law and crime, Orwin and Clyde shot at as bullets whizz past Aurelia and Huruk. Their vehicle blazes through the street while Clyde punches out shockwaves of air at the mob members. Trailing to the warehouse, they pass through several streets and waves of bullets.

Behind the veil of warfare to mask any moves or sound, the keys to the cell are gently placed on the wooden chair in the corner. The barred door slowly swings to being closed again as Cypher makes his way down the stairs, pistol in hand. Speaking aloud, his voice was cold and soft. "You don't know me. . .and I don't think you should keep trying to. I might be the death of you next time, and I don't think I'd be able to forget your face."

4

Between Fire & Ash

1.0 | Distant Memory: Heaven in Hell

After losing consciousness, my mind fell into the shadows. Descending past the curtains that I'd been warned of all my life. Maybe they were right — maybe I should've listened to Teacher Haz,

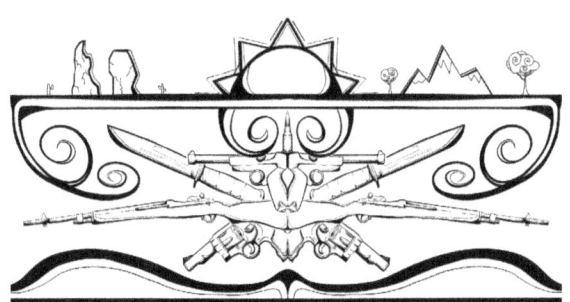

Zeyvn, even Rakesh with everything he's done. The former tried to reason with me and the latter showed a glimpse of what was behind it. But now, despite everything — *I'm here*. And though I know I'm wrong, I can't help but feel right — knowledge is not sin. So as I fall into depths deeper than I could've known, I'll do as I said. I will continue beyond the end and discover the undiscoverable.

My body feels numb as I descend through an airless void. The way I cannot breathe, it's as if I'm submerged in an ocean — lungs crushed by the pressure, not enough to kill me but enough to make me uncomfortable. Though my body does not feel the pain, my mind does. I can feel the way they're disconnected from one another. And as I continue to think to myself, rejecting the realization of where I am, my form is slammed down onto a bed of grass. With my face pressed against the blades, I pick up my head to look around confused.

"Why is this place beautiful?" I whispered to myself.

The sky did not exist, but neither was it just black, there was truly nothing — the absence of substance that not even darkness can describe. It is beyond words that we've made to tickle at the skin of this idea. Ineffable, void, nothing — I don't know, but it was oddly comforting. To know that there was zero existence beyond the scope of my eyes, it gave me peace. Like being in a mothers embrace, feeling like nothing could touch you as she sang to your ears. This place was her arms, her voice, her eyes.

But where is the daylight coming from? This place basks in illuminance but it is sourceless. No stars to see so I may even *hope* that it's night. So I'm left pondering its existence or rather the lack of.

Not knowing what to do, being in a place removed from our world, I reluctantly stood to walk around. Perusing the winding landscape, I traveled across grassy plains and forests while heading toward the distant mountains which peaked over the horizon. **They stared at me**. There were many trees, both miniscule and mountainous. Ripe fruit hung from their branches and vines, this place is how an adult remembers the stories told to them as a child. The fairytales whispered to them before bed. Where I am, it's like clear memories that never existed. But as I took in the wanderlust of it all, that's when I noticed the disquieting details. The nature here felt far more alive than what our world allowed us to see. Leaves flowed like hair. Roots curled like fingers. Vines swung like arms. Branches waved like hands. And the dirt. . . the patches of dirt I began to see in the otherwise flawless grass that spanned for miles — I could see faces in them. But am I just boggled by the situation? All these things were so faint, am I making it up? In truth, the forest seemed normal. Maybe I'm playing tricks on myself.

I find myself second-guessing the thoughts that circulated in my mind, something that doesn't happen too often. Everything was so subtle, but there was horror in the detail. It was covered by silk sheets and hidden behind lavish curtains. This place was undeniably beautiful — confusingly so. If I hadn't seen those crumbs, the allusions to something **else** here, I may have believed that this was *it*. Aslia, Hearteth, Emparse, Varhal, perhaps even the ancient religions and their afterlives too. But no, there's something strange about the God that's made this place — it doesn't feel right. It doesn't *feel* like I should be here. So there must be something in this world, something to prove that notion right. This had to be the works of those three Hollow Titans. But which one? With nowhere else to go, I moved forward.

Eventually I came across huge waterfalls that poured into glistening lakes. For a moment, I noticed the animals around. They avoided my every step, lurking in the distance and never showing their full selves. The creatures varied between tiny and massive, fantastically beautiful and powerfully striking. Though, what made me envy them was that they got to live in this paradise. Each eternal day they spent here must be bliss. Sinking their teeth into fresh food without worry of their next meal, sleeping while knowing they'll wake, and even living without the fear of death.

"Wait. What am I thinking?" Life is best lived with death as a consequence, sleep is best earned with a day well spent, and a meal is best eaten by a stomach that knows its worth.

"What the hell is going on with me?" My hands don't feel like my own, nor do my thoughts. This must be an effect of this place, a way to lure in victims — I know what I saw in this forest. The beauty it shines with now faded for a split second, I could see the faintest traces of depravity. But, why am I doubting myself? Is this hesitation mine? Or has it been instilled in me? I- I need to go. . . deeper or back? I'm not sure. But I need to go. The animals are growing less wary of me — more curious. As I stand here they lurk closer. Though they only seem to move while out of my sight, I hear their feet moving. It's gut wrenching to think that they may know what I'm feeling too. These are not just beasts, they are something more.

My walk turned into a brisk jog, and oddly the animals around me began to match my hurried steps. Their trots and scurries became that much louder. Feeling my heart race, I shifted to a sprint and unfortunately, they did the same. My legs kicked against the ground as hard as they possibly could and despite my efforts the creatures gained on me.

With my vision narrowed to the safe path ahead, I dashed between thin trees and through lush bushes. I'd inevitably be caught at this rate, a spell will be the only thing that'll save me. With how many I hear, there's a horde at the very least — multiplying by the second as they track me down. I can't tell how many of them there are, some are larger than trees and others smaller than rabbits. There may be as many of them as times I've blinked in my lifetime.

Calming myself so my breathing steadied, I saw a clear straight path in front of me and closed my eyes — with no choice I recited words to the storm spell I used in Printon. But then that suffocating feeling returned. I couldn't speak. My hand finished waving as I turned around to the swarm behind me. My back suddenly slammed into a tree once the spell failed. And as I came to an abrupt stop, those elegant creatures grew closer. Leading the charge a goat-like beast emerged from the foliage, breaking past distant bushes and revealing more and more of itself. Its horns curved at a violent angle, growing into its own eyes as the tips stuck out from the ears. Reaching its head forward, the beast's long snout opened to reveal a row of teeth belonging to a monstrous wolf. Throwing myself out the way, its bite ripped through the tree behind me — it did so easily, as if it was made of plastic. Whipping its gaze down to me, it repeatedly lifted its front legs up and slammed them into the ground like a startled horse. I backed up frantically to try and get up but the creature didn't leave me any room to stand. This panicked dodging didn't last long either, eventually I got caught in a bush, accidentally throwing myself into it while avoiding the beast's hooves. And as I tried to stand, it was as if the vines wrapped around me, holding my body to the ground. Now before me, I could see the creature in its entirety. Silver fur that blindingly shined in the sourceless light, the body of a lion with the legs of a horse or goat, and a long tail that waved around with its own mind. Its hooves then rose up to crush me, but instead it stayed frozen in that stance. Something stopped them. That's when I heard it.

A voice that belonged to an entire choir. It was layered upon itself perfectly, giving it an ethereal quality — especially as it seemed to have no body. The voice shot out from every direction from the dirt to the trees and asked me if I knew why I was pulled here. Obviously, I didn't know the answer. But to avoid any discord between me and it, I slowly stood while staring at the hooves above me. Looking around I searched to see if there was anything to look at, anything to speak to, but all I saw was more curious creatures — each one was bright in color, they had silver or completely white fur and or feathers. They seemed close to the myths and folktales I've seen and heard of in my travels. That only tells me that these things can exist with us, an eerie thought that I unfortunately have to pocket.

The voice then noticed I hadn't answered, that my hands were trembling and my eyes were darting around. Asking another question, I only nodded in response. I simply couldn't stomach the words.

At first I didn't notice anything, it was eerily quiet as all the eyes on the horizon stared at me. The only thing that made noise was the wind which rustled the forest, not even the breathing of these beasts filled the void. However, that changed once all their heads turned to someone else. All at once, the faint noise of a single head turn was amplified to an uncanny swoosh of the wind. Shifting my head to look as well, I saw a being of the same bodiless force of the sky. Its silhouette was sexless and because it wasn't filled in it felt like it could be anyone. Such a thing invoked the feeling of seeing a loved one and a stranger, all at the same time. A harrowing sense of deja vu. The Voice before me then walked forward, the creatures all bowed their heads in respect — as knights or subjects would to a king.

Seemingly noticing my puzzled face, it created a pair of starry eyes for me to look at. It then asked me a peculiar question. *'Your insatiable thirst, is it love or fear?'* A bit confused, I turned to the creatures around me. It must be talking about my curiosity, no? If so. . .which is it? Staring into the only stars in this realm, I answered. "Fear", my voice was a bit rough as the adrenaline settled. I soon realized which of the three this being was. The Void.

I was taught to never look at the Sun, Moon, and Void solely as its namesake. What we see with our own eyes is merely an interpretation of what we can understand. There is greater meaning in those things above our reach, so I can't help but wonder. What exactly do you Titans really represent? I do not know the others, yet I recall Rakesh cherishing not the shadows but what was behind it. So there, I found you. "Mages seek the end of things, where everything eventually leads so we may get ahead of it. It's an honor to finally be here, to meet you myself."

"The being behind black curtains"

"Timeless Whispers"

"Hollow Heart"

"Veratrox"

I've heard your many names across many peoples. Even as I journeyed across the world, from great cities to modest towns — the names have appeared as local stories or urban legends. In the worst cases people gathered to form cults or religions based on what a single man had seen. You'd think they'd write off the claims of a crazy man, but no — they listened. I always wondered why, what did these people see? What made their statements true to them? But now I see it. Our faiths are our own interpretations of you and the others. Of course they wouldn't keep the parts deemed as hellish or sinful, but that doesn't make them unreal. You are true neutral, no matter what the others see in their filtered lenses — you do not care. I don't think you can.

"So what is it that you seek? What keeps the cogs turning? Is it your Seraphics, do they do your bidding and push out your true message?" As the speaker of the conversation shifted between Veratrox and myself, all the animals and beasts turned. That's when I looked up to notice something. The pitch black sky wriggled. Staring closer, there were thousands of beasts — appearing more monstrous than animal-like despite their uncanny resemblance. In shape, some of them looked identical to the beasts down here. . .but they were rotten and withered — held together by threads of decaying flesh. The longer my eyes stared locked onto the void above me, the more I saw. A world just like the one down here, but completely black with specks of scattered white — bones of the creatures which clung onto death. This only feeds into my theory, this place itself shows both sides of this Titan and how much it doesn't care for either. Just what is your game?

It then answered. Telling me that what is done with its strength has little to do with itself. That what it seeks is only to give — to supply those who want with what they need. A chance. *'Because in my realm, a realm that cannot be, anything can.'*

"You want me to believe you had nothing to do with the Seraphics? That they **all** chose to serve you? I would've assumed the beings above Gods would've been better liars." As I was about to continue, emerging from the ground, the paintings from the museum appeared in front of me. The land itself regurgitated the artworks while branches from above reached down to hang them up. Staring at the canvas, the first one created in this set, the picture of war hadn't changed too much since being burnt. However, the middle of it had. Instead of a wall of warriors meeting in the center with bloodshed and loss streaked across the image — there were open hands. Both sides reached out to a small black box, fighting over such a tiny object and shedding lives for it. And while I pondered the value of the box again, Veratrox spoke.

'As the first flame was sparked, I created darkness. And as man created war, I gave them reason.' Staring at the array of paintings, the Black Box was the center of each one. I couldn't tell if it was the same one or not. And it didn't matter whether it was glory, peace, wealth, or power which they sought out — that **thing** was always there. The fact that such a small object has moved history along for all this time was devastating to learn. I've heard time and time again about the good parts of the wars — the aftermath. The chaos was like a fire which spread across a dying forest. It destroyed everything indiscriminately, returning all which grew to ash and from those remains sprouted a world one step evolved from the last. This cycle has repeated since the first breath was taken. So where does it end, at the last?

'I merely react to the causes you all perpetuate, and like the others I have grazed my fingers across the world — we do so in hopes to continue it. If nothing else, remember this. I am the end of your actions.'

"So you're saying that everything you've done has been a reaction? To us? To what **we've** done? But are we not reacting to you and to Magic itself?" My eyes stare into its stars. Looking around I can feel a tingle roll down the skin of my arms — something was rapidly approaching.

'You are not the first to question us, nor shall you be the last. And each time you will be given the same answer. This world is an endless cycle, one that is moved by the living within it. We are but the cogs you push to keep it moving. And I, the end of it all, will return you to the beginning.'

"Does that mean the Seraphics are the ones closest to you? The ones with their hands on the brass that is the cog, pushing it directly."

'They wander to us unknowingly, as you have. You're now burdened with this knowledge, and whatever you do now will push along the gears of the world. Those who find value in History, Progression, and Truth always eventually stumble to us. As for Mages, you've been trying to find the Truth and thus you have been given it. But by your very nature, you want more.'

"You believe I'll push along this story of yours? I don't think I'll do so willingly. After everything I've been through I do this only for my kind, what was lost and what is left."

'Even so, your actions will push it forward regardless of intention. I apologize, but there is no choice for any of us. Even your death will act as a propellant. Only breaking the cogs could ever stop the meaningless cycle.'

"They say you are hollow yet you apologize, you show opinion as you call it meaningless. I don't know what was written about you, Veratrox. And I never will, but I know whatever I scribe shall be different. I see you, better than anyone else has so far. Even them."

Across the sky, four streaks of ethereal essence raced toward me like shooting stars. They were all made from that substance Veratrox himself consists of. Very clearly, these were the Seraphics that move the Cog of the Void.

My feet felt like they were stuck in place, my eyes and head were the only things to move to see everything going on. Approaching faster than I could react, the four of them landed around me — they were all dressed in dark colors with very different aesthetics. Rakesh was here in his abbot attire, his eyes were pure black and so were the others — they all were Husks. The man next to him had on modern clothes, they were worn to rags and draped over him like a cloak. But more odd was the baseball cap he had on, it didn't seem to match the rest of his outfit — not to say it was put together with thought, it just stuck out to me for some reason. Regardless, it was obvious this man was from Northridge.

Then there was the closest person to my right. They seemed rather androgynous despite the masculine frame they had. Maybe it was the masquerade mask they wore atop their gothic suit, but they had a veil of mysteriousness around them — one that I could find myself trying to solve if given the right motives. However, with their choice of attire and the lavish umbrella they held above their head, this person was from Vola. There's only one city I know that's known for both constant rain and its gothic style, Peratar — the Flooding Stacks. And finally, the woman dressed elegantly for the cold. There's no doubt in my mind that she's from Mastonov. Though it doesn't snow, that place is known for its chilling winds. She's likely the Seraphic Zevyn had mentioned before.

"Ain't you that lil' mage I been hearin bout?" Said the Seraphic from Vola. Along with the genderless look, their voice was deep and sultry. A bit of rasp cutting portions of their accent into gravel — like Veratrox but in a more plausible way, this person could be anyone. As they spoke, I could see silver grills that outlined their canines. They glistened as if hit by the moon and the diamonds laced upon its frame glowed like lights. Folding their umbrella and planting it on the grass like a cane, the Seraphic turned to Rakesh and smiled.

"So this is one them variables in ya passion project. I gotta ask Rakesh, how's that going? Because by the looks of it, we **all** still stuck." Their sneer remarks were said with confidence — it was clear that the Chalice wasn't just for the Abbot. But for all of them. Rakesh then turned to look at them as his hands were held behind his back.

"I don't see *you* trying to do anything, and **don't** try to paint me as wrong for creating potential prospects — we all have Husks around the world. You think I haven't seen *your* passion project? You don't seem too hurried to leave your hunting grounds, especially not with your little candles roaming around the world — these **pests** are a nuisance resembling the roach I see you as."

"*Roach*? Aren't you the lil' bug that's goin round the world — tryna break that spell them mages helped put on us? All that burning for what? Only thing you got was some more pets to add to your collection."

"They're **not** pets." Rakesh angrily spoke. "I'll take your **tongue** for belittling them."

"Put that damn hand in my mouth and I'll fuckin bite it off." Though they smiled, it was clear that they too were getting angry — their teeth clenched as the two of them slowly walked toward one another.

"I oughta eat your bitch ass n shit you down a *fuckin pit*." The white fur around the neck of Vola Seraphic waved around like the tips of a flame. It seemingly fused with the person's skin as if the fur became theirs — it then grew down their back and arms while going up and around the head. Their upper body became a bit larger as the fur suddenly came to an abrupt stop — the strands hardened to appear like withered and bleached branches. The face of the Seraphic was tucked away in the fur, obscured by darkness — the only thing that could be seen was the shining grills they had. Some villages saw it as a sickness, others a curse. Regardless of the true nature, this was lycanthropy.

"Such vulgarity coming from a *beast*, **how fitting**." Rakesh then summoned his black tendrils from within his sleeves. A large amount splurged out from his back as well, forming into multiple pairs of wings belonging to several different animals — he rose slightly up to meet the other Seraphics gaze.

While all this happened I stared at the other two Seraphics, but they weren't where I last saw them. Turning my head slightly, I jolted backward in fear. They were beside me already. The Mastonov Seraphic drew closer, leaning her head toward me.

"There's one of us from each major landmass, and now there's you — a boy born in the middle of the world, atop tha spire of mages. I truly do wonder what tha Moon has in store for us, what do they see in our future?"

"What?" I asked. I had no idea what she was talking about, to me it felt like gibberish with how bombarded I felt with information. "Anyway, this isn't Veratrox's true form is it?"

"Of course not, tha real thing cannot be understood. Though, that hasn't stopped some from wandering into places they shouldn't. A small portion of people find themselves meeting eye to eye with our lord and the others. . . oh how I wish to be so lucky."

"Then what is this place we're in? I was of the assumption that **this** was Vertrox."

"No, no. This realm is but a portion of our lord. Tha real thing would break us if we were to see it. Tha greatest glimpses we have are tha Sun, Moon, and Void. Those celestial bodies are like tha eyes of tha Titans. Not in a true sense but in a way, yes?"

"Yeah. . . sure. So after everything I've done to reach this point, I find you four. Great. I can only assume all of you are evil, I can feel it radiating off your skin. Is Veratrox's power corrupting? If so, it looks like I'll just have to fight against it."

"Fight against it? No, please my friend don't do something as silly as that. This is your reward for getting here. You sought the end of tha Mages and you have reached it, this is where it all leads — it's exactly what you wanted!"

"This? No, my conversation with your lord was enough for me. And with everything I've learned, I think I know where to continue the path of my kind. I'll break the cogs, find out what lies beyond this **meaningless** cycle."

The face of the Mastonov Seraphic twisted from glee to complete disgust and anger. She immediately spawned a blade of light and shot it forward, piercing into my chest. Right after, the Vola Seraphic turned their head and raced toward me like a wild animal. Leaping forward before I could even react, a clawed hand slashed deep into my body and sent me flying into a tree, cracking it as it splintered into tiny bits. Thankfully, I didn't feel any pain but it was obvious that my brain was starting to lose function. Everything became blurry, this form was about to die. With just my eyes I looked over to see those two Seraphics racing after me, one filled with rage and the other like a predator spotting its prey. But before either of them could reach me, Veratrox spoke out. '*You may be the most interesting part of this cycle, but know that no matter what happens. Your path will lead back to me.*' I shifted my eyes to look upon the stars. "I know, I'll be seeing you soon."

Pulled up into the shadows which I dropped through, my mind returned back to my body. All the fatigue I once had hit me like a truck. As I jolted up from unconsciousness I immediately went back down. Turning my head to Aurelia, I noticed she was still asleep. Should I even try and explain any of this? This was worse than my first couple of visions. And I– I feel myself falling asleep again. . .

2.0 | He who remembers, regrets

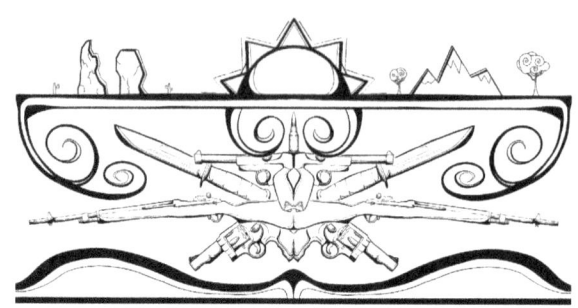

Breathless, with sweat dripping down to blood soaked streets Soren whips his head toward the horizon as the Sun hangs high. Completely distracted, Uval suddenly jumps in front of him to block a barrage of blades. Yelling out to the hero, the Ogre asks him if he's tired. "YOU DONE ALREADY, SOREN?!" Several seconds pass before he turns to answer — his mind and eyes fixated on something in that general direction. "ARE YOU WORRIED FOR OUR FRIENDS?! I AM SURE THEY'VE MADE IT ALREADY!" Uval says while pushing away the Midnight Candle rogues with a single swipe of his arm.

"No, it's not that. . ." Turning to Uval, a wall of rangers emerge from the nearby alleys to separate them from the rogues. Blood spills as havoc is spread, but everything seems to blur in Soren's eyes. A terrible feeling grabbed at his throat. "Did. . .did you not hear that?" He asked. "Hear what?" Uval said while turning to him, finally getting a bit of a break from the fight. Taking several breaths in and out, he tried to conserve his energy despite the time they've spent in this battle. Nearly an hour at this point.

Soren's head whipped around, looking at someone as if they whispered in his ear. But nobody was there. His eyes widened as he heard screams of people that no longer lived. History flashed across the battlefield, each gunshot he heard brought up a terrible memory. Each an isolated moment that brought his hands to a tremble. Unable to turn to look at him, Uval spoke out to Soren as his focus was forward. "Ah, I see now. You need to go my friend, this place is becoming too close to our past."

Breathing in and out, Soren looked forward at Uval's back. He remembered charging through the trenches behind a group of Ogre's, the explosion and bullets that were scattered across the ground like fireworks. But worse, the sound of the dogtags he collected jingling in his pocket. That chime rang clearly in his ears. Clasping his hands around his head, Soren smacked himself a couple of times to try and focus. Looking at Uval, there was an unsteady focus in his eyes. "I'm fine. The war was hard on all of us, I'm sure even you have your gripes."

"I do, but they are not tha same as yours. I do not loathe or linger on tha past as most do, I am just confused. This bloodshed no longer excites me. But no matter what is going on in our heads, we will win that battle as we have every single one before. Have faith in that at tha very least."

In the middle of their conversation at the front of the fight between ranges and rogues, Dario sprints past them while yelling out. "YA'LL DONE TALKING, OR AM I GONNA HAVE TO DO THIS MYSELF?!" His arm shifted to sand as he formed a blade with it, sending a horizontal slash into the crowd in front of them. While looking at one another, Uval and Soren nodded as they marched in behind Dario. The battle between both sides continued on several fronts, and as the Midnight Candles met the rangers at a stalemate, it seemed clear that Luminel had the numbers advantage. Along with two war heroes fighting alongside them, the rangers couldn't help but cheer aloud as they pushed the battlefront forward. While this burst of confidence ran rampant through the hearts of the fighters, screams shot out from the rangers who pushed far into rogue territory.

In the jumble of battle, where sides mix, some of the armored rangers began to fall. A wave of defeat swept down toward the frontline as Uval jumped into battle. Landing in the center of many rogues, Uval launched the ones who stood near him with a swipe of his arm. That's when he noticed the rangers in front of him falling, his head immediately looked down as he felt millions of tiny vibrations tickling the ground. The street shook as it became cloaked in a veil of darkness. It climbed atop rangers and as it reached Uval, it wriggled and crept upon his armor. Confused, the Ogre swept at the black substance, but as some of it was pushed away more took its place. His confusion turned to frantic swatting as it swarmed around his helmet, completely covering him. Millions of onyx spiders filled the street, and though most of them were real, some of these spiders were shapeshifting rogues — undoing the transformation spell upon themselves, the rogues stabbed at the rangers who were felled by the creeping nest.

Seeing all of this happen, Soren took a step back. Yelling out to those holding the frontline, he screamed for everybody to retreat. Dario then turned to him, "Did you turn back then? Is that why my brother took the box instead of you?" In Soren's mind, everything around him was blurred and muffled. The rangers that sprinted past him, the distant wave of rogues and spiders approaching — nothing was clear except for Dario. In this moment, he couldn't distinguish this battle from the war — to Soren, it was one in the same.

"W-what? How. . . how do you even know that?" His words rolled over his lips like an unsteady river. Everything abruptly became clear to him, the shock of it made him blink his eyes several times and shake his head. Dario then turned his head confused and sprinted past him. "What the fuck are you talking about?!"

Soren then stood there, his feet stuck on the cobbled bricks of the street. He looked over to Uval as he raged about — desperately trying to kill the spiders and rogues that swarmed him. Clenching his hands till they bled, Soren took a step forward as the wave of black approached. Marching forward into the great mass, the youngest hero pushed through the spiders as if it was fog. Hundreds of bites formed on his body as venom mixed into his blood.

Both his movement and vision began to fade as he powered through. Reaching out blindly, all he could see was the scramblings of black surrounding him. Very quickly his legs began to give out — dropping to the ground as millions of legs crawled over him. Desperately reaching across the ground he found the body of a ranger, scanning the corpse he whispered, "I'm sorry." But whether to his knowledge or not, every ranger consumed by the black wave was already dead — filled with paralyzing venom and finished with blades of bone. His mind began to panic as his hand wandered around for the man's gun. Soren then dropped down further, his elbows slamming onto the ground while squishing the bugs underneath him.

'*You should've died. Not them.*' His teeth gritted as his fingers ran across the stone. Crawling through the wave, Soren searched for other bodies, hoping they had their gun with them. '*You're no hero.*' Finally finding another corpse, he scrambled about while searching. It was getting hard to breathe, his throat slowly closed. '*Admit it, a quick death is too sweet for you.*' Losing his sense of touch, Soren felt something vaguely hard. Eventually finding the bolt handle, he pushed as hard as he could to stand. '*You're not allowed to die here. You haven't done enough yet.*' Rising up he swiped at the spiders on his face and shot several times with the rifle. The bullets pierced the fuel tanks of several nearby cars as gas began to pour out onto the street. His knees wobbled, causing him to fall back onto a street lamp. Leaning against it, he stared up at the flickering bulb.

Down the street hundreds of people ran from the wave. Rangers sprinted and grabbed hold of whoever they could find. A mother and daughter were trapped in their home, as a huge fragment of the house blocked the door. A father carried his wife and baby, running desperately down the street. A lone boy cried out for help, tears falling with every yelp. Pointing the gun up, Soren pleaded aloud. "Will this be enough?"

A gunshot rang out and flames soon consumed the street as a wall of smoke rose in its wake. A massive portion of the black wave bursted into ash. Rising from the fire, Uval stood as he looked over to the citizens in the distance. Everyone stood shocked as the rangers went around to secure their safety. The Ogre's gaze slowly shifted to Soren as flames completely consumed him. His eyes widened as he jolted into a sprint to go and grab the Hero. Breaking through a wall, Uval placed Soren onto the floor gently. His eyes shook while looking down at him. His lips quivered as he tried to speak. "You– you won't let something like **this** kill you right?!"

2.1 | The Fall

Firemen and their trucks surrounded the flame to control the spread of it. This proximity consumed a large amount of a major street, every building, streetcart, and car were devoured by the teeth of fire. On the

edge of this border, surrounded by families who cried tears of joy and rangers who took a breath of relief, Dario stared toward the hole which Uval made. A handful of worries entered his mind, he hoped Soren was alive if not for his life, but for the secrets he had buried in him. Taking a step backward, he was about to turn away to go help transport some of the injured but he saw something in the distance.

"Who the fuck?" He whispered to himself. As the firetrucks shot tons of water from their cannon like hoses, manmade rain poured down onto the flames as daylight shone done upon it all. The fire became more and more spread out, allowing safe spaces to form as the flames were slowly being put out. Looking between these segments, three rogues began to march toward Uval and Soren. They were dressed the same as the others but had silver jewelry all across their body. Ankles, wrists, and necks were laced in dazzling pieces — especially the larger man, their limbs were much larger than the cloak they wore even though it was as big as a tarp. Leaning down, the huge rogue tilted their head to enter through the hole Uval made. Seeing them walk in, Dario's eyebrows furrowed as he made his way over.

Entering behind the silver-lined rogues, the Hunter saw Uval standing between them and Soren. Fists and weapons raised, a moment before another brawl. Tapping his blade against the stone bricks, Dario alerted the rogues of his presence — turning to look at him, the two normal sized rogues readied themselves to fight the Hunter instead. The huge rogue smiled as he looked to Uval, his teeth were plastered with shining silver.

"I thought we would never meet. You cannot believe tha joy I feel — to finally see you in front of me again." Confused, Uval tilted his head.

"Another fan? I do not remember you."

"Tha great Ogre does not know me. . .of course. I fought against you in tha war. You felled me in battle, bringing me to a knee and ripping tha power from my armor. Leaving me to die, exposed to the war — a natural cause on tha battlefield I admit, but that is not why you disgust me. It was when I heard you speak as you fled from your victory. Oh great Ogre, such a warrior does not belong on tha side of peace — return to Mastonov. Where you belong."

"I won't be going anywhere. My home was destroyed in preparation for tha war, my family and friends were left to die in tha freezing winds to make room for forts and walls. War is no longer my place — my place is here, with them."

"Who? Are you talking about your little group? Don't you know that Destiny's Call is a mask for that little rat, Rakesh? He sullies tha title of Seraphic — he is nothing compared to our leader. This *family* of yours is a coverup for his mistakes, don't you realize — you are all victims. Not even your armor can protect you from that."

"It does not matter what you say to me. I won't be going anywhere." Uval slowly squatted down to prepare himself to charge.

"Then it seems like I'll have to drag you back. Ready yourself, for I no longer **need** my armor." The large rogue took the same stance as they both ran toward each other. A massive impact shot out as they startled grappling. Though their movements were minimal and strained, you could feel the intensity radiating in the air. The building cracked as the floor splintered from it.

"*WAR* IS ALL YOU HAVE, OGRE! RETURN TO IT!!" Screaming aloud, the rogue was slowly pushed backward as Uval grew angrier with every remark. As manmade rain fell, dousing the flames outside, the two ogres pushed their way into the street. Seeing that he was getting overpowered, the rogue shifted their hand positions to make use of Uval's forward momentum. Without anything to push against, Uval fell forward as arms wrapped around his chest. Lifted into the air, the rogue paused for a moment before slamming the unpowered suit of armor down into the ground — his smile grew wider as the street fissured from the impact. Standing up as Uval recovered from the blow, Vertur the Ogre walked around him smiling.

"You've grown *WEAK!*" He yells while punching Uval in the helmet as he tries to stand. "I THOUGHT THA GREAT OGRE COULD BRING ME TO MY KNEES AGAIN, GIVE ME A WARRIORS DEATH — BUT LIKE THIS?! *YOU ARE NOT THA MAN I REMEMBER!*" Kicking forward, Vertur's foot planted on Uval's armor and sent him crashing into a wall opposite of Soren. As the dust settled, Uval looked past his enemy to see Dario struggling with the other rogues — his arm cut and turned to sand as they whittle down at what's left. Falling to the ground, the Hunter tried to reform himself to no avail.

One of the rogues relentlessly carved into his body, the more sand he tried to gather, the more was cut. The other walked past him, taking a blade to Soren as he laid there helplessly.

Standing above him, the rogue looked at his melted skin. Placing the sword to his neck, they whispered. "If anything, this is mercy." Back on the street, Uval screamed out for them to stop as he stood and rushed over. But before he could fully make it, Vertur stepped in front of him and planted another punch onto his helmet. In anger, Uval retaliated with his own punch which landed on his face. Drawing blood from the rogue's lip, he smiled, finally feeling like this was a proper fight.

"So that's what fuels you now, huh?" His silver teeth glimmered as his face was shrouded in darkness. Vertur chuckled before speaking again. "I admit, we are lucky he sacrificed himself earlier — **maybe** we would have been in trouble if he was still awake. But know that when I defeat and drag you back to your real home, I will kill him and the rest of your new family."

Screaming out in anger, Uval charged at Vertur as they began to exchange blows. Most of their attacks landed cleanly on one another, causing waves of pressure to blow out nearby flames. Their battle would constantly shift forward and back, the oppressor changing from one person to the other. As Uval backed up, he'd grab hold of nearby objects. Welding it to his arms to use as a weapon. Streetposts as baseball bats, cars as clubs, anything he could carry. When Vertur backed up, the sheer battlelust he experienced seemed to power him. The more of it he felt, the more his feet sunk into stone beneath him. Uval would have to find larger and larger things to strike him with, it seemed like the man was getting heavier with every ounce of fun he experienced during the fight.

During this, the rogue who held their blade to Soren's neck paused. For a moment they thought Soren was speaking — a strange mumbling was heard from his lips. These mumblings slowly shifted into an angry and feral growl as Soren opened his eyes. Opening his mouth, it felt like every other noise in the world halted — even the echoes of battle outside weren't there. Soren and Soren alone could be heard as he screamed out. A call for help, a warning to his enemies. The desperation to be set free, the need to make his life worth what it cost, it could all be heard in the cracks and shrill echoes of his voice as it exploded out into the city. He then rose up, faster than anyone in the room could react. Blood shot out from his wounds and the fragile flesh tore as he held the blade once placed on his neck. Swiping it toward the rogue, they barely managed to react fast enough to block it with their spare shortsword. Pushed backward, Soren continued on. Swiping at the rogue with precise and fast strikes, his form looked like it was taken straight out of a handbook. But when he realized it wasn't working, he did something unorthodox. Throwing the blade forward, he forced the rogue to block it with their weapon as he charged. As it was parried, he grabbed their lead arm and swept the legs. Falling to the ground, he placed a foot on their chest and plunged two fingers into their neck before the rogue could speak to say a spell. Grabbing both of the weapons as his enemy slowly choked to death, his head whipped over to look at the other rogue and Dario. Standing up, he began to walk toward them.

"Are you. . .alright? You don't seem to be in control of yourself. . ." Dario said while reforming his body. While he and the rogue were caught backing away from Soren, the Hunter took the moment to swipe at them. However, it was as if the rogue knew he was going to pull something sneaky. Easily the surprise attack was blocked as Dario was then kicked away. Approaching the lone rogue, Soren started to sprint forward.

Every slash was followed with another that lagged behind, their blades flowed like water as they clashed repeatedly. Slowly Soren ramped up in speed and power to overpower the rogue. Thinking to himself, Dario believed that the Hero may have been gifted with an ability too — at the very least he must've gotten a boost in strength. One more powerful than him and Clyde, maybe closer to Uval. Eventually one of the attacks slashed their throat and in that moment, it appeared like another version of the rogue emerged from their back like a butterfly to a chrysalis. Exploding out from a dark liquidity substance, an unhurt rogue stepped out from the body that fell to the ground. Moments later, both dead bodies on the floor disintegrated into their own shadows.

Taking another step back, the Silver Rogue used their magic again to leave behind a clone of themself. It raced forward to just get slaughtered by Soren, its head falling to the ground as the Hero ran at them. Frantically the Silver Rogue formed more clones. Noticing Soren's wounds worsening with every move he made, they realized that tiring him out was the best option at this point. Killing him by their own hands no longer felt possible.

Confused by his extreme change in demeanor, Dario stood there while watching the Hero dismantle body after body in an attempt to reach the Silver Rogue. Soren created a literal path of blood and bodies as he gruesomely killed each and every clone in his way. Realizing something, Dario raced forward and stepped between them — blocking Soren and his blades with his own. As their swords bit into each other, Dario looked the hero in his eyes. His voice strained from the strength he had to use to hold him back.

"Even if you get him, you're gonna end up killing yourself. You're clearly **not** in control right now." Pushing down even harder, until Dario's knees buckled from the weight of his strength, Soren stared back into his eyes and spoke with gritted teeth.

"Who said I wasn't in control?" Swiping his arms to the side, Soren blew past Dario and continued forward — blood leaking from his skin with every step. While in a full sprint, the Hero culled the line of clones that attacked him. Each cut exploded with a firework of blood and guts.

Chasing after him, Dario tried his best to stop Soren. The more he continued to fight, the worse his condition got. As the Silver Rogue dove into windows and broke through doors, they used the propulsion of creating another clone to get past these objects with ease. Yet still, each version of them was cut down as Soren pursued them. Reaching out to the Hero, Dario grabbed onto him several times but was shrugged off. And as the Silver Rogue rushed into an enclosed room with no exit for them to escape through, Soren forced their back to hit the wall. Smushed between two people who wanted to stop him, the Hero yelled out in anger while looking at a shattered mirror in the room. At the same time, the Silver Mage whispered a spell as clones poured out from himself, and in the fissured reflections Dario reached out to Soren. Shifting completely into sand, the Hunter surrounded him as the room filled with clones.

Stuck in a sand coffin, Soren screams out in rage — his dissonant voice matching the cracks and booms of Uval and Vertur fighting just outside. "LET ME OUT!" He roared. Raising the blades, Soren stabbed at the sand in an attempt to dig his way out. Like a hungry lion, caged behind iron bars, he desperately tried to leave. All this excess energy began to pool up at the bottom of the sphere of sand in the form of red viscous blood.

"*LET ME BE THE HERO!*" His voice crackled out like lightning, lighting up the dark sky as it blew apart the landscape. "*PLEASE!*" The rageful wind in his voice poured with rain. Tears formed in his eyes as he began to gasp for air, hyperventilating from the storm which brewed in his mind. "**I HAVE TO MAKE MY LIFE WORTH IT!**" The young man wailed.

Bursting through the sand, Soren raced forward — the clones slashed him but he slashed back. In mere seconds, the room began to erupt in flurries of red. Until one single Silver Rogue was left. Hit a foot to their chest, and two blades at their neck, the rogue looked up to Soren. His eyes whited with tears pouring down. A deep grimace filled with layers of loathing. As a cold wind brushed past the city of Luminel, Soren exuded a white smoke from the sides of his mouth. The Hero's skin was hot to the touch and oddly some of his wounds were healed, most notably the burns. Crossing his arms, the Silver Rogues head dropped to the ground. Right after, Soren did too. His knees slamming onto the floor as his body leaked blood. Once he went fully limp, the Hero stayed upright in a kneeling position. Feeling the toxic effects of those spider bites, he whispered while fading into unconsciousness. "I- I know it should've been me. I don't. . .I don't know why **I** survived. It's not fair. . .it's not fair at all."

Walking toward him from behind, Dario stared out into the street. Uval fought desperately against Vertur but nothing more seemed to work. Despite his attacks previously wounding the rogue, they do no more than tickle the man now. Forced to back away, Uval was put on the defensive — a position he'd never grown accustomed to.

Seeing an opportunity to exact his revenge, Dario raised his blade and placed it to the side of Soren's neck. His hand shook with the decision at the edge of his sword, holding it so firm that it cut into the hero's skin. Dario's face scrunched together as he tried to force himself to take advantage of the situation, to do what he'd been dreaming of this whole time.

"YOU HAVE NO RIGHT TO CALL YOURSELF A HERO!" Pulling back the sword, he stared at Soren's neck intensely. Everything began to feel overwhelming for the Hunter, nothing besides this decision existed as he stood there with wide eyes. Breathing in and out until a hand gently held onto his. Turning to the person next to him, his head whipped over to see no one.

Staring out into the empty room, the blade dropped from his fingers as someone walked in from the doorway. Turning his head again, he saw Cypher walking in. Suddenly, the Archer stopped as he stared at the current state of the room. Seeing him hold a rifle, Dario knew there was a chance he'd just die here.

"I only have two questions for you." Said Cypher. "How did you beat him, and was he *really* trying?" Raising the gun toward Dario's head, the Hunter raised his hands and turned to fully face him. "I-I don't. . . I can't–" With his mind boggled, Dario struggled to answer his questions, but that didn't matter to Cypher.

"Unforturnately, this isn't my gun, or my bullets. This round is gonna have to enter your skull if you don't answer me." Hands still up and mind still hazy, Dario fell to his knees. Stuttering over and over again, Cypher began to grow impatient.

"There's too much going on for me to get stuck on this — I can't even tell if that loudmouth behind you is alive or not. But in one minute, I'm dragging him out of here no matter what happens. You know what I mean don't you?"

Dario nodded.

2.2 | The Rise

Pushing out from the building filled with tension, we find Uval further down the street as he backs away from Vertur. After throwing several cars and trucks at the rogue, Uval turns to sprint into a nearby tower. Chasing after him, Vertur looks around to see a huge and empty lobby room.  Standing in the center, he looks up to stare through the glass skylight several floors up. Shifting his eyes back down, he thinks to himself. 'No way tha Ogre climbed up that fast. Scared are we?'

He chuckled aloud and smiled. *"**HIDE N SEEK**?!* AREN'T WE A LITTLE TOO BIG FOR SUCH GAMES, UVAL?!" Suddenly a chair was smashed against his head, turning around he saw Uval sprinting through walls — throwing random items while circling him.

"THIS IS YOUR PLAN?! YOU BORE ME!" None of the tables or benches had any effect on Vertur, but as soon as he exclaimed his boredom, Uval sprinted forward while snatching one of the marble pillars to use as a bat. Smashing it against Vertur, the rogue bled from his nose as his head was knocked backward.

"THERE YOU ARE, OGRE! C'MON, MAKE ME BLEED **MORE**!" Throwing a combination of punches after yelling, Uval backed up instead of engaging. This enraged Vertur as he roared out. *"**WHERE ARE YOU GOING?!**"*

Sprinting back to the outskirts of the building, Uval sprinted through more walls and gathered things to throw. Chucking small items once more, he waited for Vertur to lose interest. "ENOUGH OF THIS GAME. THIS IS NOT THA OGRE I REMEMBER!" A massive stone slab was suddenly launched at Vertur, as it broke on his skin Uval appeared behind it with a straight punch. The metal fist landed right on the rogue's face as a cracking noise shot out, he'd broken the man's nose. Leading up with a combination of punches, going from ribcage, chest, to chin, Uval backed away as Vertur blindly swung his arms out to try and grab him.

"**NO MORE OF THIS!**" He yelled as he began to sprint forward, chasing after Uval. Leading the angry man through the building, the tower began to lose its stability shaking with every step these men took. Uval came to a stop in the middle of the lobby. Seeing him stand his ground, Vertur grew happier. As his smile widened, his feet sunk into the ground as he walked toward Uval. All the loose objects nearby began to scrape against the floor, slowly they were pulled toward the rogue.

"FINALLY! *LET US BATHE IN THE GLORY OF BATTLE!"* Sending out a punch, Uval slipped the attack but felt a massive shockwave explode out as Vertur's fist came to a stop. It was a slightly slower than your average punch, but it cracked the air like a metal whip. After dodging the straight, Uval lifted his leg and slammed the bottom of his foot on Vertur's thigh. And though it did no visible damage, Uval would continue to target his legs. Every narrow dodge he'd risk the same attack over and over again. Their interactions shattered nearly all the glass in the tower, broke almost everything support beam in the building, and shot out tank-like explosions into the air every second. Dodging his punch again, Vertur held out his arm instead of reeling it back. So as Uval lifted his leg to kick, Vertur swung his extended arm, clocking him in the side of the helmet. But despite the ringing in his ears, the rattling of his brain, Uval committed to the kick. Landing it again, he smiled — the Ogre had figured something out with his power.

Dazed by the strike of the battlelusted Vertur, Uval wobbled backward and shook his head a bit. Backing away from the rogue's reach, he started to sprint around the building once more. Seeing him just walk away, Vertur angrily took a step forward, but as he tried to lift the leg that Uval kicked over and over again, he realized that it was stuck in the hole he made himself.

Running beside the unbroken walls and pillars, Uval lifted his arm to break all of them as he sprinted past. Yelling out to the mirrored image of his past. "THA WAR IS IN THA PAST, WE HAVE NO CHOICE BUT TO MOVE FORWARD — WE ARE **MORE** THAN BATTLE!"

The entire tower began to collapse as Uval took out the remaining beams of support. Sprinting out, he turned to Vertur as he stared up to the skylight. The walls smashed into each other, tightening the spotlight that shined on him until everything went dark. He smiled crazily as he watched all the destruction fall upon him. Whispering under his breath, Vertur opened his arms as if accepting this new age of war.

"*Burtor fi ir Kosehr*"

"Weight of the World"

As Uval exited onto the street, he turned to see the entire tower crumbling to rubble. Backing up to witness everything in its entirety, he waited before moving on. Though he didn't hear his whispers, he saw his smile. Looking off to the left and right, several small papers and leaves were blown by a wind Uval himself couldn't feel. Oddly, they flew right into the piles and piles of stone. Beginning to worry, he looked around to make sure there was nobody nearby before running — realizing it was empty, Uval began to sprint away. As he did, the rubble suddenly condensed and cracked more. The pile became smaller as a deep hyena-like laugh echoed from within it. As the cackling became louder, the pulling effect became stronger. The pile started to become dust while the radius became larger — dragging nearby buildings to the ground as Uval himself felt the tug of gravity. Feeling his feet slip from the ground, he had no choice but to weld them down onto the street. Turning his head, Uval saw the remains of the tower get pulled into a single point and vanish. In the center of this force, Vertur stood as a being a pure black. Other than his silhouette, his only other distinguishable feature was his fanged silver smile. Anything pulled into Vertur's voidskin would disappear as if entering a portal.

With the radius growing larger, the bricks that Uval was welded to weren't safe either. Picked up from the pull, the Ogre went sliding backward. He yelled out in fear, but even his voice was dragged away. Digging his fingers into the ground, Uval desperately welded himself over and over again — but each time the foundations which he laid upon were uprooted by the stronger force.

In a stroke of luck, Uval managed to grab hold of a metal pipe which stuck out from the ground. Looking up, he saw the steel wires which the cablecars used to get around. It swung wildly and struck him in the helmet — scratching the emerald glass and blurring his vision. Waving his free arm around, he tried to find the wire as he felt his joints popping from being pulled. Strained more, both skin and muscle began to part until he finally grabbed the wire. Welding himself to it, he pulled against the force with all his might.

"This'll be the only armor you'll ever need!" A voice of someone he missed yelled out to him, a memory fading and falling into the void. One hand then the next, he didn't care if blood started to pour from every fiber of his being, he yelled out that he couldn't die. Though his voice was silent, that scream rang out in his mind and summoned flames within his arms.

"*WAR IS OVER!*" He reached as far down the line he could, dragging himself forward as he screamed into the void.

"*THE OGRE IS DEAD!*" The armor on his body began to finally crack, small bits and pieces were ripped off. While shedding the metal, Uval continued to pull with all his might.

"*I AM UVAL LOTRENSKY!*" His legs shed the weight of home.

"*SON OF UTHRA LOTRENSKY!*" His chest shed the weight of loss.

"*TRAITOR OF MASTONOV!* His arms shed the weight of war.

"*KNIGHT OF DESTINY'S CALL!*" And as his hands became free from the only option ever given to him, Uval chose to fight for a reason he felt like *he* chose. Now without his armor, the one thing he chased after, Uval continued on — pulling forward as his hands gripped the metal wire. Knowing that Soren needs his help, that everyone needs his help, Uval pushed as hard as he could — until it all suddenly stopped. Dropped down to the ground abruptly, Uval appeared unconscious for a single second until he took a deep breath in. Feeling the air fill his lungs, he jolted up in shock. Scanning around for Vertur, he found him standing in a huge crater where the tower once stood. This massive bowl spanned a handful of building lengths as the rogue was found kneeling in its center. Seeing that he was drained of energy and battlelust, Uval the Knight sprinted down toward. Leaping into the air, he landed on the rogue and struck him down several times. This continued as blood spurted out with each punch, then Uval realized that he was already unconscious a couple strikes ago. He hadn't protected himself, or rather he couldn't. Vertur ran out of energy. Realizing that the others were still in danger, the Knight sprinted back out the crater as fast he could.

3.0 | Open Eyes See All

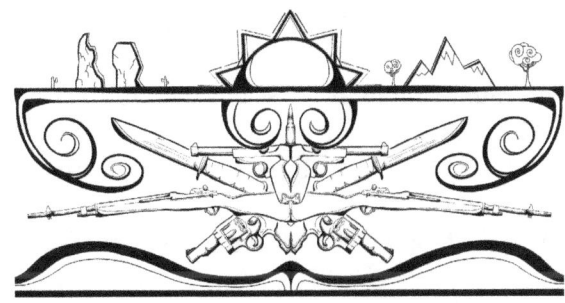

Moving with reason in each step, Orwin paces around the warehouse. Gathering several guns and small ammo caches they grabbed on the way here. Orwin prepared to breach the cathedral and meet up with the others. Cleaning the blood off one of the guns he carried, he turns his head to look at Clyde. Still near the truck, the young man grabs hold of Aurelia and Huruk, slowly and carefully placing them between a huge stack of wooden crates. Opening some of them up with a crowbar, Clyde looked inside to see tons of random fabric with peculiar designs. Placing them on it like a bed, he made his way back down to Orwin. Breathing in and out, he scanned their surroundings to make sure they weren't followed.

"We seem to be good, but I hope the same can be said about everybody else." Clyde gestured to the noises in the background. The blaring alerts, gunfire, and doused flames, were all quickly overshadowed by the sound of a building crumbling. The cracks and crushing noise of it echoed out like a booming drum, it was so intense that you could feel it in your chest.

Both Clyde and Orwin turned their heads to the direction of the sound, looking at one another afterward. "Eh, nevermind — hope is overrated, let's just go fuckin check." Nodding to acknowledge him, Orwin then raised a brow. "Do you even need one of these? With your powers I figured you didn't."

"Magic is cool and all, but a bullet is still damn good. If you're offering, I'll take a gun." Throwing him a pistol, the two began to make their way back into the fray. Sprinting past blood soaked streets, their feet splashed in puddles of red. While heading to the cathedral, Orwin counted the bodies on each side. Based on corpses alone, the Luminel rangers seemed to be winning.

"I've always hated working for these guys." Clyde said while looking down to the Midnight Candle rogues. His eyebrows scrunched together as he ran past them.

"I have a feeling that after all this, nobody else in Luminel is gonna have to worry about them." Stepping onto the main street leading to the Cathedral, they stared past the vendor shops and lavish street lamps to see several rogues bombarding the front gate.

"I sure as hell hope so." Clyde furiously said under his breath.

Knocking on the large doors, the rogue began to chip the material in hopes to make a small gap. As one of their swords pierced through, one of them walked into a nearby shadow. As their figure disappeared a small black spider exited in their stead. Turning to watch their transformed ally slip between the crack, the rogues shifted their head to see the arachnid get smushed underneath Orwin's boot. Before they could react two chained daggers flew out from within his sleeves as Clyde jumped in from behind him — arm pulled back for a wild haymaker.

From the interior of the grand hall, Queen Eldora stood in front of the stone monolith. In her hands was an articulate and radiant blade. Dressed in armored clergyman robes, she prepared herself for the knocking doors up ahead. Hearing the chaos outside shake the entrance till dust fell from hard to reach crevices above, the rangers to Eldora's left and right went into a half circle formation in front of her. Armed with rifles which they pointed, and blades which they stowed, the men steeled their nerves for eventual battle.

Queen Eldora yelled out, her usual soft voice boomed out commandingly. Behind her chant, the men screamed out with pride – their back foot slamming into the ground like drums.

"WE SHALL LIVE TILL DUSK!"

"WE SHALL LIVE TILL DUSK!"

"AND FIGHT TILL DAWN!"

"AND FIGHT TILL DAWN!"

"LET THE SUN GUIDE AND THE MOON PROTECT!"

"LET THE SUN GUIDE AND THE MOON PROTECT!"

A shockwave of air suddenly blasted open the front doors as a rogue rolled through the central aisle. Running in, Clyde ran forward to deal with the straggler while more rushed in from behind. Using his chains to keep them at bay, Orwin slowly backed up. Turning his head slightly, he saw the Queen and gave her a nod — giving one back, it seems she was willing to put their differences aside. At least for now. Yelling out, Eldora and her men ran forward. Unloading their rifles into the crowd of rogues that began to swarm the front, they donned their blades and marched in head first. With full suits of armor, though they were much slower, these men were closer to knights than rangers. They could withstand a plethora of strikes as they dealt their own, and with Eldora behind them, it felt as if their stamina was limitless.

Bringing her sword up, the Sun shifted so it could glisten upon the blade. Immediately, Orwin and Clyde opened their eyes wide — they had felt the touch of the Sky. With honed pupils they fought fiercely, hacking down the rogues as more and more swarmed the cathedral. Blasts of air, bullets from rifles, swinging daggers, nor empowered slashes could fell all of the Midnight Candles which collected at the doorway. Yelling out to Clyde, Orwin swung a church pew with all his might. As he released it toward the horde, a shockwave impacted the back of it and sent it flying with even more of a punch. Like modern artillery it blew a hole in the swarm.

"THERE'S NO END TO THEM!" Clyde yelled while rapidly punching several concussive blasts.

"I'VE GOT AN IDEA!" Orwin said while throwing his chains over to him. "YOU'RE STRONGER!" Catching it, Clyde looked down at the weapons confused.

"HOW– HOW DO I USE THESE!?"

"JUST SWING THEM!" Yelling back instructions, Orwin became immediately swarmed without his weapons. Cuts formed all across his arms as he held them up but none were killing blows. Suddenly the gashes stopped as the swarm passed him by, looking up he saw the rogues were ignoring him — looking to the person before himself, he saw a Silver Rogue waiting. Quickdrawing the pistol on his hip, Orwin shot twice. But before the bullets hit, their body shifted into a dark mist. It then traveled to him with haste, reforming into the rogue as a bone blade shot out from the cloak — cutting Orwin's chin. Narrowly pulling his head back, the Showman could feel the tip of the sword cut from lip to neck. Raising his gun, Orwin shot again. Seeing them shift to mist, Orwin swiped at it with his hand in hopes he'd disrupt it. It didn't.

Instead the fog moved forward and wrapped around his torso. Reforming, the Silver Rogue had their legs around his waist as they now held a dagger. Stabbing it into his back, Orwin screamed out in pain while grabbing the arm. Flipping them off of him, he slammed the Silver Rogue into the ground. Immediately after, they turned to mist once more.

"Well this is getting fuckin annoying. . ." He said with darting eyes, trying to keep track of everything going on around him. Exploding out from the stampede to his sides, a rogue stabbed at Orwin. Being prepared he ducked the attack and broke their wrist, stealing the sword he sunk it in their chest. But as soon as the weapon struck skin, the Silver Rogue reformed and swung their blade at Orwin's head — saving the man he was about to kill. Jolting backward out of pure instinct, the Showman was a moment away from falling into the horde behind him. Then suddenly from above, his chained daggers were seen glowing bright like the sky as Clyde slammed them down.

"*INCOMING!*" He yelled out as he swung them downward like a hammer. A massive shockwave exploded out, toppling the rogues behind Orwin as he got his footing. With more room to maneuver, he stuck out his blade as the Silver Rogue ran forward, wildly swinging as Orwin parried and blocked. However, with every riposte Orwin did, the Silver Rogue vanished into black mist. Using their ability, they covered their lack of experienced swordplay. Growing frustrated, Orwin continuously backed up. When the Silver Rogue appeared, he would parry and counter with seemingly no chance of landing a blow himself. And when they tried to reform atop him he'd dash away. Dragged into a stalemate, Orwin processed a plan and continued to play along.

Pulling closer to the tall glass windows behind him, Orwin put his nondominant arm backward to feel for the wall. Thinking he was cornered, the black mist reformed and the Silver Rogue thrusted with their blade. Turning his body to narrow his profile, the blade struck the wall instead of him. Swinging his sword as a counter, the Silver Rogue dispersed as usual.

Orwin's hand then gripped the curtains behind him as he ripped them down. The golden and silver stitched designs fell upon the mist, dispersing it to the point where the Silver Rogue was forced to reform — now trapped underneath it, they flailed about with their sword in an attempt to escape. Staring down at the rogue, Orwin's mind passed through the days where his lover began to forget him. When a vibrant home became quiet, when his answers became theories, and when his prayers became forgotten. Plunging the sword into the fallen sheets, blood spurted onto his face as he recalled his first conversation with Rakesh. In the dark and rainy streets, where he was told about the Midnight Candles and their leader — Xilia, the Eater of Virtue. A foul creature disguised as a person, better known as the one who consumes all that is good. Whether it be physical or not, where there is hope and joy, Xilia watches with bared fangs. Plunging the sword deeper, Orwin makes sure the rogue is dead before moving on. His eyes stared through his eyebrows in sheer frustration as a veil of determination was cast over his shoulders like a cloak.

Ride along with a band of misfits, battle against Rakesh and Rangers, give away his treasured weapon — there weren't many things that would stop him from finding the leader of the Midnight Candles. Taking a life was certainly not one of them.

Sprinting back into the fight, the rogue's numbers were thinning — no longer needing the chains, Clyde tossed them back to their rightful owner. Catching them, Orwin swung them around like a meteor hammer. One hand controlled the length as the other swung the blade around. Twisting it around himself, the rogues that approached became confused — they didn't know where or how to attack Orwin with it swinging around him like a shield. In that hesitation, the chained blade was hooked around the Showman's foot and then kicked out. Plunging into one of their necks. Pulling it out, the others raced forward.

'Too many at once. . .' He thought to himself. Swinging it wide, the chains wrapped around one of the approaching rogues and completely ceased their movement. As they fell to the ground, Orwin took out his pistol and blade. Shooting the first couple who ran at him, he threw the empty handgun at the next one he saw and used it as a distraction. Slicing across the rogue's stomach, they dropped their weapons in an attempt to catch the guts which fell out. Moving past the dying man, Orwin continued to dismantle the remaining rogues that charged into the cathedral. Thinking to himself, he turned his head to look at Queen Eldora through the corners of his eyes. 'You must've heard those Magic whispers too, your orisons aren't just for show. I haven't broken a sweat being in here.' He then turned back to the remaining rogues as his steady walk turned to a sprint. 'I must've been praying to the wrong Gods.'

The battle would continue until the dwindling number of rogues became zero. Though Eldora, her men, Clyde and Orwin took a substantial amount of damage their spirit alone remained unbroken. However, the Queen knew that undoing this empowering effect she's bestowed upon them would send them into a shocked state. All the stamina lost and energy they used would pile up on them all at once. And though the others thought the battle was over, Eldora was given hints in her dream that there was more to come. She remembers a fanged grimace, a silver one that attracted rage and fear. "I know you're here. . ." Eldora whispers to herself as she stares out the open doors.

3.1 | Glisten then Dry

The Sun stares down at the chaos in Luminel, most of it having died off already thanks to Soren and the others. The erupting flames were slowly extinguished, put out by the firemen who drove through turbulent streets in their trucks. The rogues and their swarms of spiders dispersed till their numbers sunk back into the shadows. Seeing victory on the horizon the rangers ran out with pride in their hearts, the sunlight beaming down on them as citizens cheered for their efforts. Meanwhile, Cypher walked down a street with a rifle in hand — in his other, the Archer dragged Dario by his collar. Walking with him, Uval carried Soren with a pained expression. One that only these three could understand as soldiers.

While they slowly make their way to the cathedral, we find a lone figure marching toward the doors. Using their closed umbrella like a cane, Xilia the Vola Seraphic approaches. Their eyes black, signaling the body is a Husk. With a mischievous and sinister smile their ears perk up as they hear something in the shadow which they cast. Yelps of pain and muffled screams for help shoot out from the darkness beneath them — and the Husk simply chuckles. Peering down into the shadow, everything goes black. The floor above appears like the surface of an ocean made of ink, and the silhouette the Husk casts on the ground is the only source of light in this sunken pocket. Trapped here, with lungs filled with liquid and a heart that'll never stop beating in this place — Sena is brought along. Her eyes blindfolded and her hands bound.

"I knew makin you was a good idea." Xilia said with a grim and forbidding tone — they spoke light of the situation, as if to make fun of it.

Back in the cathedral, everyone stared at the blinding light that shone in front of the building. Seeing a silhouette slowly come closer into focus, they took a bow before fully entering. Xilia the Husk then opened their coat jacket as several creatures slithered and skittered out from their pockets. A long and thin green snake with warmtoned marbling going down its scales made its way across the tiles. Creeping behind a bench and out of sight, in its place rose a rogue with the same pattern and colors on their wispy cloak. Going to the opposite side, a gunmetal gray huntsmen spider did the same thing, and a rogue rose up from the shadow with a cloak looking similar to the creature they were. Both of them have many silver adornments like Vertur, likely a symbol of rank between the Midnight Candles. As the light dimmed to expose these three intruders fully, everyone else in the room got prepared to fight.

"Oh fuck. . ." Clyde says as his hands tremble. Walking down the aisle with very little concern for the dangers, the Husk responds to him. "You finally decided to go against me, Clyde?" Hearing their voice, the young man takes a step back. He stared at his boss, the one who turned his debts to a trap. Stammering on his words, he uttered nonsense.

"Ain't that a bitch, after everythin you done did for me you choose now? You one opportunistic fucker aren't you? I already ate your lil sister's hearing, you don't think I'll take somethin else too?" The Husk smiled wide, their question was obvious — of course they would.

Turning their head, they find Orwin staring with a stern glare. As the Showman's eyes widened, the Husks grin grew wider. Jumping over a wooden pew separating them, Orwin sprinted toward Xilia — winding back the bone blade he'd taken from the rogues. Swinging toward the Husk, a green blur launched between them as the Serpent Rogue blocked his attack with two daggers — they dripped with a glowing emerald venom, each drop sizzling upon hitting the floor.

"*You*. . ." Orwin said, his teeth gritted with a furious grimace. Moving with the Showman, all the rangers in the room slowly marched around the rogues and the Husk. Surrounding them completely, the Husk bent down to a knee — seemingly giving up.

Stood at the elevated podium, atop the stairs before the obelisk, Queen Eldora stares down at them. Her mind becomes dizzy from prolonged use of the power she bestowed upon her men, but regardless Eldora attempts to drag out what little energy she has left. Masking the anxiety creeping onto her shoulders, she speaks out to the intruders. Her voice echoing in the chambers with the confidence a queen should exude.

"You have plagued my kingdom with petty crimes for years, like an infestation your candles have been a nuisance. So why — why bring forth an onslaught after nearly a decade? Even my mother didn't think such a thing was on the table." Raising their head to speak, the Husk looked the Queen in her eyes.

"This has been a long time comin ya majesty. There is just SO much love n care put into these here relics of yours, and they've only grown sweeter since the war's end. But as for the trigger for such a beautiful display of violence today, you need not look any further." Their gaze then turned to Orwin as he seethed in anger while pushing against the Serpent Rogue.

"One of them is here with us now. . ." The room paused as the rangers hesitated, their attention slowly shifting to Orwin as their weapon remained pointed at the real enemy. But to them, the difference was becoming foggy. However, Eldora knew differently.

"You're right. . ." She says while pointing the blade at the Husk. "I'll see that as your admission of guilt — *now prepare for your judgement*." Every ranger, even if they doubted Orwin, did not doubt the Queen. Taking a step closer, their weapons tightened the circle around the Husk and their rogues. Seeing that things were about to escalate, Xilia reached down into their shadow. Pulling out Sena and holding her by the neck, the tension in the room tightened but did not dare to snap. Everyone stopped.

"Oh? What happened?" Xilia says while smiling, fully knowing they now had the upperhand. Walking further down the aisle, the Husk dragged the blinded and bound woman along with them. Stepping up to Eldora, no one dared to make a move — not even her. The Husk walked past Eldora as she lowered her blade, sweat dripping down from her brow.

"A hostage, really?" She said while sucking her teeth. "It seems you wanted to skip the fighting, fine then — let's have a conversation." While maintaining eye contact with Orwin, the Husk spoke to the Queen.

"The items lining the walls, you wouldn't mind if we took them off your hands would ya?" Her eyes narrowed while looking at him, hands tightening around the handle of her sword.

"I wouldn't mind, as long as you spare her life and leave this city — you do that, and those items are yours. But I promise that I'll hunt you. Never again will you sleep easy."

"I highly doubt that. . ." The Husk pushed Sena over to the Queen and made their way down the stairs. The rogues then walked past the rangers as they shared a hateful glance. Going to the glass boxes, they began to pry them open with the Serpent Rogues daggers. As Eldora held Sena, she softly asked if she was okay while unbinding her hands. During this, the Queen stared over to her men — giving them a nod to strike. But before they could pounce, the Husk spoke aloud.

"These will be delectable treats. . ." Sena, still blindfolded, ceased her cries and grabbed hold of Eldora — her strength was inhuman as with one hand she lifted the Queen, with the other she swiped away the blade. The ornate sword bounced down the stairs and slid toward the Husks feet. Bending down to grab it, they stared at the obelisk as sunlight shined down upon it. "But ain't there something else sweeter around here? I heard you had an archive of sorts, I'd love to see how that history tastes."

Walking up to the obelisk, the Husk peered through the angled hole as light shined through it. Curiously, they put the blade through the crevice and it began to reflect it in all directions like a torch. Beneath the pillar, the sound of sliding stone muttered out like whispers.

"How'd you know how to open it?!" Eldora says with a strained voice, still struggling to keep the enchantment on her men. As the large circular platform the obelisk was on began to descend, slowly revealing a spiral staircase, the Husk responded.

"It's a secret — between me and your predecessors. And I plan to keep it that way, your majesty." Suddenly, the Husk looked up to see the glass ceiling shift and rotate like a massive golden gyroscope. The colored glass became stacked on top of one another, creating an indented and curved shape. This focused all the light down the entrance to the vault. Reaching out with a single hand, the Husk sizzled in the intense beam of sunlight. Pulling it back in the shadow, they looked down with an angry smirk.

"Those dirty fucks. . . even in death you try and outsmart me." The Husk then whips their head around to the front doors after feeling someone's presence. Cypher alone stood between the tall frame. He had told Uval to watch their unconscious company as he went in to scope out the situation, "But if you hear my gun fire, you take Soren and that kid out of here. By no means should you come help."

"But tha others might need me, I can still fight even without my armor. . ."

"It's not about the armor, Uval. You're tired, and I'll be damned if I have to drag you out once we win."

". . .are you sure?"

"Mostly. I can't have you dying out here too. Soren, despite his injuries, has stabilized. But we don't know how long that'll last. So please, **go**."

Quickly lifting his rifle faster than anyone in the cathedral could react, Cypher aimed directly at Sena's blindfold as she held up Eldora. Walking forward, the Spider Rogue suddenly leapt at him with blades baring at him like fangs. But before they could land, Clyde had met them in the air, punching them away and starting a brawl between rogues and rangers. As the battle began, the main actors on the stage didn't take part in the chaos. Continuing to walk down the aisle, Cypher stopped halfway while still aiming at Sena's head. During all of this, the Husk spoke out to her.

"Dear, if anyone takes a step onto these stairs, tear the queen's throat out."

Cypher's finger then softly touched the trigger. Walking in front of his gun, Orwin stood between them. That's when Cypher realized who this woman was.

"Put the rifle down." The Showman demanded. Unmoving like a statue, the Archer responded.

"Do you not see what's going on? Her claws-"

"Her **hands**. Don't describe her like some sort of monster."

"You're blinded, Orwin." Cypher put a hand on his shoulder, trying to move him out the way but the Showman stood his ground. Pulling his hand off him.

"By what? *Love*?! I haven't known that feeling for years — you and the others should know at least that much about me."

"No. You're blinded by something I've only grown to know recently, **regret**." Scoffing at his claim, Orwin scowled at the man before him.

"And what would *Heartless Cypher* know about regret? It took magic to make you conscious, don't go around thinking you've lived like the rest of us." Peeking over Orwin's shoulder, Cypher could see the Husk whispering something as they raised their hand to the sky. Slowly the clouds around began to darken — shifting to block the sun.

"That's right — I've killed and slaughtered people my whole life without an ounce of regret. No faces to remember meant no nightmares to wake from. And even if *some* people can be seen in these eyes of mine, that doesn't mean I've changed. But I can feel it now. . . something isn't right."

Pointing his bone sword toward Cypher's neck, Orwin used his other hand to lower his aim to the ground. "You're gonna have to kill me to get a clean shot."

"We'll see about that." Orwin swings down with his blade, forcing Cypher to block with his gun. Pushing back the sword, he kicks the Showman in the stomach — pushing him backward as he takes aim at Sena. Seeing him do so, Orwin races forward and reaches out with his sword, hitting the tip of the barrel and sending his bullet askew. During all the havoc occurring in the grand hall, Eldora stares at Cypher as she turns her head to look up. Dark clouds slowly gathered to block the light.

"SOMEONE-" She yells out. "STOP– STO. . .*stop*" She begins to drift off, her mind succumbing to sleep as her body continuously loses energy. Her eyes barely stay open as her head tilts on its own — staring at Cypher and Orwin fighting, she can only hope it goes well.

Forced backward as Orwin approaches with his sword pointed forward, Cypher turns his head to take a glance at what was behind him. Turning back, he ducks to avoid a horizontal slash and reaches down to pick up one of the many swords scattered across the ground. Swinging it at Orwin, the Showman easily catches the blade with his own. With two hands opposed to Cypher's one, Orwin is easily able to use his leverage on the sword to overpower him in the bind. The Showman's blade then scrapes down the side of Cypher's as the edge plunges toward his neck. Bringing his rifle to his own shoulder, using it to help brace the gun to block the attack. The shock that shot through the rifle went straight into his shoulder as the blade cut into it. Pushing down harder, Orwin slices further into the gun in an attempt to reach his neck — his sword a mere inch away from his skin.

Abandoning his rifle to survive, Cypher kicks Orwin in the stomach again, but this time he knew it was coming. Bracing for the impact, the Showman eats the attack without being pushed back and raises his sword to strike again — the rifle was stuck to the blade from how deep it was cut. In the moment he took to start swinging downward, Cypher moved forward instead of backing up — using Orwin's angry and exaggerated form to cut a shallow gash across his chest. As Cypher passes him by, the Showman smashes the gun onto the ground and it breaks into several pieces. Quickly turning, he chases after Cypher as he sprints toward the stairs. Stopping right before the steps, he pulls out a pistol and points it at Sena — his head turned to Orwin as he breathes heavily. Abruptly halting, he looks to Cypher and holds up his hands, dropping the sword as his eyes widen.

"Aren't– aren't you trying to change? Why. . .why kill an innocent woman, Cypher? She's clearly been mind controlled, or– or forced to do this. . .just lower the gun. You can learn to be human and make mistakes but please– please, just don't let it be my wife. . . I'm begging you."

Eldora sank deeper into sleep. Her vision constantly shifting from black to blurry as she witnesses the scene before her. But the thing that woke her back up was the sound of a gunshot. Eyes open fully, her head jolting back as she looks at Cypher's pistol. Smoke fizzling from the barrel as she slowly turns her head to look over her shoulder. Sena was laid out on the floor, with a bullet hole straight through the center of the blindfold. Slowly it unravels now that it's split. Suddenly from behind her, Cypher grabs hold of Eldora's shoulders as she watches Orwin desperately sprint to his wife.

"Why. . ." She whispers as she stares at Orwin as he holds Sena in his hands, tears rolling down his face. Softly speaking back, Cypher responds.

"I didn't know I was broken, and now I know I'm not fixed. I can't see everyone's face, but there are some exceptions. And when that happens, I'd rather burn this faceless world to ash than learn what loss is — you happen to be one of those people now. I can't let you go that easily. . ."

Holding his wife, Orwin's hands grip onto her as if he was trying to grab the little life she had left. But his hands soften once he realizes that she was already cold — then in the middle of his break, he realizes something as he stares into her eyes. His despondent emotions slowly shift to fury.

"Did you know?" He asks while lifting the bone blade he picked back up before running up here. Plunging it into Sena's chest, his face scrunched together as his hands shook. He was killing something that resembled his love.

"**DID YOU KNOW**?!" He yells, turning to Cypher with his head. A deep scowl filled with droplets of sorrow is smeared across his face. As he looks away from Sena, Eldora looks over to see her pitch black eyes as she begins to dissolve into black matter — sinking back into the shadows. Cypher then rises back up to his feet as Orwin does, they walk to one another. Facing off before turning to march toward the Husk.

"We both know my answer doesn't matter."

3.2 | Bloodshot they stare

A battle between the sides commenced. Among the trinkets of Mystcalls history, the armored rangers fought alongside Clyde. Battling the two rogues became a bout of speed, the Spider and Serpent both dashed around the rangers while striking at their joints — slowly the men were  brought to their knees. Struggling to hit them, Clyde sent out blasts of wind to no avail. They moved too fast for him to track properly, let alone for his attacks to hit. Running out of options, he scanned the room to see Orwin's chains wrapped around a dead rogue. Breaking the circular formation they were forced into, Clyde sprinted out to it. Suddenly a blur of green sped toward him from the right. Sending a shockwave that direction, he managed to send the Serpent Rogue off course, buying him some more time. Reaching toward the chains, he unraveled them as he turned to find the rogue again. Spotting them, the Serpent Rogue squatted down — coiling like a real snake would. Swinging the chains around as fast as he could, Clyde built up momentum and force within them. Yelling out to the rangers, he told them to brace for impact.

Slamming the chains into the ground, a massive shockwave exploded out, throwing everyone in the grand hall backward. Standing up at the same time, the Serpent Rogue and Clyde rose as the rangers managed to quickly restrain the Huntsmen Rogue in the confusion. That's when Queen Eldora finally couldn't take it — drifting off to sleep, she fell on the ground as everyone affected by her prayers felt the fatigue they'd been building this whole time.

Clyde dropped to his knees as the strain in his muscles made it feel like the fibers were going to rip apart. Similarly, the rangers all collapsed under the weight of their own armor. Thankfully, the rogue they apprehended had already been restrained with cuffs and a muzzle.

Up top, beside the dwindling and magnified light, Orwin suddenly fell to a knee whilst in the middle of a sword stroke. Falling short of his attack, the Husk chuckled and swung their black hooked claws toward his neck. Stepping in front of him, Cypher halfsworded to block the strike. Their nails then tore through the middle section of the bone blade and cut into his chest. Without wincing at the pain, Cypher took both parts of the sword and jammed them into the Husks torso. Smiling more, Xilia responded to his gall in kind. Stabbing their claws in his ribs, the two of them stared at one another as blood leaked from Cypher's lips.

"I guess this is just how far mortal men go. . ." The Husk says while smiling, their silver plated teeth glistening in the light behind Cypher. Then slowly, they began to turn until the light was behind them instead.

"You fight like an animal — you rely on your regeneration a little too much. Even Rakesh was more of a threat than you." With the bone fragments jammed into the Husks body, the slashes they had didn't seem to heal.

"This weak lil body doesn't matter much to me anyhow, I can make more given time. Besides, I was only tryna stall." Cypher turned to see the state of the battle behind him, everyone but the Serpent Rogue was on the floor. Turning back he could feel the Husk beginning to physically overpower him, slowly lifting him in the air as their claws dug deeper into his ribcage. Blood poured from his mouth as he smiled with redstained teeth.

"Me too."

While still on the ground, Orwin swung his blade as hard as he could. Slicing through the Husks legs, Cypher dropped to the ground. As soon as his feet touched the tiles beneath him, the Archer smiled. Lifting the Husk up, Cypher ran forward and jumped into the spiral staircase. Falling several carlengths, he slammed the Husk onto the floor — cracking the stoneslabs at the bottom of the entrance. The intense sunlight, though only a sliver of what it once was, shone down upon the both of them. Hitting the Husk, it began to fry its skin, weakening it enough for Cypher to pull out his broken sword — plunging it directly into its skull afterward. Breathing heavily, he stared down at the Husk as it had a shattered bone blade in its face. All its healing had stopped, and the sunlight began to obliterate what was left. Blood and sweat dripped down onto the decaying Husk as its hands fell from Cypher's torso and onto the floor. The body then smiled as its fingers stretched to lay its palm flat on the ground. Whispering, the Husk melted to black sludge. Pushing the blade deeper, Cypher desperately tried to end them. But after realizing that he couldn't do it fast enough, back up the stairs.

"I give all this form has left to offer."

"Take everything and grant me what I am owed."

"Nurtrar Fris"

"Natures Wrath"

Sprouting from the Husks planted hand, lush grass erupted up from any and every surface — spreading out at a rapid pace. These blades were dull gray, with vibrant glowing tips. Growing outward, it easily caught up to Cypher and passed him by. Extending out further, the grass spread throughout the cathedral and even to the surrounding streets. As it came to a stop and as the Husk began to dissolve back into its own shadow, random blades of grass grew at blinding speeds. Shooting upward like spears with the width of a truck, they dug into the ceiling as rubble fell from each sprouting column. As these blades struck an object, whether big or small, it ceased to grow taller and instead explosively sprouted out in a flurry of branches — this force was strong enough to tear through stone and pierce into steel.

Helping Orwin up to his feet, Cypher ran to Eldora and carried her in his arms. Running down the stairs and through the collapsing hall, huge fragments of the painted ceiling descended. History and art crashed onto the wooden pews and glass containers. Midway to the front doors, Orwin dashed off to the side. Sliding underneath branching blades of grass, jumping over mounds of rubble, and dodging falling fragments, he reached out to Clyde as he kneeled motionless — his body lacking the energy to even move.

"MOVE YOUR ASS!" Orwin yelled as dust trickled down onto Clyde. Looking up as he sprinted to him, a massive crack fissured through the ceiling above him. "DON'T YOU DARE GIVE UP! C'MON KID!" While Orwin raced toward Clyde, Cypher did his best to carry Eldora out of the building. But as the cathedral became more and more destroyed, the path to escape thinned. Huge mounds of rubble blocked their way, forcing Cypher to climb up with the Queen on his back. Reaching the top, the pain in his ribs echoed agony throughout him. For a moment, Cypher faltered — this and the commotion going on caused his foot to slip. With all his weight going forward, he wrapped himself around Eldora as they both tumbled down the jagged stones. Smashing down onto the rocks several times, they plummeted to the bottom as Cypher let go of her out of exhaustion. Laid with his belly to the ground, he clawed at the floor and pulled himself to her. Stones falling all around them as he looked up to see one falling straight down atop the both of them. Without blinking, he stared death in the face — his only regret being, 'I wish your Gods were right.' Then from his right, breaking through the splinters of arcane grass, three of the rangers sprinted out. Jumping over both of them, the rocks smashed against their armor. Whispering with a strained voice, one of them speaks to Cypher.

"I don't care who you were or who you are — **get our queen out of here**." Pushing the shattered stones off of them, one of the rangers were completely limp. Dead from the impact. The last two followed Cypher as he pushed through his own limits to carry Eldora out of the building. Staring out to see the grass extending just shy of the nearby buildings, they continued their escape as blades of grass shot upward — skewering one of the rangers and causing them to burst apart as the branches exploded out.

Sprinting past the grassline, the remaining ranger and Cypher completely collapsed onto the floor. With the sounds of sirens blaring behind them, they stared at the falling cathedral as a crumbling wall suddenly blasted open. Sprinting out after it, Orwin and Clyde screamed out in terror. They both landed in the glowing grass but no longer had the strength to move — the last thing they managed to do was warp Orwin's chains around themselves as its end was thrown as far as it could go. As the moments passed, the blades of grass continued to randomly pierce upward.Iin any of these passing seconds, they could be skewered like the ranger before them. With no one to pull them to safety, they laid there helplessly.

Uval was far away, staring at the cathedral fall as he sat in a hospital room beside Soren and Dario. Huruk and Aurelia remained unconscious, hidden in the crates they were left in. And Cypher struggled to move as blood gushed from his torso. But even so, he could see the look of desperation across Orwin's face — he had to try. His body shook as he slowly stood, one of his arms held his body as he limped forward. A foot dragging behind him as he yelled out, pushing himself for just a bit more strength.

"WHY!?" Cypher screamed out while reaching the edge of the grass. The end of the chain was merely a couple of steps into it.

"*WHY DO I CARE ABOUT YOU?! WHY DO I CARE ABOUT ANY OF YOU?!*"

"***DAMN THIS HEART OF MINE!***"

Taking a slow and painful step onto the grass, Cypher gambled his own life for a chance to save theirs.

"*NONE OF THIS MAKES SENSE!*" His foot slid across the blades as he pushed for another step.

"*THIS WON'T GIVE ME WEALTH!*" He took another step and leaned down, grabbing the chain and pulling with the strength he himself didn't have — but made.

"*THIS WON'T GIVE ME COMFORT!*" Taking a step back whilst pulling, Cypher could feel his legs starting to give out.

"*THIS WON'T GIVE ME **ANYTHING** I NEED!*" His limping leg then buckles as he falls out of the grass and onto his back. Bracing his good leg on a nearby streetlamp, he pulls till his skin turns red and blood leaks from his nose.

"*SO WHY AM I DOING THIS?! IF THIS IS WHAT IT MEANS TO HAVE A HEART, THEN **I HATE IT.***"

Reeling them in, Cypher slowly began to pass out. His clenched hands lost their grip but many more took his place. Surrounding Cypher, a mixture of random citizens and rangers helped pull Orwin and Clyde to safety. Fully lying on the ground now, Cypher turns his head to see a crowd and several ambulances surrounding the Queen. As Eldora is swept up into one of the trucks, his eyes fully close. 'Is any of this even worth it?'

4.0 | The Dust Settles

Opening his eyes, Cypher stares at a man of marble who stood atop a fountain. Feeling the bandages under his shirt, his eyes traced the falling water that poured from their tilted vase. With a 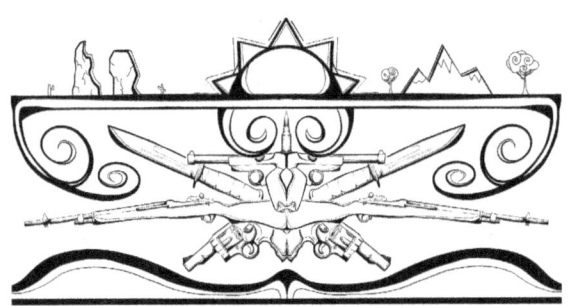 stream of thoughts passing by him, Cypher looked into the statue's eyes and saw how blank they were. Though the maker of this marble man etched detail into the rest of the body, wrinkles to skin, dimples to cheek, the Sun which shined its light upon the garden revealed how empty their gaze truly was. His vision then blurred, the ocean in the distance becoming clear to him instead. Staring past the brimming garden around him, Cypher let his mind wander off the cliff he sat by.

"How's the royal treatment treating you?" Eldora asked as she approached from behind, taking a seat on the metal bench beside him. His eyes stayed locked onto the horizon as he spoke. Butterflies and brilliant petals swept by, carried by a soft yet stern gust of wind.

"It's better than I could've imagined." His tone was somber and quiet. Though not strange for someone like him, Eldora found the look in his eyes odd. Leaning back as staring off to the horizon with him, she decided to stay a bit longer than she planned.

"Then why don't you seem happy? Is this not what you've wanted? You have plenty of food to eat, a comfortable bed to rest in every night — this is it, right? Not to mention the rest of Destiny's Call that's in my care. You all can stay as long as you need or want, it's the least I can do for the people who rid the city of those bastards."

"They destroyed your church, stole the valuables in its grand hall, and caused havoc throughout the streets. Not to mention, they're still alive."

"Yes, yes — and it was you all who sparked the fire in the museum, blah blah blah. I understand that. And I have anger for each and everyone of you for it. But seeing you all fight alongside us was enough to win over the people, and though I'll never forget your actions, I can appreciate the ones I'd rather talk about. That includes saving the vault."

"I assume Huruk spoke with you then."

"Of course, once he woke from his bed the first thing he did was march through the mansion's halls trying to find where the rest of you were. The second thing he did was march to me. After talking, I assured him that I would give you all access to the vault's contents in due time. That being a couple weeks ago now, I think it's time."

Cypher's eyes finally shift to look at Eldora. "And Soren. . .how's his condition?" Letting out an exaggerated sigh, the Queen leaned back — stretching her arms and legs before answering. She seemed oddly peeved at the topic at hand.

"He's. . .doing better **now**. It was already a miracle that his body stabilized in the condition it was left in, but recovery seemed completely out of the picture. Frankly he should've died from all the toxins in his system, and I don't even know how he got out of that fire with no burn marks. Modern medicine could only do so much for the toxins, then Huruk showed up. . ."

"I see. You're upset science is being beat out by his spells. Your pride is almost as big as your heart."

"As painful as it is to admit that, it was more painful to see Huruk fully knocked out every morning. He'd wake, check on everyone to see if they were alive, go to me to gauge if today was the day I'd let him into the vault, then he would go to Soren and use his magic. He wouldn't even say a word either. It was a short routine, one that started in the morning and ended in the morning. Frankly, as nice as it was to see him care about you all – it was fucking annoying to see his minutes of consciousness defeat the days of work my nurses and I have poured and injected into you all." Cypher chuckled very slightly, under his breath it was barely noticeable.

"He really got to you, huh? And that's why you came to me to say that you'd let us into the vault — the Queen of Mystcall didn't want to speak to Huruk herself."

"I take what I said back — I won't admit anything unless it's in a court of law. But anyways–" Eldora stands and turns to him with a hand held out, her smile bright like the sun and eyes dazzling like the moon. "Let's go get that weird mage of yours."

"Don't forget about Uval, Orwin, Aurelia, Cly–"

"Yeah, yeah – them too. Don't ruin the moment, just grab my hand."

"Sorry."

4.1 | The Smog Clears

"Did **I** have to be dragged along?" Aurelia said while looking over to Cypher. He then looked to Eldora, Huruk, Orwin, and Uval – then back to her. "Yes." After his succinct response, the group continued to walk toward the aftermath of the battle. The cathedral, now shattered to pieces, remains a focal point for Luminel. Hundreds of workers pick up and load the chunks of stone onto large dump trucks as cranes haul away the segments they can't carry. And even though they were asked repeatedly not to by Eldora, thousands of citizens come in and out by the hour, helping wherever they can. Children walk around with their parents, both with hardhats on while plucking and cleaning the smaller bits. And teenagers and adults alike do their best to reform what's been lost.

Staring off to a nearby crowd, Orwin softly smiled as he saw the little girl he and Clyde saved. Picking up a stone a bit too large for herself, the young lady pushed as hard as she could to bring it to a nearby worker. Smiling with a job well done, she turned to her parents and pretended to fight bad guys that no longer existed in this city. Seeing her trying to copy the way he fought, Orwin turned away, his soft smile didn't fade though his eyes lowered in somberness.

Walking down a clear path where the cathedral's aisle once was, many of the citizens and workers turned in disbelief. Cheering out to them, Destiny's Call was praised for the victory they themselves couldn't recognize.

"Why are they cheering for us?" Aurelia asked. Looking at her with a confused look that immediately disappeared, Orwin responded.

"Oh right, you and Huruk were unconscious that whole time. By sheer coincidence, we managed to rid Luminel of a criminal group despite trying to commit a crime ourselves. They just don't know the whole story, so don't let it go to your head."

"Didn't plan on it." Speaking while looking around, Aurelia noticed the dark spots in the rather bright crowd. Among the people who cheered for their efforts, celebrating them like heroes, there was a portion of people who very clearly doubted them. Some citizens believed this was a sham, a way for Destiny's Call to revise their public view. And in a way, though not on purpose, it was. At this point, weeks after the battle, a month after Printon, though a bit skewed, their credibility in Luminel managed to somewhat persuade the masses into believing their story. That Rakesh was not a part of Destiny's Call and that they were set up as his scapegoats. Though some believe them, others don't. Public opinion on the group became a mixed bag. The main reason this positive view was pushed out in the first place is because of Clyde, he'd spent many days writing and sending out articles of their story. Soon his words would spread across borders.

Seeing the newspaper, the larger portion of the country supported Destiny's Call, believing in them based on the credibility of their past labors – especially the renowned soldiers. Though very few of them would support them like how Clyde does, they welcomed them to their towns.

Then the other half, smaller but more potent in their emotions. These people believed the group should be brought to trial, if not imprisoned outright in the Damned Heights. Distrust was an easy feeling to latch onto, and that's exactly what people did.

Stepping down the spiral staircase, Eldora led the group to its bottom. Before them stood a door outlined by braided roots, flourished by rainleafs and brilliant insects. Grabbing hold of the brass link affixed to its surface, Eldora opened it. A cold breeze swept past them as they walked in, the light inside brighter than they imagined. Shutting it behind them, Eldora looked to the group — seeing their faces struck with awe brought a smile to her own.

Their heads constantly turned with darting eyes, they couldn't believe what they were seeing. A tall room with a spire in its center, books lined its curved surface all the way up to the ceiling. Above them was a massive circular window segmented in thirds with three distinct designs shown in the mosaic glass. Each one has a hand holding an item — a blank sheet of paper, an ornate fountain pen, and a bottle of ink. Looking back down, they saw that the walls did not confine them to this space — they were open, simply just railings as they looked out to a view that feels as if it doesn't exist in this world. They were far up in the sky, the ground itself distant and blurred miles below them. Erected up, thousands of cuboid pillars stood tall among the thin forest. Then beyond that, on the horizon, mountains of green just like the land beneath.

Rightfully confused, Huruk opened the door and stared up, making sure they hadn't been teleported without knowing. But they weren't. More confused he began to walk around the ancient and massive gazebo. However, he suddenly was stopped — pressed against an invisible force as he wandered too far. Looking around, his eyes eventually went up. Poking the force with his hand, Huruk saw that the segmented design they were under began to glow.

"Cheeky bastards." Slowly piecing things together, Huruk saw that there were three doorways attached to the three largest pillars of the room. This place had been literally cut into these thirds, seemingly only accessible from the other doorways that exist somewhere else in the world. Taking one last look at the blank paper mosaic above them, the Mage sighed while heading to the books. "After all this, **something** good better be in here."

Aurelia then raised a brow and turned to Eldora, "By the way, as you know we originally came here for these books. But we only figured that out because we heard that they were being transported here — does that mean that some of them were missing?"

"No, I just lent some of them to the researchers in Printon. There was some stuff in here that I believed could help with their studies."

"If you don't mind me asking, your majesty." The shock of everything wears off and Aurelia remembers who she was talking to. Bending the knee, she continues. "What exactly was so important that you had to ship off these books, even if temporary?"

Eldora then tells her to stand and helps her up, looking over to Huruk and Cypher to see if they could hear her, she whispers. "Medicine and recovery–" Speaking normally again, she clears her throat. "We found a way to stabilize severely injured people without bringing them to a coma. This minimizes the risk of memory loss and other factors."

"Then why is Soren in one? Did you not use this on him?"

"Actually, we don't believe he's in a coma and we never used the new injection on him either. He might just be sleeping."

"For days? Weeks??"

"Yes. . .it's hard to explain but nothing indicates Soren is in a coma other than his lack of consciousness for a prolonged period – otherwise, he's just sleeping. It's like he's hibernating, but instead of waiting for winter to pass he's waiting for his injuries to heal. We believe it's more of a mental thing as to why he's not waking. He's healthy enough to do so, but scans indicate heavy stress and anxiety. It's like Soren is having a nightmare he can't wake from."

"That's. . .terrible. Is there anything we could do to wake him?"

"Not at the moment. He has to choose to wake up. We think that he can still hear us if we talk in his ear, sometimes his body reacts to voices but not physical touch. I'd suggest talking to him every now and then — that Dario kid has been doing it pretty much every night, trying to wake him up."

Catching everyone's attention, Huruk yells out to them. "FOUND IT!" With excitedly shaking hands he lifted up a book to the Sky while stood at the many desks that lined the room. Rushing over, they all gathered round to hear what he'd discovered.

4.2 | Ancient Flames

In wars long past, the Seraphics were known as the Angels of Triumph. Beings with the strength to change the tide of a battle with their presence alone. They would descend onto bloodsoaked fields by the handful, and whoever's side they chose to fight on would undoubtedly become the victors. However, to the unfortunate souls who had their spears and swords pointed at them — the Seraphics were reapers. Calling cards of death that signaled your end as a warrior, and your beginning as a martyr. This would go on for ages, the Seraphics eventually being called many things under various religions and beliefs, but seemingly randomly they chose the victors of the wars. It was only until the more recent generations where the leaders of the world decided it was enough. They had to treat these Angels as people, not descendents from the Titans. Eventually this called for a meeting between the crowns, one that forged the very room Destiny's Call stands in now. However, this idea didn't bode well with the nation who the Seraphics had aligned with at the time. Northridge rejected a seat at their table and claimed victory, scoring the black box that when opened, ushered in a wave of technological advancements in their cities. As for the other crowns, they confided in one another and forfeited their thrones. Some say it was the cost of the vow they had cast on the Seraphics, others say it was out of shame. But no less, the Angelic beings were bound by the blood of the rulers — now trapped in their borders which they once governed.

Slowly as time passed, people found ways to slay the Seraphics. The main one used was natural weapons like horns, tusks, fangs, talons, and claws. The second of three was sunlight. Both of these combined sent shivers of mortality into their skin when struck. So as the Seraphics dwindled into obscurity, they became more legend than real. However, with the new age unlocked through the last war, it appears Rakesh and the remaining Seraphics have found the way to unlock their arcane shackles.

The red ichor that flows through those past rulers' veins. Their blood and vow were imbued into the Linking Chalice, making their essence the key to freeing the Seraphics. But with their bodies long withered, Rakesh looks to their descendants for freedom. Being one of the rulers of the modern day, Destiny's Call looks to Eldora for answers. Responding, she tells them that she only ever knew a piece of this story. The part where the Queen gives away her crown was told to her by her late mother. She had given it to one of her trusted maids, her only ask was to not let the throne be taken by any wicked man. Since then, she had vanished into obscurity, living her life as she brought along her husband.

"They were madly in love, and even with the state of the world, a family was something she herself couldn't sacrifice. It's very likely that her descendants may still live in Mystcall. We have to find–"

Cypher then interrupted her. "I killed them already, it was a job I'd taken for Rakesh. It happened on the train from Everen to Printon. Though I can't confirm that it was her descendant, we can at least assume Rakesh has gotten to one of them already."

"Then that brings our lose condition to one out of three." Orwin says while sighing. "Not that I'm any better. I gave him that chalice."

"And I should have your head for that." Eldora says as a joke, but nobody took it that way. "Not actually. I don't forgive you, but I won't kill you for it. Your punishment will be getting it back — that's a royal decree." Nodding his head and crossing his arms, Orwin slightly smiles. "Yes, ma'am."

"In Mastonov–" Uval says after thinking for a bit. "There is a folktale that tha old kings are buried in Korstivolo."

"And what is that?" Aurelia asks.

"An icy mountain, deep in tha northern wilds of the country. It is surrounded by dangerous beasts and murderous tribesmen — but worse is tha trip to scale tha summit. At least that's what my grandpops used to say. He told me to look across tha horizon, and to send my prayers to tha mountaintops in hopes tha kings may hear them."

"Wait, you could see this mountain from your town? So you know where it is right?"

"Vaugely, yes. But does that mean I want to get there? No not really, but I will if I must. Will I must?"

"Most likely, sorry bout that bud." Aurelia says while patting him on the arm. "Hold on, where the hell is your armor?"

"I no longer have nor want it."

As those two bantered with one another, Orwin interrupted, asking if it's even worth it to head over. "I know Mastonov is cold, but is it cold enough to preserve a body this long?"

"Tha mountain ranges in tha country have a ground level higher than most."

"So the elevation is damn high huh?"

"Yes, ice forms on tha things up there — snow would be a blessing to see in its stead."

"Yeah, nevermind–" Orwin says while looking back at the group. "I think it might be good to head over. But, I do also know where the last few drops of blood could be. Obviously in Vola for the remaining ruler, but in Peratar specifically — the Flooding Stacks. From what I can remember, it used to be the capital. But that was a pretty long time ago, a couple generations that vaguely matches up to the timeline we got going. For many years it was completely abandoned and destroyed until the Kastaro family built it back up despite the long lasting curse upon it."

"Curse?" Huruk asks.

"Yeah, nobody knows if it's a natural occurrence or if the city was inflicted by a spell, but it almost always constantly rains there. Pouring until the water floods the lower levels. By daybreak it empties and the cycle continues till night. All I know is that there's a massive labyrinth underneath it all, and several ancient vaults to boot. Though that's not much to go off of, there has to be something there. However, I do know that bastard Xilia is there. Another Seraphic. I want them personally dead. . ."

"Then that settles at least one thing." Cypher says while staring at the book on the table. "We'll have to leave the country, at the very least we won't have to deal with Rakesh's real body. Just potentially his husks and the other Seraphics out there."

"Okay, here's the thing though." Aurelia places her hands on the table and looks around to the group. "If we just go after these one at a time, we could lose the other."

"Even so." Uval argues. "Without all three of tha ruler's blood, the vow is still intact. Besides, I want to show you all the good parts of Mastonov."

"As much as I would love that, I still stand with my idea. We know that Rakesh has Husks all over the globe already. He could be far closer to getting the blood than we think. If he prioritizes getting one of them and we just so happen to choose that one — we could potentially be risking both. After all, we're starting a race late and blind."

"I don't really understand what you mean."

Chiming in, Orwin tries to reexplain. "With his Husks, Rakesh has the ability to be at two places at once. Probably a lot more than that actually. At the very least, from what Huruk has told us, the Seraphics don't seem to be on good terms. Especially not Xilia and Rakesh. I'm gonna have to side with Aurelia, I think it's smarter to split up. We have enough people to do so."

"That might be the case." Cypher says. "But who's going where? I haven't heard back from Clyde or Dario, so let's just keep them out of the conversation for now."

Uval raises his hand. "I am clearly going to Mastonov, and Orwin to Vola. So let's start there — I would like to take Soren. Other than me, he is the strongest combatant. We will fight lots going to tha mountain."

Orwin rejects his claim. "First off, why are we doing this like we're picking dodgeball teams? And secondly, I'm taking Soren. With his current condition, do we really think dragging him across an icy hellscape would be ideal? There are renowned hospitals in Peratar, go ahead and choose somebody else."

"Okay fine, then I choose Huruk. It would be nice to have him around making fire. Go ahead, your turn."

"Let me think. . .the guy that shot my wife in the face or literally anybody else. Yeah, I'm gonna go with Aurelia. Also I'm kidding, mostly — I know that version of Sena was a Husk. The real one is still alive in this city. Also, we have to remember their abilities. None of us knew that they could make Husks look like other people, we gotta start checking eyes."

"That leaves me with Cypher then, your marksmanship will gather us food and Huruk will cook tha spoils. This works perfectly for me."

Waving her hand between the both of them, Aurelia interrupts. "With that settled can we go? This place gives me the heebiejeebies. Besides, we should check in with Clyde and Dario to see if they're coming."

"Wait. . ." Uval says. "How are we even getting to these places? They are across borders and oceans, we'll need at least two planes." Everyone then slowly turned to Eldora.

"You guys really are scum you know that? *Sigh* I'll get you the planes." Uval and Aurelia cheered gleefully as they hugged her while Orwin and Cypher chuckled to themselves. Huruk was too deep in the books to care about anything else but regardless, Uval wrapped his arm around him and Cypher then shook the both of them in excitement.

"WE'RE GOING ON AN ADVENTURE! THA PERFECT TRIO!!"

5.0 | The Sky Opens

With luggages at their side, Destiny's Call stands on a long stretching tarmac runaway. Two identical aircrafts sit dormant behind them. Shaped closely to a dragonfly, the planes sport two large 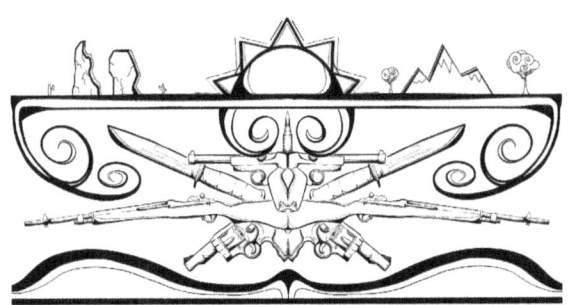 engines with propellers affixed to their front. Above them are the main wings, spanning out with a width longer than the plane's length. Made with a mixture of metal and cloth, the batshaped wings are accompanied by a secondary smaller pair at the end of the vehicle. The front of the plane also has two levels, the top smaller than the bottom. The lowest level is meant for room and board, walking down to its end it leads to a lounge with a reinforced glass wall. Similarly, the room above is fully enclosed and has all the mechanisms you'd need to maneuver this metal beast.

Greeting each other goodbye, Uval and Orwin — the self proclaimed leaders of these groups tell one another to keep in touch as best they can. Boarding the planes, Aurelia rolls Soren over while following her leader. Accompanying them, Dario, Clyde, and his little sister tag along for the ride. Though his little sister and Dario are just following him, Clyde has his own personal reasons for going. As much as he wants to help his heroes with their mission, he also wants to finally leave Luminel — adventure across the world to document the important changes everyone should know and remember. To him, this is his dream. And it starts with Destiny's Call and their story.

As for Dario, he no longer understands what he wants to do. He no longer believes it's to kill Soren – so with no option in his mind, he follows to eventually talk with him when he wakes. To figure out what really happened to his brother. To see if it differs from what the reports say.

While boarding, Huruk looks over his shoulder to see Cypher staying behind as he talks to the Queen, turning away he looks down to the book she lent him – the Mage recognizes that look in his eyes. 'He can see now.'

Looking to Eldora, Cypher carries his luggage in one hand and a pristine rifle in the other. It is ornate and seemingly carved with etchings the Queen put herself. His fingers rub against the grooves she made as he speaks out with a lively eyes.

"I want to say thank you but that's been said by us a hundred times by now."

"Especially by Aurelia, once she remembered I was the queen she started speaking all proper to me. I'm glad you don't do that."

". . .I do have something else to say though."

"I'm listening."

"That turn of fate you said, was that it?"

"It wasn't. But even though the Moon didn't outright show you all as heroes in my dream — that doesn't mean you can't do good. My people are proof of that."

"I feel like you've seen more about us than you've said."

"I have."

"And you won't tell me will you?"

"Not at all."

"Why?"

"Some things are better learnt than told.

"I don't understand. . ."

"Well, you're not supposed to know everything."

"Then how do I move forward without direction?"

"Sometimes you have to just listen to your heart, feel where your feet want to walk. Then take that step. Not everything has logic attached to it, and it doesn't have to."

"That doesn't seem like a sound way to lead a kingdom."

"It isn't, that's why you learn to use both your mind & heart. So, where do your feet lead you?"

"I don't know. . . staying here I'll have plenty of food to eat, a bed every night, and it's now safer than ever."

"But?"

"But for some reason I want to keep going. I want to see where my travels take me. I want to know what lies for me at the end of it all. Even if I starve some days, stay awake some nights. I want to keep going."

"Then don't be afraid, have faith in your feelings and walk."

". . .thank you. I'll never forget your face."

"You better not."

www.ingramcontent.com/pod-product-compliance
Lightning Source LLC
Chambersburg PA
CBHW080839250626

47161CB00009B/3121